SWEETHEARTS
CAN BE
MURDER

Connie Shelton

Books by Connie Shelton
THE CHARLIE PARKER MYSTERY SERIES
Deadly Gamble
Vacations Can Be Murder
Partnerships Can Be Murder
Small Towns Can Be Murder
Memories Can Be Murder
Honeymoons Can Be Murder
Reunions Can Be Murder
Competition Can Be Murder
Balloons Can Be Murder
Obsessions Can Be Murder
Gossip Can Be Murder
Stardom Can Be Murder
Phantoms Can Be Murder
Buried Secrets Can Be Murder
Legends Can Be Murder
Weddings Can Be Murder
Alibis Can Be Murder
Escapes Can Be Murder
Sweethearts Can Be Murder
Holidays Can Be Murder - a Christmas novella

THE SAMANTHA SWEET SERIES

Sweet Masterpiece	*Sweet Payback*
Sweet's Sweets	*Sweet Somethings*
Sweet Holidays	*Sweets Forgotten*
Sweet Hearts	*Spooky Sweet*
Bitter Sweet	*Sticky Sweet*
Sweets Galore	*Sweet Magic*
Sweets Begorra	*Deadly Sweet Dreams*

Spellbound Sweets - a Halloween novella
The Woodcarver's Secret

THE HEIST LADIES SERIES
Diamonds Aren't Forever
The Trophy Wife Exchange
Movie Mogul Mama

CHILDREN'S BOOKS
Daisy and Maisie and the Great Lizard Hunt
Daisy and Maisie and the Lost Kitten

SWEETHEARTS CAN BE MURDER

Charlie Parker Mysteries, Book 19

Connie Shelton

Secret Staircase Books

Sweethearts Can Be Murder
Published by Secret Staircase Books, an imprint of
Columbine Publishing Group, LLC
PO Box 416, Angel Fire, NM 87710

Book layout and design by Secret Staircase Books
Cover images © Anna Kraynova, Borzywoj, Ayutaka
First trade paperback edition: February, 2021
First e-book edition: February, 2021
* * *
Publisher's Cataloging-in-Publication Data

Shelton, Connie
Sweethearts Can Be Murder / by Connie Shelton.
p. cm.
ISBN 978-1945422935 (paperback)
ISBN 978-1945422942 (e-book)

1. Charlie Parker (Fictitious character)—Fiction. 2. New
Mexico—Fiction. 3. Missing persons—Fiction. 4. Con artists—
Fiction. 5. Women sleuths—Fiction. I. Title

Charlie Parker Mystery Series : Book 19.
Shelton, Connie, Charlie Parker mysteries.

BISAC : FICTION / Mystery & Detective.

813/.54

To you, my readers—I cherish our connection through these stories.

Acknowledgements:
Dan and Stephanie—each of you contributes and makes my writing life so much easier and so complete. I love you. I also owe a huge debt of gratitude to Shirley Shaw, my editor emeritus. Thank you for the many years when you dropped everything to read and correct my manuscripts. My writing is much, much, much improved since you came into my life.

And to my beta readers who catch the many little things that my eye misses: Marcia Koopman, Sandra Anderson, Paula Webb, Isobel Tamney, and Susan Gross—you are the best!
Deepest gratitude to all.

Chapter 1

Now

Yesterday wasn't the hottest Fourth of July on record, but it might have been close. And for me, having just visited England a month ago, our dry New Mexico heat felt blistering. Well, maybe that's a little dramatic. My middle brother lives in Phoenix—now *that's* a blistering heat. Anyway, when I awoke to the sound of the air conditioner humming away at seven a.m., I knew it would be a hot one and I would need to dress accordingly. I rummaged through the closet for lightweight cotton pants and a T-shirt, not especially worrying whether the outfit was strictly color-coordinated or not. Aside from checking in with and putting in a couple hours at the office, I had no big plans all day.

Drake has been away for six weeks on a fire contract. He gets two days off out of every fourteen, so he'll dash home for the weekend and we'll manage some quick hot sex and a leisurely brunch before he has to rush back. My older brother and business partner, Ron, is on the dream vacation of his life—he and Victoria and two weeks on Kauai—and there's slim to no chance I'll receive as much as a text message. It isn't often they have a stretch without his three boys, but the kids are doing their own thing at Disneyland with their mother. Our part-time receptionist, Sally Bertrand, cuts her hours even further during the summer months with her own two kids at home, which I don't mind since the office should be fairly quiet without Ron there.

Long story short, I've got lots of time to myself these days and my biggest plan is the vague notion that I'd like to repaint the guest room. Sometime. Not today.

Showered and dressed, I meandered toward the kitchen where Freckles met me with eagerness in her step. I pressed the button on the coffee maker and let her out the back door, keeping an eye toward the break in the hedge where the dog loves to race if she hears any signs of activity over at Elsa's house. My elderly neighbor and her live-in caregiver both have our little spaniel spoiled rotten.

From the doorway, I kept an ear tuned to the progress of the coffee maker while I watched the dog. She finished her business before the female voices from next door perked her floppy ears right up. Her head cocked and she made a run for the hedge.

"Freckle-baby! What you doin'?" It was Dottie Flowers, Gram's wonderful caregiver and constant companion.

Loving baby talk came through, and I could imagine the pillowy black woman as she bent to tickle the dog behind the ears and sneak a treat from the pocket of her apron.

I pulled the door closed and padded barefoot down the porch steps and followed the sounds.

"Is she bugging you, Dottie? Sorry."

"Oh, not at all. I just stepped out to pick us some tomatoes before it gets too hot."

"It's your day off. I could do that," I said, noticing that Dottie wore one of her church dresses.

"Don't you worry. It'll take me two minutes and then I'm off to help out at the vacation Bible school. They got me teachin' a class of ten-year-olds. Ol' Dottie getting a little slow for *that* bunch, I tell you."

I laughed at the image of Dottie riding herd over kids that age, but I had no doubt she could do it. For someone in her sixties, she kept going strong. She and Elsa had planted a full garden in the late spring and I often heard the two of them chattering away as they exclaimed over the progress of the beans or the squash. They'd already harvested fruit from the cherry and apricot trees and made more jam than we could eat in two years. Dottie kept Elsa as young as any ninety-plus woman could be. She'd been a godsend to our family.

"So, Miss Elsa had her breakfast," Dottie said, leading the way toward the tomato vines. "Lunch is no problem. Her friend Iris comin' by to pick her up and they having lunch out somewhere. Then Miss Iris promise to bring her home and get her settled. She'll take her nap, so not much you'll need to worry about, unless you want to come by late this afternoon."

I watched as she deftly pulled three ripe tomatoes from

the vines and placed them in the little pouch she'd created by gathering up the edges of her apron.

"I'll make a salad for dinner tonight and invite her over," I said, knowing full well that Elsa ate little or nothing in the evening if she'd had a big lunch.

"Here, then, you take these." Dottie held the apron out toward me and I picked up the tomatoes.

"You sure you don't need them?"

"Look at them vines. It's all I can do to use 'em fast as they get ripe."

She convinced me. Plus, the scent from the ripe fruits was already tempting me into considering a tomato and coffee for breakfast. Or maybe not. I called to Freckles, who leapt to attention the moment I said 'office.' Next to Elsa's, my workplace is the dog's favorite spot to be.

I wished Dottie good luck with the Bible school kids, and she told me she'd do fine once she got out of there at noon, changed her clothes, and joined up with her bowling league friends for the afternoon and evening. We exchanged a warm hug and I took my tomatoes and my dog home, where the kitchen was filled with the enticing scent of Ruta Maya dark roast.

An hour later, tummy filled with two cinnamon rolls, I carried my iced coffee into the Victorian house we now call our office and followed Freckles' lead toward the reception area.

"Anything on the agenda today?" I asked Sally.

"I've got your billing all sent," she said, leaning back in her chair and lifting her shaggy blonde hair off the back of her neck. "I'll put those in the mail on my way home." She nodded toward a few envelopes on the corner of her desk.

I had prepared the client account statements yesterday

but left the actual sending of the electronic statements for this morning. Sally was quicker at transmitting them than I was anyway. And for those few clients who still required paper bills sent through the mail, she had printed, folded, stuffed them in envelopes and affixed the postage.

"Any calls for Ron, or anything else I need to know about?"

She shut down her computer and shook her head. "Nope. He did a pretty good job of letting his regular clients know he's away. I put two messages on his desk, people with general inquiries who seemed content to wait a couple weeks to hear back from him. I made it sound like he's out of town on an investigation."

"Good idea." When people want a private investigator, they generally don't want to hear the guy is sunning himself on the beach in Hawaii. We're in a business where people tend to think their particular problem transcends all rights of the investigator to have any time to himself.

Sally picked up the outgoing mail and headed toward the back door, while I grabbed my laptop case and my coffee and took the stairs to the second floor. My office felt stuffy and I nudged the thermostat on the modern-day central air down a notch. I was in the process of booting up my computer when the front door chime went off; someone had just walked in, and I couldn't ignore it the way I did when I knew Sally was at the front desk.

Freckles raced ahead, as she always does, and I heard a female voice exclaiming over the dog before I was even halfway down the stairs. A teenage girl stood in the reception area, clasping a folder to her chest as she bent to accept doggie kisses on her fingers. She wore skinny jeans, a turquoise tank top, and white linen jacket with elbow-length sleeves, and her honey-brown hair draped straight to her shoulders. A tiny white purse hung from a thin strap that crossed her body. I guessed her age to be somewhere around a junior in high school.

When she spotted me she stood straight and smiled, showing perfectly aligned teeth.

"Hi, can I help you?" I asked.

"You're a private investigator, right?" She shifted the inch-thick folder to her left arm, seeming uncertain as to whether she should shake hands or what.

I quick-debated whether to go into the whole spiel about how I'm really the accountant for the firm and my brother is the PI. Why bother? She was probably here to ask for donations for the school band or something. I just gave a nod.

"Good." She stood up taller, easily five-foot-eight in her flat sandals. "I want to hire you. Oh. I'm Cassandra Blake. Well, Cassie."

"Okay … um, Cassie. What's the nature of the case?" I could see it now—girl who wants to find out if her boyfriend's cheating.

"It's a missing person case. The police worked on it for a while, but they gave up. I was just a baby at the time, but I've read the entire case file a bunch of times." She patted the top of the folder.

"Let's go in the conference room. May I take a look at the file?"

She handed me the folder and followed my lead toward the old house's former dining room. I switched on the overhead lights and ushered her toward the long table where she took a seat facing the foyer. She declined my offer of a soda or water or coffee, apparently wanting to get right to business. I sat at the head of the table and opened the file for a look.

At a glance, it did seem to be a copy of an actual police investigation. There were the usual initial report forms—a woman named Jennifer Blake reported missing, now more than fifteen years ago—and several pages of what appeared to be witness statements. I didn't spend much time on the details; if we took the case Ron would want to read everything in detail later.

"Who's Linda Arnold?"

"My grandmother. Jenny Blake is my mother. Well, I don't remember her at all. I was only a year old when all this happened."

"So Jenny went missing and Ms. Arnold reported the fact …"

"Right. The police didn't really seem to question very many people, and no one has worked on the case for years now. I just need to find her, to find out what happened and why she left us. And I need to bring her back."

From the slimness of the file, I could tell the case hadn't gone far. I've seen murder files easily eight or ten inches thick, filled with all the various witness statements and interviews with suspects. The detectives in Missing Persons had clearly made an effort here, but it must have gone nowhere. I was intrigued.

I closed the folder and looked directly at Cassie, giving her the respect of a legitimate potential client. "Our private investigator is away from the office this week, actually until the eighteenth of the month, so what I can do is tell him about your case and if he's got time on his schedule we'll be in touch." Not to mention, I wasn't actually sure we could take on a minor as a client.

Her bright smile faded. "Oh no. I was hoping … Well, I guess I didn't explain well enough. This is urgent. Grandma is really, really sick. This is the most traumatic event of her life, and she shouldn't have to leave for heaven until she sees her daughter again."

Oh boy. I had no idea how to answer that one.

"Oh, I can pay for your service," Cassie said, mistaking my hesitation. "Grandma has a little money in the bank, and I know this is how she'd want to spend it."

I felt a tug in my heart. "What about you? After she's, um, gone … won't you need the money to live on?" And how was that going to work? Here was this young girl who would be left alone, possibly to become a ward of the state. "Are there other relatives?" I asked as gently as I could. "Where will you go?"

"There's an uncle and his wife in Colorado." She didn't elaborate, and I noticed she didn't say 'my uncle' or give much indication how she felt about them.

I felt myself wavering toward this kid who was about to lose everything familiar to her. She only wanted one thing: to find her mother. How could I say no?

Chapter 2

Cassie pulled a checkbook from her purse and insisted on writing a check for a thousand dollars to retain our services, even though I explained that I would need to call Ron and get his okay. I didn't even address the fact that she'd be winging it with me, at least for the first couple of weeks, not to mention the very slim chance that someone who'd been missing for fifteen years could actually be found at all. At some point, I would have to bring up the possibility that Jenny Blake had been dead all this time.

"I won't deposit this until I at least get the go-ahead from my partner," I told her as she handed over the money. "At that time I may need to have your grandmother sign a contract. I'm not sure how that works—we've never had a client under eighteen before."

She smiled with a lot more confidence than I felt. "It's

going to work out fine," she said, standing and shaking my hand. "You'll find her, Charlie."

I walked her to the front door and we stepped out to the covered porch. "How did you find us anyway?"

She pointed toward the small sign on the building. "RJP Investigations. I've seen this place for years. We just live on the next block over, and I've walked past here a hundred times. My friends and I have ridden our bikes and played on this street since we were little."

Such a normal girl, considering the trauma in her early life and now facing the loss of the person most important to her. I wished her luck and told her I would be in touch once I knew more.

Something about this girl, I must admit, had drawn me in. Maybe it was the fact that she was now near the same age I was when I'd lost my own parents. Elsa had taken me in and finished raising me. Cassie was faced with losing her grandmother; I couldn't imagine how off-the-deep-end I would have gone had I lost Gram at that age. I walked back into the conference room, sat down, and opened the file on Jenny Blake.

The initial police report was fairly basic: Jennifer Blake, age twenty-one, had been home alone with her one-year-old daughter. Her mother, Linda Arnold, reported that she went to the house on Sixth Street to get the baby while Jenny attended classes at UNM. When she arrived, the baby, Cassandra Lynn Blake, was quietly playing in her playpen, alone in the house. The front door was unlocked, which Linda thought odd. Jenny's car was in the driveway, her purse was where she normally kept it, on a hook with jackets near the front door. Linda had called out, then searched the entire house and backyard. Assuming Jenny had popped over to a neighbor's house she waited a few minutes, then left Jenny a note saying she had Cassie and was heading out to a scheduled pediatrician's appointment.

When Linda and Cassie returned an hour later, everything was exactly as she'd left it and that's when she knew something was horribly wrong. Jenny had not moved the note Linda had left for her, had not taken her purse or car, and by now she would have been late for class. The only thing Linda spotted out of place on the property was a cigarette butt at the foot of the front steps. No one in the family smoked.

Linda called the police, who told her that an adult is not considered a missing person until they've been gone 48 hours. Just sit tight, they said, she'll come walking in at any time. Linda called Jenny's friends, especially eager to talk to Laura, who was in her accounting class at the university, thinking maybe her daughter had ridden to school with Laura, maybe she'd been in a rush and forgotten her purse.

Laura said no, she'd had no plans to drive with Jenny that day. She had missed her in class but assumed something came up. She asked if the baby was all right. Linda had no reason to think Laura was lying. Her concern seemed genuine enough, according to what Linda told the police.

There were other interviews, along with notes from the detective who had eventually come to the house at Linda's insistence. But I'd read enough for now to know that I wanted to try and help this family. I calculated the time difference and figured I could catch Ron at the crack of dawn, well before he and Victoria would head out for a day of whatever they were planning. They'd only been on the island two days, and surely their inner clocks were still operating on mainland time.

"Yep, we're up," were his first words when he heard my voice. "Don't tell me there's an office emergency already. Please don't tell me that."

"No emergency. Just a question." I gave him the basic one-sentence synopsis of the case, ending with the fact that we were being hired by a sixteen year old.

"Get the grandmother to sign the contract," he said. "Nothing should come back to bite us legally if it's her name on the paperwork. And make sure the check clears the bank."

Good old Ron.

I heard Victoria's voice in the background and spent a couple of minutes chatting with her. They were enchanted with the island, she told me, and couldn't wait to follow my recommendation and take a helicopter flight to get the whole overview. She asked about the best places to eat and to buy gifts to bring home, but I'm afraid I wasn't much help there since I hadn't been to Kauai in a few years.

"Don't expect too much," came Ron's voice from a distance. "That case is fifteen years old already. Those are the tough ones."

"Tell him I said thanks," I told Victoria. "And reassure him I won't disrupt your vacation time again."

She laughed and told me to give Drake and Freckles each a hug.

I hung up and put the Blake file back in order. Upstairs, I got on the computer and created a new version of our standard contract, filling it in with Linda Arnold's name and address. Tucking that into the folder Cassie had given me, I bribed Freckles into her crate with a doggie cookie, locked up the office, and set out walking. It would have been easy to justify hopping in the car for the short two-block trek, given the hot day, but I could use the exercise.

I stuck to the shady side of the street and located the address on the next street to the south, a block over and one block west of our office. They say horses sweat, men perspire, and ladies glisten. Even so, I was feeling more than a little glisten-y by the time I climbed Linda's porch steps and tapped at the door.

Cassie answered and her smile widened. "You came!"

"Is your grandmother home?"

"She is. She starts the mornings a little slowly these days. She's in the recliner in the den. Come on in."

I followed her through a generous-sized entryway, noting a formal living room to my left and a hallway leading to bedrooms on the right. This house didn't appear nearly as old as our Victorian, most likely dating to the 1940s or '50s. It had the substantial feel of the homes of that era, without the cookie-cutter floorplan so prevalent in later subdivisions. Straight ahead was the den, a good-sized room with a stone fireplace, parquet floors, and cushy furniture. A sliding glass door led to a backyard full of shade trees and flowering shrubs, and I could see past a built-in bookcase on the far wall into the kitchen. The stove and fridge had last been updated sometime in the '80s.

A recliner chair in one corner faced a large TV set diagonally across from it, and the woman with graying blonde hair pressed a remote control to switch it off. She looked older than her sixty-some years, but I supposed that was due to her illness. A side table near the chair held at least a dozen pill bottles.

Cassie introduced me to her grandmother and offered me something to drink. I told her a glass of water would hit the spot right now.

"Pardon me for not getting up," Linda said, lowering the footrest so she could sit somewhat more upright. "I find that I get a little woozy sometimes when I stand."

"No problem at all." I perched on the corner of the sofa nearest her chair.

"Cassie told me who you are and said she had gone by your office this morning."

"Good. Did she mention that we might not get a lot done on your case for a couple of weeks? My partner is actually the licensed investigator and he's out of the city right now."

A tiny crease formed between Linda's eyebrows. "I know my granddaughter is hoping ..."

"I understand. And I'm happy to review the old case and work on locating people we might talk to. So it's not as if there won't be any progress at all."

Linda's face relaxed into a smile when Cassie walked in and handed me a glass with water and ice.

"Sweetie, wasn't today the day you were going to change the bed linens?"

Cassie took the hint to leave us alone. She flashed me a smile and headed in the direction of the bedrooms. I pulled out the contract and a pen, and Linda glanced over the two-page document before signing.

I thanked her, then patted the police file. "Is this something you've had all along?"

"No, actually. At the time, all those years ago, I just let the police do their business and when they stopped working the case, I guess I pretty much gave up hope. Cassie's the one who took the initiative now. She filed the request and got this copy of their investigation. I thought I'd done a good job of making provisions for her, in case something happened to me—which now, it has. But she's …" Her voice trailed off. She cleared her throat and pointed to a shelf behind the flatscreen TV. "You'll need a picture to show your witnesses. I'm afraid that's not the best, but it's what I can give you now, without having to dig through a lot of old boxes."

I stepped over and picked up the framed 5x7 photo of Jennifer Blake holding baby Cassie on her lap. Both were dressed in pink sweaters.

"She'd bleached her hair," Linda said. "Wanted it lighter, like mine, not the rich brown from her father's side."

"I'll leave the frame with you, if that's okay."

Linda nodded, seemingly deep in thought.

"Cassie sounds very hopeful that we can locate her mother, at least that's what I took from our conversation this morning."

Linda nodded. "Let me give you a little background. It might help you understand the girl's viewpoint. Jenny and Ricky married young, way too young to my way of thinking, but they were determined. They were high school sweethearts, both graduated and got jobs. Well, his was sporadic work—musicians are like that. He played with a band that was actually starting to be fairly well known here in town. Jenny worked in an office and decided becoming an accountant would be a good career choice. She was always good with numbers, and she liked office work."

I had to smile at the parallels. My own skill with numbers was what led a university professor to suggest that direction for me. I couldn't say that I loved office work, but the computer presented no big challenge, so that was the path I took.

"I encouraged Jenny to get her degree. She would get better jobs and could open her own office as a CPA one day—that was my thinking. What I didn't say was, she would need a decent income after Ricky bailed on her. Which he did. When Cassie was born a year or so later, he decided fatherhood wasn't much fun. Going on the road with the band was more to his liking."

She sighed and shifted slightly in her seat. "I *really* tried not to say 'I told you so' to my daughter, but it was there. She heard it enough from friends and other family members who had seen doom in the marriage."

I nodded, sipped my water, and let her continue.

"I tried to talk Jenny into moving herself and the baby in here with me. I've got plenty of space and all … But she was so fiercely independent. She wanted to stay in her own little rented place. Secretly, I think she always hoped Ricky would come back. She loved him blindly. I kept my mouth shut and just tried to help out where I could, mainly with childcare while she worked and attended classes."

"I read your statement and the police report," I said. "So, on the day she disappeared, Jenny was supposed to go to her university class?"

"Yes. I got to the house to pick up Cassie and take her for a checkup, and Jenny just wasn't there. I was surprised at first, then puzzled—well, you read the report. I asked the neighbors if they'd seen her leave or if they had talked to her that morning. No one knew anything. I called a few of her friends. Their names are in there—I gave everything to the police so they could follow up. At first they didn't want to. You know how they can be. But after I stayed all day and that night at Jenny's house and she didn't turn up, well, I had to insist to the cops that something was really wrong."

"I'll read through it all and see if I can locate the friends, maybe revisit the trail the police worked on."

She nodded.

"What about any other avenues? Did you put up fliers around the neighborhood? Try to get the TV stations involved, anything like that?"

A sigh. "Yes, some. I suppose I could have done more. The problem with getting media attention was that there was simply no sign of violence or any reason for them to think a crime had been committed. Do you know the phrase 'If it bleeds, it leads'? That's what they learn in journalism. The news reporters aren't interested in stories unless there's a promise of violence. Look at the way they cover anything—a natural disaster, a political race, a disagreement between groups. It's only interesting as long as there's an angle that involves a battle of some kind. Once the problem gets solved, or gets happily resolved, it's over for those guys. Sorry—didn't mean to start on a rant."

She shifted in the chair again, trying to get comfortable, then gave me a piercing stare. "Can I be frank with you?"

"Of course. Please do."

She glanced toward the hallway where Cassie had gone, then lowered her voice. "At the time, I really thought Jenny might have decided to go off with Ricky. Maybe she had gotten her fill of motherhood. Ask any woman with an infant. It's hard. It's exhausting, especially if you're doing it alone. I didn't want to believe my daughter would ever abandon her baby—I still don't think she would have—but that thought must have crossed everyone's mind. What if Ricky had come to the door, begged real hard with that winning smile and those baby blue eyes? What if Jenny just plopped the baby down in the playpen and walked out the door with him?" She gave a shrug.

It could have been a possibility, and she wouldn't have been the first to do it. "But without her purse, without packing a change of clothes, anything?"

"And that was the main reason I never voiced that doubt to anybody," Linda said. "Plus, it didn't fit with what I'd witnessed. Jenny loved that baby. I can't imagine what might cause her to turn her back and walk away. Not willingly."

I heard the sound of a washing machine running in the background, and I glanced toward the hall to see if Cassie was returning. No sign yet.

"Let me ask one more thing, Linda, and then I'll let you rest. Do you believe Jenny is still alive?"

"My granddaughter wants that more than anything. But with not a single word, in all this time?" She shook her head sadly. "Probably not."

Cassie met me near the front door as I left, and I wondered how much of the conversation she'd overheard from another room. We stepped quietly out to the porch and she reached out to touch my arm.

"Please find her. The doctors only hinted at it, but Grandma probably only has a month or two, and my uncle is already making plans to move me to Colorado in time to start school in August. Charlie, I can't stand the idea!" Tears gleamed in her eyes.

I swallowed a lump in my throat. "Cassie, if her condition is that bad, a big change is coming for you, no matter what."

"I know." Her head hung, her hair hiding her face like a curtain. "But I don't *know* Uncle Ted. And Aunt Myra is just *so* unfriendly. They don't want a kid now. All their children are older, grown and away from home. I just want my mom."

This time I couldn't swallow at all. I squeezed her hand and managed to mumble that I would do my best, before my vision blurred and it was all I could do to navigate the porch steps and head in the right direction down the street.

I'd bitten off a huge chunk of responsibility by taking this case.

Chapter 3

Back at the office, Freckles was ecstatic to see me, which lifted my mood a bit. The one thing I could do to feel better about the situation was to dive right in and start searching out whatever clues I could pull from the file. Then I would see who I might track down to question. Sometimes people remembered little things that hadn't come to mind at the time.

Who was I kidding? Memories typically don't improve with time. I could only hope to ask the right questions and learn something the police had not been able to ferret out.

I decided it couldn't hurt to start online, browsing back to see if there had been any mention of the investigation at the time. Despite what Linda had said about the lack of interest from the media, it was always possible some beat reporter had got wind of the disappearance, perhaps through the police department, and there might be a piece in the police blotter section.

This was about the time print newspapers were scaling back, but they hadn't quite given up yet. So, what I discovered was a combination of articles reproduced from the print editions and some decidedly dated versions of the classifieds and other sections. I entered the date of Jenny Blake's disappearance and scrolled through the news for that and the following three days, leaning forward to see if I could spot even a tiny blurb.

It had been Thanksgiving weekend, so the feel-good stories all had to do with the traditions of getting together with friends and family, best turkey recipes, and the inevitable challenges of crowded airports and flight delays. The front page story in the Albuquerque *Journal* had been about a blizzard that roared through the state, and a resulting multi-car pileup on I-40 east of the mountains. I entered Jenny's name as a search term, went through the pages carefully, and still didn't find anything. Frustrated, but not surprised, I shut down the laptop. There was still the file folder Cassie had given me.

I stared around the quiet office and decided to close up early. No point in sitting here to read through a folder I could take home with me. I had no one here or at home to make plans with, and maybe a big plate of Pedro's chicken enchiladas would hit the spot. I locked the front door, set the answering machine, hustled Freckles back out to the car, and headed toward Old Town.

Two blocks off the plaza sits the best kept secret in the city, a tiny restaurant that seats about a dozen people. Pedro makes margaritas to die for and his wife Concha is known equally for her red or her green chile sauce. And they bend the rules a little about letting me bring the dog inside.

Freckles and I took our usual corner table. I declined the margarita in favor of iced tea, this being midday and me having a lot of reading to do this afternoon. Within minutes there was my plate of green chile chicken enchiladas and a basket of chips I could share with my pup.

"Drake is still away?" Concha asked when she emerged from the kitchen, dabbing rivulets of perspiration from her face. She sat with me a few minutes since no other customers were present, not even Manny, who is always a fixture on the last stool at the bar.

I nodded. "Busy fire season this year. I'm hoping the monsoons will start soon."

She glanced up at a wall calendar with the Virgin Mary on it. "Two, three weeks. By the end of the month, it will."

I smiled at her certainty, hoping she was right. I've been out with Drake on many of his helicopter jobs, but fires scare the poop out of me, I'll admit it. There's a low-grade tension running through me every hour of every week he's out there, and I'm always thankful to see the seasonal rains show up.

Concha patted my arm and stood up. "He'll be fine." And she disappeared back into the kitchen without another word.

I finished my lunch, chatted for a few minutes with Pedro as I paid my bill, and nodded hello to Manny who walked in as I headed out.

It wasn't really on my way home, but I detoured a couple miles out of the way to drive past the house on Sixth Street where Jenny Blake had been living with her baby daughter fifteen years ago. I had no idea what it looked like then; today it seemed an ordinary small house with white siding and a blue metal roof, neatly tended front yard behind a waist-high chain link fence. A driveway ran along the south edge of the property and an older Mustang sat there, probably in the very spot where Jenny had left her car parked on the day she vanished.

Random thoughts meandered into my head—what had happened to her car, her furniture, her personal belongings, when she never came home? Most likely the rent ran out and Linda had no choice but to pack up everything and take it to her place. I could make a list of items that might provide clues and ask Linda about them.

My big lunch was settling well and I felt a nap coming on as I steered into my driveway. A pearl white Lexus pulled to the curb in front of Elsa's about the time I reached my porch, and I paused to watch Elsa's friend Iris emerge from the driver's seat and circle to help Elsa out and see her to her own front door. I waved, glad to see my neighbor was home safely but not wanting to get involved in a conversation at the moment.

I allowed myself a twenty minute doze on the couch before getting back to my new case. Brewing a cup of cappuccino and icing it down to a good frigid temperature, I settled at the dining table with the police file, a yellow notepad, and my laptop.

I began to read, determined to start by making a list of every name I came across in the folder. The place to begin was at the beginning, with Linda's initial report to the police. Although I'd glanced through it quickly at the office, this time I made notes.

Chapter 4

Then

Detective Ernie DeAngelo watched the blonde woman sign her written statement. Another mother who couldn't believe her daughter would leave town without a word. He couldn't tell her how often he'd seen this. A baby at home, a twenty-one year old who could think of a lot more fun things to do with her Saturday nights than to change stinky diapers or wipe crusty oatmeal off the food tray, and she runs off with the first guy who shows an interest. But the guy doesn't want to be a daddy. And face it, the girl doesn't really want to be a mommy either, now that she's had a taste of it. And here was poor grandma, about to be stuck with all the chores her daughter didn't want to do. And she hoped the police could solve it all.

He glanced down at the name on the report form.

"Thanks, Ms. Arnold. As I mentioned, we can't officially start working the case until … Jenn …, um, Jennifer has been gone forty-eight hours."

The woman started to sputter a protest.

He held up a hand. "But—but that doesn't mean I can't start making a few calls. Did you list all her friends on that paper?"

"I think so," Linda Arnold said. "Jenny has a lot of friends. I tried to remember them all."

"See there? Most likely someone called her up and suggested they go out, and she'll be back home before you know it. It's probably someone you didn't think to call yet."

The look on Ms. Arnold's face told him she didn't believe a word he said. Frankly, he didn't believe it either, but it was the standard line, the thing they had to say until it became obvious that their victim was *not* coming right back home.

The good-looking woman in her late forties wanted to keep talking, he could tell, but they'd been through everything she could tell him about yesterday's events. Once they started to repeat themselves, it became pretty obvious that these types needed a friend to commiserate with, not a police officer. He gave her the department version of "don't call us, we'll call you" and began subtly walking her toward the door.

At the end of the hall, she stopped abruptly and he nearly bumped into her.

"I thought of one odd thing that I forgot to tell you," she said, turning to aim her vivid blue eyes at his face. "Gosh, I don't know why I didn't remember *this*."

He gave her a polite smile that he hoped didn't convey *get on with it*.

"There was a cigarette butt on the ground, right at the

base of the front steps. I just know it wasn't there the day before. It was bright white with a tan filter, not all dingy like it might have been there a while. Whoever came to the house and took Jenny away must have dropped it yesterday morning."

"A cigarette butt. Do you know how many people smoke? And most of them drop the butts before they enter a house, with smoking protocol being what it is nowadays."

She gave an impatient nod. "I know. Detective, please don't treat me like I'm stupid. I'm just telling you—no one in the family smokes. I can't think of a single friend of Jenny's who smokes. It was dropped by a stranger. And if you get over there and pick it up right away there could still be DNA or prints or … something … couldn't there?"

He conceded the point that there could be trace evidence on the discarded piece and he promised to go by the address she'd given. "Don't go over and pick it up yourself," he said. "People want to be helpful, but your touching it could change things."

She gave him another of those don't-call-me-stupid looks, turned on her heel, and left.

He sighed and walked to his desk in the squad room. Truthfully, the woman's story did intrigue him. It was just a touch off from the usual scenario, in which the young mother would drop her kid off at grandma's for the weekend and then pull a vanishing act. In those cases, they always packed their clothes and took whatever was important to them. Even a young woman who met up with a guy in a bar or somewhere, at least she had her purse with her.

Yeah, this case was different.

He ran a thumb across the folders in his Inbox on

the desk. His caseload was light right now, relatively, and Linda Arnold was right. The sooner he collected any trace evidence, the fresher it would be. Plus, he had to admit he was eager to take a look around inside the house. Ms. Arnold had given him a key and told him to check it out. Didn't seem as though she had anything to hide anyway.

He glanced at the clock. Nearly lunch time. Eh, why not? Grab a burger, drive by the house on Sixth Street, and scope it out.

Forty minutes later he wadded up his Lotaburger wrapper and tossed it into the back seat of the plain government-issue car before heading up Menaul. He found the house on the east side of the street, in a block of small homes where the majority were most likely rentals. Jennifer Blake's place seemed well-kept, with white siding and blue trim.

DeAngelo pulled to the curb and got out, scanning the neighborhood's activity. On a late-fall weekday, kids would be in school, parents at work. Other than a noisy car chugging down Fourth, a couple blocks away, it was so quiet he could hear the birds in the trees. He caught movement at the mini-blinds covering a window across the street and one house to the south. So there was a neighborhood busybody. Ernie had told his previous partner there was one on every block.

Once they officially opened the investigation he would get back here and ask some questions. For now, he casually strolled up the driveway that ran along the south side of the white and blue house and lifted the latch on the short chain link gate. A sidewalk led to a screened porch, and he immediately spotted the bright white of the cigarette Linda Arnold had told him about.

Dipping his hand into the left-hand pocket of his tweed jacket, he pulled out a zip-top plastic bag and a slender pair of tweezers. He purposely turned his back toward the house where someone was watching him, holding the specimen up for a look. No lipstick stain, no sign that the butt had been dropped and then stepped on. It was in pristine condition. He dropped it into the baggie, sealed it, and slid it into his pocket.

For show, he went through the motion of tapping on the screen door. It rattled loosely on its hinges. He opened it and stepped onto the screened porch, crossed to the front door into the house, and rang the bell. No response. No surprise. He tried the doorknob—you never knew—but it was firmly locked.

Well, Linda Arnold had given him a key and permission. Didn't need a warrant to follow up on that. He used the key and stepped directly into the living room. Hardwood floors, yellowish paint on the walls, thin flowered curtains over the front window, a narrow bay with barely a window seat. The furnishings were early-marriage, dorm-room, or rental—cheap stuff with plenty of wear. Brown sofa, wooden side chair, laminate coffee table and end table. The newest thing in the room was a playpen in bright colors for the baby. A set of hooks near the door held a couple of jackets and a purse hanging by its strap.

The mother had said her daughter left her purse behind. Once this became an official case and he had a warrant he'd go through it.

He could see a refrigerator through a doorway near the end of the couch, so he walked into the kitchen. Again, simple furnishings—a laminated table with three chairs. Why three? Who knew? Older, outdated appliances, the kind you didn't mind putting in a rental so they wouldn't get stolen or trashed. Linoleum flooring that must have been in place since 1960, but it seemed clean enough although worn thin in places. The countertops were clear, and the baby's highchair had been wiped clean of spills. Linda Arnold's handiwork? Maybe.

Beyond the kitchen was a small bedroom decked out with a crib, changing table, rocking chair, and pastel chest of drawers (filled with baby clothes, he discovered). A second door in the room led to a larger bedroom. A bathroom branched off it.

At a glance, nothing in the bedroom seemed out of place. The closet held jeans, shirts, sweaters, and a bulky winter coat. Purses lined the shelf above the rail, shoes were thrown a little haphazardly on the floor below. A large suitcase stood in one corner, surely the bag Jennifer Blake would have taken with her if she'd packed up with the plan of being gone a long time. He made a note to ask the mother if Jenny owned a smaller suitcase or two. She hadn't mentioned any.

A bureau in one corner held a stack of textbooks, basic accounting and a tome on the US tax code. A laptop computer case leaned against the chest.

The main bedroom had a second door that led back to the living room. Kind of a strange floorplan, he thought, but ideally suited to the single mom and her one child. He took his time and retraced his steps through the series of rooms, scanning the spaces carefully. No sign of violence or struggle. The whole place was tidy, if not spotless. Just the type of environment that fit with what Ms. Arnold had told him—Jenny lived a quiet life with her child, worked part time, and attended university classes. He would need time to search the computer, and that would cross the line where he needed to be officially working on the disappearance. And right now, it had been slightly more than twenty-four hours since Jenny went missing.

DeAngelo walked to what would be the center point of the house—the side of the living room near the playpen— and stood there quietly, getting the feel of the place. He swore sometimes he got—for lack of a better word—*vibes* about places. In a twenty-year career he'd learned to pay attention, so he stood there now, listening, faintly sniffing, feeling the air on his bare hands. Nope. Nothing came to him.

"Doesn't mean there was or there wasn't anything that happened here," he muttered to the empty room. The fact that his neck hairs didn't rise or his heart didn't beat faster didn't mean anything. Ernie DeAngelo had been a cop long enough to know he had to follow the evidence.

One cigarette butt. Some evidence.

Chapter 5

I yawned and stretched. Somehow the afternoon had disappeared as I read through page after page of the investigative notes. If only there had been some clue that jumped out at me—but no, there wasn't. I picked up the yellow sheet of paper from the police report, the one where Linda Arnold had written down names and phone numbers of all her daughter's friends. At least I had a photo, one of Jenny holding baby Cassie on her hip. Unfortunately, the shot was too far away to get clear details of Jenny's face. Linda hadn't wanted to part with any of the few studio portraits she had left.

Also in the folder were pages from a pocket-sized spiral notebook, the kind with a curly wire at the top. They were filled with bold, angular writing which I assumed belonged to Detective Ernie DeAngelo, based on the small set of initials EDA at the top of each page. I carried them to our home office and turned on the printer/copier. If something happened to remove the police file from my possession, I would at least have a good starting point toward following the same trail the cops had taken fifteen years ago.

Above the whir of the copier, a light tapping sound drifted into my consciousness. A familiar tap and I went to the back door, where Elsa stood with a plate of chocolate chip cookies.

"Dottie's not around, so I baked," she said with a hint of an evil grin. "I had a big lunch with Iris and I was in the mood for dessert."

I knew Dottie was trying to get Gram to cut back on her sugar intake, but habits of ninety-plus years are hard to break. Besides, what the heck—past a certain age, I think we should be allowed to do what we want. When you're in the final leg of the race, does it really matter that you extend it by a few extra months or years? Have fun, I say.

I chuckled along with her and invited her in. Cohorts in crime, we decided to put on a movie and treat ourselves to popcorn and cookies. I'd had a big lunch too, so this evening would be our trip into decadence. Freckles settled at our feet, alert to the fact that Elsa doesn't always notice when she drops popcorn kernels. We chose a chick flick and cozied into the corners of my living room sofa, but it turned out we had both seen the movie.

"Did I tell you Iris says she's been going out with a real hunk?" Gram said, out of the blue.

I muted the sound and just let the movie keep running. "What? No. When did she meet him?" I was having a hard time associating *hunk* with anyone in the geriatric set.

"At bingo, three weeks ago." She nodded and passed the popcorn bowl over to me. "I guess he was the youngest thing to walk in the place in ages. All the ladies were so jealous when he sat down next to Iris."

I laughed at the image. "The youngest thing … so he's what, sixty?"

"Ho-no, more like forty."

"Really …?" I must have been staring.

"Well, I don't know. I can't guess ages anymore. She says he's quite the hottie."

"Have you met him?"

"I was there, that day at bingo. Got a real good, long look. She's right. Total hottie. And they've been going out every night. Tonight, she says he's coming to her house for dinner and most likely staying over. She bought a sexy, lacy red thing to wear."

Ew. I didn't even want to imagine that. Iris, from what I could tell, was shaped about the same as most eighty-somethings. Red and lacy clothing somehow didn't fit the picture. But who was I to say? "Sounds like she's having a good time. Good for her."

"He's been dropping hints. She thinks he's going to propose."

My clutched popcorn went flying, but the dog took care of them. This bombshell went a lot further than Iris just having a good time. "Gram, she wouldn't actually marry someone that much younger, would she?" A niggle of worry went through me.

"She's pretty crazy about him."

"But marriage? Seriously?"

"She says he wants to take care of her in her old age. Not that she's there yet. Seventy-two isn't old at all."

Take care of her ... Was I being overdramatic by giving it a sinister meaning? I set down the popcorn bowl and turned on the couch to face Elsa squarely.

"Listen, Iris has money. One look at her car and her clothes, and I know she's not some helpless old lady living on the edge."

"Well, of course not. Harry made a killing in oil futures, way back when. The man was an investment wizard and he died leaving Iris set for life."

"Exactly." I looked into her eyes, but she didn't seem to be picking up my clues. "This new man—what was his name?—he could easily have noticed the wealthy widow who seemed a little lonely."

"Jeffrey something. But Iris? Lonely? Why, the woman has more friends than you can count. She's on the boards of a bunch of charities, and she gets invites to all the important fundraisers—including the governor's."

Yes. Every single one of them wanting her money. I took a deep breath and resisted the urge to lecture. Iris was a grown woman. Surely, she had close friends and relatives looking out for her interests. And at least Elsa wasn't in the same position. She owned her house and had a little something coming in from social security and Mr. Higgins' retirement, but nothing in the way of real wealth. And she certainly wasn't flashy about it, not in the way Iris seemed to be.

"Just tell her your nosey neighbor recommends that she have her attorney draw up a prenuptial agreement. Certainly, Iris has an attorney who knows her circumstances."

"That's a good idea. I'll tell her." She turned to face the TV screen again.

I had the distinct feeling she was humoring me, but

at least I'd done my bit by making a sensible suggestion. I unmuted the sound and we watched Kate Hudson's fictional love life unfold toward the inevitably mushy happy ending.

Headlights flared through a space between the front drapes and a couple minutes later there was a quick ding-dong at the front doorbell. I had a feeling I knew who it would be, even before I opened the door.

"I thought I'd find you here," Dottie said, smiling across the room at Elsa. "We 'bout ready to head for home and get ourselves tucked in?"

Elsa popped up from the sofa, spry as anyone half her age. I had to admire her spunky way of facing old age.

"I walked on over when I saw there wasn't lights on at the house," Dottie said. "But I got my little flashlight here to see us back across the lawn."

She took Elsa's elbow at the door, and I watched them negotiate the porch steps and move away. When I turned back, Freckles was eyeing the near-empty plate with the enticing bits of cookie crumbs.

"Uh-uh, you," I warned. "Not even crumbs of chocolate for you."

I picked up the plate, carried it to the kitchen, and handed the dog one of her own biscuits. On the dining table, my phone rang. Drake, checking in after his day's work. I told him briefly about the new case that had come into the office, but I could tell he was tired and not all that interested. After ten minutes of catching up, we wished each other a good sleep and ended the call.

I glanced at the police file and list of names and numbers I'd left scattered about earlier in the evening, thinking I could go back to them. But, frankly, no one would welcome a phone call this time of night from an investigator, and the day was catching up with me. I locked up and settled the dog for the night, resolving to read a novel for a while before falling asleep. I managed two pages before my eyes slammed shut.

Chapter 6

Canvassing a neighborhood is not a favorite thing to do but sitting on surveillance is worse, and I totally understand why my brother hates doing either. He's more of a computer research guy. Certain cop friends have actually admitted they like canvassing, questioning people about what they saw. They say a lot of interesting stories come out. I hoped that would be true this morning.

A car sat in the driveway at the little white house on Sixth Street, so I figured what the hey, I would stop in and see if they knew anything. A young woman answered, so young she might have been Jenny Blake fifteen years ago. I could hear a toddler jabbering in the background as we stood at the door, she just inside the screened porch, me on the bottom step outside.

Not surprisingly, the girl said she'd never heard of a

missing person who once lived in this house. She and her partner and their child had only lived here six months, and she'd heard from the landlord that the couple who was here before had occupied the house for three years. There seemed no one remotely tied to Jenny's case, but I asked for the name and number of the landlord on the off chance he might have owned the property that long ago.

I had no clue what information he would have, even if he did, but it was one loose thread I could tie up. I stepped out the short chain link gate and looked at the homes on either side. No vehicles at either one, but I took a chance and rang the bell at the place to the south. Two rings, no answer. Moving on, the next house down the street yielded the same. From the notes in the file, I recalled the detective had tried this same maneuver and hadn't much luck then either.

I crossed the street, studying address numbers. One of these places had produced someone who spoke to the cop back then, a woman named Mrs. Donna Chacon. The detective's notes had been basic and sparse, so I assumed he learned nothing here. But it was worth a shot. I saw a curtain move, oh so slightly, at a window one house to the south and across the street from Jenny's

If Donna Chacon was elderly then, she was nearly ancient now. She took a while in getting to the door with her metal walker, and the poor thing could barely raise her face to look at me, so bent was her spine. I gave my spiel about being a friend of the family who once lived across the street, the young woman who had gone missing some fifteen years ago.

She let me talk, without giving any indication of wanting to share information.

"Anyway, according to the investigation at the time, the police officer said he talked with you?"

"Fifteen years … How time gets away." She didn't seem inclined to invite me in, which was probably a smart thing on her part. When you can't move fast, it's not a good idea to let a stranger come too close.

"I'm trying to help the family, hoping to piece together what happened that day when Jenny Blake disappeared. Do you remember that day?"

Her head wagged back and forth slowly. "Not really. I remember the day the cop came by. He was kind of a cold one. Just questions, questions, real quick. Like that old TV show, *Dragnet*."

A memory sparked for me. My father used to watch that one.

"Do you recall what he asked and what you told him?"

She shifted her weight within the framework of the walker. "Not exactly. Something about a girl with a baby who lived over there." A gnarled finger pointed toward the Blake house. "Guess she left but didn't take the baby with her? He wondered if I'd seen anyone around the house two days earlier."

"Do you recall if you did? See anyone?"

"You know how hard it is to remember something from two days before?"

I smiled sympathetically but left the question open. This was the neighborhood busybody—then and now. She would have noted details, and a visit from the police would have cemented those memories. I pulled out the photo of Jenny and Cassie and held it up to the screen door.

She fidgeted a little more. "I do remember the girl—I guess she'd be called a young woman—and I remember the baby. When she moved in, there was a man. They made a cute couple, her with her belly out to here," she said, indicating a basketball-sized shape. "I suppose they were dirt poor; rented the house and the furniture, and everything they had fit into their two cars. Well, his was a small pickup truck. His gear was mostly guitars and amplifiers. She had a big blue suitcase and boxes that probably held dishes and such."

I nodded, hoping to keep her talking.

"That's about it. I remember the day she came home with the baby all wrapped in a pink blanket. A month or so later, he took off—the husband, boyfriend, whatever he was. Packed up the pickup truck with the musical gear and I never saw him again."

That fit with Linda's account.

"Oh, wait, maybe I saw him a time or two. Never did go inside for long. They'd have these discussions, him standing out on the steps there. I don't know if he was asking to come back home or wanted her to go with him … or maybe just bringing her a little money. She never looked very happy to see him."

"So, that day in November right before you talked to the cop. Did the man come around that day, the day they're saying she disappeared?"

"Sorry, I didn't see that."

Did my face register skepticism? It must have.

"That cop gave me the same look, ma'am. I'd caught the flu or a really bad cold. I remember not feeling like talking to him at all. So, my guess is that I was in bed that day, or indisposed. I didn't see the girl leave, didn't see the man come by, didn't see anyone around that day."

"Thanks, it helps. Could I ask one more thing? Do you

remember the last time you did see the ex-husband come around? Was it close to that time, or had it been a while—weeks or months?"

"Oh, at least a few weeks. I think. Well, I'm fairly sure but I could be mistaken. You know how it goes." She tapped the side of her head, making me think she was talking about her memory going. I couldn't be sure.

"And later? After the girl disappeared did the ex-husband ever come around again?"

She shook her head. "I guess the rent came due the end of the month, right after Thanksgiving, because the girl's parents came over in their minivan and packed up all the personal stuff and took it away."

"Did you speak with them at all?"

Another head shake. "Never met them, actually. I figured out the blonde woman was her mom because of all the times I saw her come by in the minivan. They always hugged, she brought gifts for the baby, stayed to babysit sometimes. That kind of thing."

Donna was becoming visibly tired, so I thanked her for her help and went on my way. Driving into the neighborhood, I'd noticed a small convenience store at the corner less than two blocks away. It was a mom-and-pop sort of place, the kind that looked like it even predated the intrusion of Circle K and 7-11 stores everywhere else in the city. The kind of place that most likely had been here a while and very likely under the same ownership. I hopped in my Jeep and drove to it.

Chapter 7

Then

"You heard the chief," DeAngelo told his new partner. "We're officially on the case."

Alan Curtis reminded him of a field mouse—pinpoint dark eyes that darted here and there as though unsure where his enemy might be lurking. Surely the guy wasn't truly a wimp—he'd never have made it through the police academy—but there was something timid about him. DeAngelo shook off the feeling.

Probably it was just the fact that this was Curtis's first day in the division. He most likely had heard of Ernie DeAngelo and his reputation for being tough to work with. DeAngelo knew about the talk. Yeah, he asked a lot of his partners, expected them to be as sharp as he'd become after more than twenty years of chasing down bad guys. He needed another ten on the force, but he made no secret that he didn't plan to spend it behind a desk. He'd tolerated the mandatory years on patrol, thrived in Major Crimes, and now saw Missing Persons as his way to shine and to end his career with a commendation or two.

He just wasn't sure this no-leads case of the young mother who'd vanished was going to cut it. Seemed almost obvious that Jenny Blake's ex must have come back and convinced her a place in the glamorous lifestyle of a musician trumped being home with a squalling baby.

DeAngelo gathered his notes and turned to his new partner. "Let's go."

Curtis almost flinched at the sharp tone. But he buttoned his overcoat and scooted in behind the senior man, following him out to the gray government car in the parking garage. Unlike a lot of the detectives, who liked having the junior officer chauffeur them around, DeAngelo took the wheel.

"I've put in for a search warrant for the missing woman's home," he said as he pulled out of the parking lot and made the turn onto Roma and then the quick turn to Sixth. "I went in yesterday with permission from the girl's mother, but to take away evidence, I want the warrant in place. Meanwhile, there are some potential witnesses we can talk to."

Curtis looked like he was about to pull out his notebook and write all this down. He switched the motion to a nod when he caught DeAngelo's sharp glance. "Right."

"You do much canvassing in the past?"

"Not really. I only did six months on patrol and it was pretty routine. Traffic stops, the occasional domestic dispute. You know." The younger man tried hard to appear nonchalant. "I was just lucky to get this assignment so quickly, especially to work with you. I know I'll learn a lot."

Suck-up. "Yeah, you will." DeAngelo slowed when they reached the block on Sixth Street he was looking for.

"I read the mom's statement. Sounds like she's going on mother's intuition and one cigarette butt as her basis for believing her daughter didn't just walk out willingly?"

"Pretty much. You heard the mumbling around the squad room after the briefing, right? But something doesn't feel right about her walking out with the ex. That kind of scenario, a woman would at least take her purse, some clothes, her computer. Doesn't make sense to me. Unless he, or somebody, came to the door, grabbed her by the arm, dragged her away."

Curtis nodded. "But no witnesses to her leaving the house?"

"Not yet." Emphasis fell on the word *yet*. "We'll take the neighborhood, house by house. Anybody that's not home this time of day, we'll come back around dinnertime. But best to start with roughly the same time the victim disappeared, which was nine in the morning. Usually, it's the same people home every day at the same time. Routines. People stick with 'em."

He pulled to the curb across from a tan stucco house with mini blinds over the front windows. "Someone was here yesterday—didn't answer the door. I didn't push it since the case wasn't officially underway. Today, we'll get her attention."

"Her?"

"I saw the blinds move when I walked up to the door there at 1604." He aimed a thumb at the white and blue house across the street. "It was a quick glimpse, but I definitely saw a female hand with nail polish and a ring with some sparkle to it. The more you do this, the more you'll realize every neighborhood has a busybody, that little old lady or man who has nothing else to do all day but look at what's going on. You watch—she'll brag about how observant she is, how she notices little details."

"Sounds like she's the one we want."

"She might be. You gotta watch out for the ones who want to embellish, make themselves star of the show, add things to their story to make it sound better."

Curtis nodded thoughtfully as they got out of the car.

DeAngelo strode across the quiet residential street and up the short sidewalk at 1607. He gave the doorbell two quick jabs and stepped slightly back to watch the front windows. No movement, no sound. He repeated his moves with the same result.

"Was there a car here yesterday?" Curtis asked.

DeAngelo shook his head. "Most likely in the garage."

For good measure, in case the doorbell wasn't functional, he gave a good, firm knock on the wooden screen door frame. Still nothing.

"Okay, we'll come back."

The two men walked down the steps and stood at the sidewalk. "All right, it's door to door now."

"Let the fun begin, right?" Curtis joked.

"It may not be fun, but it's going to become one of the most important parts of your job." Rookie.

At the chastisement, the meek mouse was back. "Yes, sir."

DeAngelo ignored him and started toward the next house to the north. For the next forty-five minutes they rang doorbells and waited on porches, with little success. Two residents answered. One was a teen who claimed to be home sick with a cold and said his mother wouldn't like him talking to anyone. Rap music thumped heavily from somewhere inside the house. All the cops could ask him was whether he'd been home the day before yesterday— the answer was no.

The second person they spoke to lived three houses away from 1604, an elderly lady with such bad hearing she asked them to repeat every question at least twice. She seemed completely at a loss when DeAngelo showed her a photo of Jenny Blake and explained that the young woman had gone missing from a house down the block. She merely shook her fluffy white head and started to close her door.

Even the veteran detective began to show some impatience. "Okay, look," he said as they entered their car to get out of the chilly wind that had come up. "I thought of one more place. It's not far, but I'm not up for walking it." He started the Taurus and drove to the next corner, making a left turn.

"If I remember from the days when my own kids were little, the wife used to like to get them out of the house now and then. We had a convenience store in our neighborhood, a little fancier than this one, and she'd take the stroller out and go buy some little thing, just to keep life interesting."

"And maybe Jenny Blake did the same with her baby? Good thinking."

They parked in front of the wide glass windows, noting two other cars in the lot. A young man in a tightly fitted T-shirt, leather jacket and jeans was paying for a tin of tobacco when they walked in, and he brushed past them without a second glance.

The man behind the counter was fifty-ish, with a tired

expression. He glanced up when they entered but sent his attention back to a clipboard with some kind of list on it until they approached and DeAngelo cleared his throat and showed his badge.

"Just a couple questions," he began, pulling the photo of Jenny from his inner jacket pocket. "Is she a customer?"

"Yeah, she comes in."

"Driving or walking?"

"Some of each. Drives a blue Celica, I think. But more often, when the weather's nice she's walking. Has a cute little baby."

"Has she been in here since Monday?"

The man's eyes went upward as he calculated that today was Wednesday. He let out a *puh* on a breath of air. "You know how many people come in here on any given day?"

Both cops waited patiently.

"Look, it's dozens, a lot of them regulars. Did any certain one of them come in Monday? Saturday? Yesterday? Hell, I don't remember. I can come closer to telling you what they bought. This one—" a nod at the photo "—she likes her candy bars. Always a Milky Way Dark. And a fruit rollup for the baby. Otherwise, she looks like any other college kid or young mom."

DeAngelo nodded slowly, as if he was giving some thought to his next question. "Was she ever with another adult, maybe a man?"

The store owner shook his head. "Not that I recall. She's probably been coming in here a year or so. I don't remember anybody other than the baby."

They jotted down his name for the record, left a business card with instructions that he call if he thought of anything more, thanked him for his time, and walked back out to the car after purchasing two coffees.

"He talked about Jenny Blake in the present tense," Curtis commented. "I suppose that's a good thing."

DeAngelo nodded. "At this point, we can't really make judgments about whether something is good or bad, just gathering facts. But that's a good observation on your part."

Curtis looked like he'd take any praise he could get right now. They sat in the Taurus, sipping their coffee, until DeAngelo's phone interrupted with an incoming text message. He set his cup in the drink holder, pulled out the phone and looked at the screen.

"Looks like the judge came through with our warrant. Let's go pick it up."

Forty minutes later they were back on Sixth Street, ready to go through all of Jenny Blake's possessions to see if they could find anything to explain her eerie disappearance. The warrant limited them to evidence that might point to an abduction—signs of violence—or to connections that would show she willingly went away with another person or persons unknown at this time.

Using the same key he'd used yesterday, DeAngelo unlocked the front door and they went inside. Curtis carried an empty cardboard box for whatever evidence they collected.

"Start with the purse and these jackets near the front door," he told Curtis as they both pulled on latex gloves. "Go through the pockets and pull out anything resembling a note or anything informative. Bag it all. Same with the clothes in the closet. I saw a computer case in the bedroom. I'm going to check that out."

Chapter 8

Now

The convenience store in Jenny's old neighborhood had definitely seen better days. Surely no one builds a business with the intent of showing off the peeling paint, faded sign, and piles of last autumn's leaves rotting in the back of the parking lot. But when I walked in, I was impressed to see bright new merchandise and clean floors. I didn't plan on giving it the real test, finding out what kind of shape the bathrooms were in.

I whiled away a couple of minutes, looking over the candy bars, until the only other customer in the place had gone. Then I approached the older man behind the counter. He looked to be in his late sixties, with a tired face that went along with the overall tiredness of the whole establishment.

"Hi. Are you Joe O'Connell?"

His eyes narrowed, obviously wondering whether I might be with the IRS or some branch of the law. Or maybe he was generally suspicious of anyone who walked in and called him by name. I introduced myself and handed him one of my business cards.

"Investigator. Huh."

"We're looking into the disappearance of a young woman from this neighborhood ab—"

"Haven't heard anything about that."

"About fifteen years ago. I believe the police canvassed the neighborhood and talked with you at the time?"

"Maybe." The non-helpful attitude was beginning to wear on me.

"They did. I've got a copy of the entire police file. Your name was noted."

Silence.

"Look, I'm just hoping you might have remembered something in the meantime. Maybe the young woman returned, maybe someone else came in asking about her?" I pulled out the photo of Jenny and the baby. "Could you take a look?"

"This girl and the baby? I recollect that someone was asking about somebody like that. Been a lot of years though."

"But you do remember her, as a customer?"

A slight tilt of one shoulder.

"Aside from the police, did anyone else come by and ask questions? She was recently divorced from the baby's father, and he might have been concerned."

And hell might have frozen over. According to Linda Arnold, Ricky Blake had cared precious little about doing right by his child. She said he'd never paid a dime in child support. But it was worth asking here.

"Afraid not. Or I don't remember. I've been parked in this store going on forty years now. My dad left me a little money and I used it to build the business. Little did I guess it would turn into a life sentence. Can't sell the place, can't abandon it, can't do anything but work, work, work."

I tried for a sympathetic expression on my face. I did fully understand how owning one's own business was far different from having a job you could walk away from. But I had to think that, sometime over the years, he might have had an offer or some other options.

"Day in, day out. People rush in, buy a pack of gum or a soda, dash back out. I'm the furniture—they don't see me. Didn't used to be that way in my dad's time. He was the friendly type who visited a little with every shop clerk he encountered."

"Times really have changed, haven't they?" I didn't personally remember a whole lot chattier time in our history, but Elsa talked about it some. My vaguely sympathetic comment warmed his demeanor several notches.

"The one thing I'm thankful for—well, two really— I've never been robbed. This is still a neighborhood of pretty decent people."

A questioning look must have crossed my face.

"Oh, the second thing is that this fall I can start collecting my social security. I'm putting the building up for sale and don't care if anybody wants to run a store here or not. My wife wants us to go live with the kids in Phoenix, and I'm gonna do it."

I gave him a smile and let him talk another few minutes about his plans. I picked up a few little items—hand sanitizer, a lip balm, and a splurgy-feeling pastry wrapped in cellophane and filled with useless calories. He brightened a little further.

"I don't suppose you remember the last time you saw this woman, Jenny, come in here?" I asked as I pulled out some cash.

He shook his head sadly. "People come and go around here. So many of the houses are rentals now, and no one stays long. I have my regulars, but never seem to notice until way later when somebody hasn't shown up for a while. Sorry."

"I can imagine. Well, thanks anyway."

I put my purchases into my purse, except for the pastry, which was likely to be gone before I got home. Out in my Jeep, I started to peel back the wrapper on it, getting a heady whiff of cherries and sugar, when my phone rang. I fumbled for a tissue to get the sticky stuff off my fingers, and tapped the screen.

"Hi, Charlie," said Elsa. "Is it okay that I'm calling on your cell phone?"

She was still under the impression that all cell phones charged by the minute and it was a luxury to use them. Luckily, I had gotten past that.

"Absolutely fine—what's up?"

"Iris just came by and she's so excited. Jeffrey proposed and they're having the wedding right away. She brought me an invitation she printed off the computers at Kinko's."

"Wow, that seems quick."

"It's this weekend at a park somewhere in the northeast heights. I told her I didn't know where that was, but she says I should bring a plus-one, someone who can drive me there. So, will you be my plus-one?"

I started my Jeep to get the AC running. My pastry was

beginning to feel a little squishy in the heat. It also gave me a few seconds to think about Elsa's request. Well, how could I turn her down?

"Sure, I'll take you. Give me the details when I get home and we'll make it a date."

Four days to put together a wedding … interesting, I thought as I ended the call with Gram and took a big bite of my pastry. In a lot of ways it made more sense to me than what so many brides did, sending out save-the-date cards a year in advance and spending the price of a luxury car just to have a 'do' with all the expensive trimmings. Save the money and all the big fuss, and get into your new life right away.

Still, a little frisson of worry nagged at me when I thought of Iris. I hoped Elsa's friend wasn't making a colossal mistake. I wondered if there was anything I could do for her, but put that aside. One, she's a mature woman who can make her own choices. Two, I don't know her well enough for this to be any of my business. Three, my life is pretty darn full already. I'd go to the ceremony with Elsa and keep my eyes open. That's about all I could offer.

Reminding myself that I was on the clock with Cassie Blake's retainer money, I decided I'd better get myself back to my computer. I might accomplish more with some online searches than by trekking around out here, trying to get information from people who couldn't care less. Putting the Jeep in gear, I headed west on Lomas toward my own neighborhood.

Stepping out onto my driveway, the heat hit me again. I scanned the sky but there was nary a cloud in sight. Concha had promised rain would come, in two or three weeks, she'd said. Our lawns were drinking gallons of water every morning, and the leaves on our trees were looking a bit limp—I hoped the weather would shift sooner than that.

Inside, Freckles lay in her crate, seemingly in no great rush to exercise. She rolled to her back, presenting her belly to me, as I crossed the room and opened the little door for her. Only after I reached in and tickled her tummy did she get to her feet and come out, giving a long leisurely stretch on the way.

It was nearly noon, but since I'd effectively spoiled my appetite for lunch with that cherry pastry, I decided I could wait for food and make better use of the time with my computer. I washed the residue of icing off my fingers and picked up my laptop, carrying it to a cozy corner of the sofa.

Maybe rather than trying to piece together the events of the day Jenny Blake disappeared, based on old, and probably faulty, memories of people who didn't especially know or care about her, I needed to look at this in a different way. Cassie and Linda seemed convinced that Jenny was alive and well somewhere. The police had been convinced she had taken off with her shiftless ex. What if both those ideas were true?

If Jenny was still in love with the high school sweetheart, and knowing her mother would take good care of her daughter, maybe the young couple really had simply hit the road together and not given Albuquerque and their life here another thought. And if that were the case, where would they be now, and how would I go about finding them?

I drummed my fingertips lightly on the keyboard while the computer booted up. Linda said Ricky Blake was a musician, so that might be a good start. Ron tells me all the time, if you want to find a person who's skipped, look toward his hobbies. People can change their names, change their looks, but they rarely change their interests. He'd often served papers for the courts, most of the time finding the subject at their favorite bar, the casino, the car races, even the library.

So, I went right into a search for "Ricky Blake musician." The little searcher thingy whirled around for a few seconds, and gave back about a million hits, but at least among the top searches I didn't see anything promising for the particular Ricky I was looking for. Maybe his name was Richard and he was using that. Good try, but I got the same results. And spent two hours of my time reading through non-related results.

"All right, what about Jenny?" I muttered to Freckles, lying at my feet. I had no idea whether our missing woman had gone ahead with her studies, begun a career, or if she really was trailing Ricky along whatever path he'd now taken. She could be remarried to someone else and have an entirely different surname—but I wasn't going that route.

I went to Facebook first. Everybody in the world wanted to share the details of their lives—why not her? I came up with more than a hundred Jennifer Blakes. Ugh. I began going through them. Jenny would be thirty-seven years old now and, yes, people do fudge their ages, so I glanced through the given birthdates of each prospect. Most got weeded out right away, and I clicked the profiles of those who didn't list a birthdate, trying to guess by their photos whether I might be on track. That took out about half the remaining prospects, being too young or too old to fit our Jenny. Hair color was another clue, but women these days were not like those of two generations ago—we can change our hair color on a whim, and many do. And most of the profile pics were not taken close enough or clearly enough to match with my file photo of Jenny. Not to mention those smarty-pants types who posted pictures of their cat or their grandchild or a cartoon avatar to represent themselves.

This was turning into a dead end, but I went through a similar exercise on Instagram until it was starting to get dark outside. Holy cow, it was after eight p.m. and I was getting a low-battery warning for the laptop. How had Freckles not pestered me for her dinner? Maybe she had. I sometimes have a way of moving through routine duties in a blur.

I got up to plug the computer into its power cord, groaning at the crick in my neck and stiffness of my legs. Sheesh. As I walked into my home office I had the thought, what would Ron do? He tracks down info on people all the time. And the answer came to me.

We subscribe to some super sophisticated professional databases that give out a whole lot more information than social media. I needed to go to the office, get his login data and try that. Gigantic head-slap.

Chapter 9

DeAngelo carried the laptop computer case to the kitchen table in the Sixth Street house, pushing aside a napkin holder, a set of salt and pepper shakers, and a child's plastic sippy cup to make room for the power cord to drape behind and plug into a wall outlet. As the older machine booted up, he hoped it wouldn't ask for a password—that would require taking it to the lab guys and probably having his case slotted in line behind a few dozen others. This would be so much easier if he could just take a peek now. When someone goes missing, there often is no time to wait for due process when their life could be on the line.

A colorful screen came up, a scene in a forest somewhere, most likely a stock photo that came with the computer itself. He waited a moment, but no little box asked for a password. He tapped the touchpad and up came icons for all her programs. Good. It looked like standard stuff—word processing, spreadsheet, email, internet browser—and one linked to UNM studies. The mother had said she was taking courses.

Curtis walked into the kitchen and set his cardboard box on the table.

"Done already?" DeAngelo asked.

"Got the purse, phone, and a few things. This thing is getting bulky to lug around. I'm going to check pockets and items in the closet now."

"I'll be a few more minutes here," said the senior man. "Go ahead, sit down and go through the purse and phone first. Those are the most likely places to find anything of value."

"Sure." Curtis did as instructed, setting the box on the floor, taking a chair and pulling out Jenny Blake's phone. It took no more than five seconds for him to announce, "It needs a passcode." Next came the purse. He dumped the contents on the table and ended up chasing down a tube of lip gloss that threatened to roll away.

"Be sure to list everything," DeAngelo reminded.

Curtis pulled out his own small notebook and a pen. "Lip stuff—whatever you call this, two pens, hairbrush …"

"That may have DNA—bag it separately." What DeAngelo didn't say was that if a body was found that was beyond visual identification, a few stray hairs might be the thing that identified their victim.

"Right." Curtis was, at least, good at following directions without argument.

DeAngelo turned his attention back to the laptop. Most

valuable, for his purposes, was likely the email. He tapped that one and got stopped by the damn password box. Okay, he could make some guesses but would probably end up locked out. Better to take it to a guy he knew. Later.

"What do you think about this?" Curtis interrupted, holding up a four-inch-square plastic container that showed bands of colored makeup inside. Eyeshadow.

"Bag that too. Smooth plastic, good fingerprints." He looked over at the collection of junk all women seemed to carry. In this case, there was also a pacifier for the baby, a little packet of wet towelettes, and a tiny box of raisins. "Just put it all into a bigger evidence bag together. Lab will go over everything. What about the wallet?"

Curtis unsnapped a fold-over flap. "Driver's license. Details match what we've been told. A debit card, one credit card, a little packet thingy of photos." He spent a moment flipping through them. "One of her with a guy—maybe the ex—and a bunch of the kid."

"Okay, bag all that. As long as there isn't an appointment card for something in the last day or two, we'll have time to go through it all later. Might as well get back to the closet and dresser drawers. Pull out anything written—receipts, notes, appointments. Well, you know the drill, right? Then we gotta check out the car."

"Yep." Curtis carefully placed the various evidence bags back into the box at his feet, then left the room.

DeAngelo stared back at the computer screen, tapped the word processor icon, and got a list of Blake's most recent documents. Most looked like school reports but the name of one stopped him in his tracks: **Me – deceased**. *What on earth?*

He opened the document, which turned out to be less

than a page long.

Jennifer Blake died of unknown causes on Monday the 24th. She was known, during her short lifetime, for being a loving daughter to Linda and Steven Arnold, devoted wife of Ricky Blake, and an awesome mom to Cassandra Blake. When asked about her dreams for her future, she had once stated that she wanted to become either a dancer on Broadway, the lead singer with a band like Gloria Estevan had done, or an astronaut. She had not yet followed through on those plans, but a girl can dream, can't she? Mainly, Jenny wanted to be remembered as the girl who loved her friends and never said no to adventure, even if it was risky.

DeAngelo sat back in the cheap wooden kitchen chair and stared at the screen. What, exactly, was he seeing here?

Chapter 10

Ricky parked on a side street, two blocks down from Jenny's place, and walked over, keeping to the alley wherever possible, looking over his shoulder the whole way. The last thing he wanted to do was put his baby daughter in danger, but he needed to see her. Getting past Jenny-the-gatekeeper was the thing, and that was his story. He didn't think his ex had yet discovered the loose boards in the bedroom floor.

Three times he'd been to the door and asked, three times she turned him away. No child support money, no visits she said. What the hell? A guy had to pay money to see his own kid? Apparently, the court saw it that way too, said Jenny, threatening him with some piece of paper she waved around in his face.

She'd taken away his key to the house when they split. "On the advice of my attorney," she told him at the time. That gray-haired bitch with the frown like iron could go straight to hell, he decided. What if he still had some of his stuff in there? But she was pretty sure he didn't. He'd packed everything valuable—his music gear—and somehow that counted as burning all his bridges. First time he came back, seven months later, Jenny had kicked a weather-beaten cardboard box out the door, onto the porch and told him that was the last of his stuff. She didn't want him leaving socks and underwear in the drawers, thinking he could come back any old time. He left. He'd better take all his crap with him. She had moved on, she said.

He had staked out the house for two weeks, knowing he would see some guy. Jenny wouldn't just *move on* alone. There had to be a guy. But he never saw one. Just Jenny and Cassie, coming and going. Her mother stopping by way too often. The woman hadn't liked him from day one.

The first time he picked up Jenny for a date, their junior year in high school, Linda Arnold had given him the stink-eye. She frowned her way through their wedding, and he never saw a woman less happy about the news she was becoming a grandmother. The old bat wanted Ricky out of the way and Jenny married to somebody *acceptable* before she had any kids.

He ducked into the unfenced back yard of the house next to 1604, standing with his back pressed to the trunk of an old elm, scanning the area for movement. Nothing. The breeze chilled the light sweat that he only now realized had broken out on his forehead. He waited a full two minutes, watchful, then edged along the side of the white house.

Her car sat in the driveway, which could be good news.

At least it wasn't Linda Arnold's. Since he'd been back in town—a week now—Jenny went somewhere nearly every day, probably work, and Linda most likely was Cassie's babysitter. Most of the times he'd done a casual drive-by during the day, it was her car parked out front and Jenny's was gone.

He'd already planned his approach. This time he had cash in his pocket and he would pull it out and show her before she had a chance to say anything about his lousy record for paying child support. Hey, the music business wasn't like others. Gigs came along whenever, wherever. When he could get with a band and they got work, he was real flush. Other times, not so much. She had to understand this wasn't like some crappy office job where the employer took money out of your check and sent it to the ex. But he would tell her that what he had with him today should at least buy him a few visits.

He wondered if the baby would remember him, and a small stab of guilt went deep. Even when he'd lived here, he'd almost never been home. Nights out, connecting with the right bands, connecting … in other ways. And Cassie had only been a month old when he got word that he could be working in Branson. Not long after, Jenny pulled that *abandonment* shit and got some jerkoff to serve him papers. What was he supposed to do?

He started to round the corner of the house when he heard voices. Male voices. Nearby. Uh-oh. He risked a peek and saw a man in dark pants, white shirt, tie, and trench coat leaning on the open door of Jenny's blue Celica. He was facing the house and another male voice was talking to him. Everything about the guy screamed *cop*.

Well, hell. He should have just broken into the damn

house when he had the chance. He'd blown it now. Ricky turned around toward the alley and ran.

Chapter 11

Now

There was no way I would sleep. I figured this out after two hours of tossing and turning. Once the idea of getting into Ron's databases online had got into my head, my mind wouldn't stop whirling over the possibilities. I put on some jeans, woke my sleepy puppy-dog and we headed for the office.

The Victorian sat quietly, lit by a couple of nighttime lamps we keep on timers, while the rest of our half-residential, half-commercial neighborhood slept. I steered down the driveway beside the building to the parking area behind, and went in through the kitchen door. A cup of tea sounded good, so I nuked a cup of water and dunked a teabag while I tried to remember the name of the database Ron preferred for searches.

Upstairs, I sat in his chair and turned on his computer. He's got a strange system of filing names, numbers, and other pertinent information. I pulled the old-school Rolodex toward me and began flipping through the cards. If I'd hoped there was something under C for computer passwords, I'd have been in for a letdown—luckily, I already knew a little something about Ron's filing system. Nothing under S for searches. Nothing under M for missing persons, ways to locate. Finally, under L (lost people) I came across NexFind. The name rang a bell—this was it.

At least he had listed his user name and password on the card. Now that the computer was booted and ready, I entered the required fields and was all set to go. I explored around the features of the program for a few minutes, getting a feel for what to query in order to get what I wanted out of it.

I started with Jenny—well, Jennifer Blake. From the police report I got her date of birth. The biggest stumbling block was that I had no social security number for her. I would need to ask Linda, and could only hope that she had it written down somewhere. How many people would know, offhand, the numbers for their kids or spouses? And a phone call at nearly one o'clock in the morning wasn't likely to be well received.

So, okay. I entered what little I knew. Work history: an office position with a plumbing and heating contractor was the only scrap of information I had; Schooling: I listed UNM, accounting major, and guessed at the years of enrollment (hoping that was correct—I could also ask Linda what high school Jenny had attended); Medical history: I only knew she'd given birth to a baby; Credit history, mortgages: I had no clue, but it didn't seem like there would be much in that area.

Face it, I think I pretty much sucked at this investigative stuff. Seeing how many blanks were left empty on the form gave me a whole new appreciation for how my brother manages to ask all the right questions and come up with detailed reports. And he does this all the time. Too bad I didn't have him here right now. I gave a shrug and clicked on the Generate Report button.

Amazingly, given the tiny amount of information I had, up came two names on the screen. One of the Jennifer Blakes was flagged with a red asterisk and a note that the age of the person was not an exact match. But the second one was good and, it appeared, was our Jenny Blake. I clicked the button asking the program to email the full report.

That opened up a whole new scramble, as everything in NexFind was tied to Ron's name and account info and the email would be coming to him. Luckily, the one thing in his darn Rolodex that was in a logical place was Email Password. I found it, signed in and there was my brand-new NexFind report. It seemed like a good idea to print it out, to have something I could show Linda and Cassie if need be, so I turned on the printer and did that.

Unfortunately, the report was every bit as skimpy as the data I had given it. The good news (or bad, depending on your viewpoint) was that a person's history seems to be on some computer somewhere for a very long time.

Jennifer Blake had co-signed the rental agreement, along with her husband Rick, for the house on Sixth Street. She'd had a Visa card issued to her but the account showed as expired and unused after the month in which she disappeared. The credit section of the report showed no other cards issued to her, no loans in her name. Her student record at UNM showed an Incomplete for the last semester she was there, and there didn't seem to be any record of her re-enrolling or of a transfer to another school.

The heading on the third page was Work History— ah, something I could follow up on. But after her brief stint as office staff at ABC Mechanical, there had been no other wages reported for her. This was not good news. No matter where a person lives, if they are working anywhere, their employers will be reporting their taxable income and paying into social security on their behalf. For Jenny to be this completely off the grid did not look promising. I felt a huge letdown when I thought of passing this information along to Cassie and her grandmother. Their beloved Jenny might have been deceased all this time.

I paced the floor between Ron's office and mine, debating alternatives.

Okay, what if Jenny really had run off with Ricky? Maybe they survived on what he made as a gig musician, earning cash paid under the table, nothing regular, on the move too much for her to get and hold a steady job of her own? Yes, I was grasping at threads, but I wanted some ray of hope I might present to my clients.

I slugged down the last of my tea, now gone cold, and went back to Ron's desk. The skimpy information from the old rental agreement contained the only scraps of data I had on Ricky Blake. I started a new search and entered his details.

His report came through with the following tidbits: He had worked sporadically, not enough to support himself, really, but his scanty work history was at least there. He'd once joined the musician's union in Arizona (note to self: check further on this), but the membership had lapsed after six months and was never renewed.

Ricky had been in rehab twice; sent there the first time after an arrest for dealing less than an ounce of cocaine. Interesting, but probably not surprising, given that a lot of people in various types of show-biz found themselves on that path. His first stint shortly after the couple split; the second time was six months after that. I compared the dates of his treatment with the dates on his work history. This seemed to be the point at which Ricky Blake had dropped off the radar.

So, had he simply quit working after his second release from rehab? Had he gone over completely to the underground cash economy, working only for those who wouldn't report it? Or had he, too, disappeared, like Jenny?

Daylight began to show through the windows, and I realized I'd been at the research more than four hours. As all the questions about Ricky and Jenny Blake began to blur my thinking, I realized I was tired. I shut down Ron's computer and went into my own office, where I curled up on my small sofa and promptly fell asleep.

Chapter 12

Curtis carried the box filled with Jenny Blake's possessions into the squad room, while DeAngelo went in search of the young whiz-kid he knew in computer forensics. Affectionately dubbed Tarantula by the detective squad, because of his unruly black furry hair and because of the way his fingers flew over computer keys like spider legs, the twenty-four year old followed the senior detective to his desk.

"We have to keep the chain of evidence, here," DeAngelo told him.

"Right." Tarantula kept the impatience out of his tone, barely.

DeAngelo picked up Jenny's cell phone and laptop, inside their labelled plastic bags, and had the computer guy initial the labels and sign the log sheet.

"Get me into these," he said. "I—uh, *we*—need to check the victim's emails and phone calls."

"Got it. You want me to …" the young guy indicated DeAngelo's desk chair.

"You can take 'em to the lab. Just give me a call when you've figured out the passwords and I'll take it from there."

"Right." Tarantula headed out of the room.

"Meanwhile," DeAngelo said to his partner. "Run a DMV check on the girl's license. See if there've been any traffic stops where she claimed not to have it with her. And run a check on her credit card and bank account. Any activity, find out where, when, and what she bought."

Curtis picked up the bag containing all of Jenny's identification and headed toward his own desk.

DeAngelo lowered himself onto his chair, feeling aches in his back and legs he sure didn't remember from a few years ago. Maybe a cup of coffee would perk him up. But before he'd even reached for his mug, his desk phone rang.

"Got you the passwords," came the young tech's voice over the line.

"Both?" He heard the skepticism in his own voice and added a "damn, you're good."

"Wanna come down here, or shall I bring the laptop and phone back to you?"

"If you don't mind …"

"Be right there."

His old mug was looking a little battered and stained these days, but DeAngelo picked it up and filled it from the carafe at the far end of the room. He'd barely made it back to his desk when Tarantula came in with his prizes.

"All set, boss. I unlocked both devices so you don't need a password to get into them now."

"Thanks. Appreciate that." See? He *was* getting better about offering praise, not being the complete curmudgeon people thought he was.

He'd heard the remarks when his back was turned. Oh well. It probably was about time to retire. Meanwhile, he'd see if there really was anything to this mother's claim that her daughter had vanished into thin air.

He started with the cell phone. Kids these days used their phones more than computers, or so he'd been told. It took him a couple of long minutes to figure out the little pictures on the screen and which ones to touch. Luckily, Tarantula had left the squad room, showing off that springy young step of his, and Curtis was on the telephone, apparently talking to someone at the credit card company.

DeAngelo fumbled his way into Jenny's phone contact list and scrolled through, looking at the names. M&D he assumed were mom and dad. Under Blake there were no names. Either Jenny wasn't close with her ex's family members, or he had none. Maybe the kid had been a loner and Jenny latched onto him from some sense of filling the gaps in his life. Women and their motives in relationships were way beyond him. He gave a quick shake of his head— no point in going that route.

Most of her contacts were simply first names, and mostly female. He would need to compare the names with those on the list the mother had given, see who she'd deemed important to contact. Later. Right now, this was recon.

He looked at Jenny's list of recent calls. Three numbers came up repeatedly. M&D, Laura, and an unknown caller. He went to the details. Long calls to mom—not surprising. The two seemed very close. One- to two-minute calls to

Laura, the friend Linda Arnold had told him was a girl in Jenny's classes at school. They sometimes carpooled. So the short calls made sense.

The unknown caller was the intriguing one. They were all from the same number. He would have Curtis check that out, see which company provided the service and whether they could determine the owner of the phone. The interesting thing was that, while she ignored ninety-percent of the calls, she actually had answered a few of them. She knew this person.

DeAngelo jotted the number on a sticky note and leaned across the desk to hand it to his partner. "When you're done with those other calls," he said.

He switched back to the main screen on the girl's phone and studied it. One of the icons was obviously for email, but he had little experience with the program and didn't know how to look at the history of messages, so he opted for the laptop. Opening the lid, he saw that what Tarantula had told him was true. He was able to immediately get into the email program without a password.

The Inbox showed seventy-six new unread messages. His eyes widened. The girl had been gone, what, a little over sixty hours now. He began the tedious task of reading through them. Within ten minutes, he began to realize Jenny Blake must have subscribed to every free offer and win-this-thing promotion she came across. At least ninety-percent of the messages came from someone offering her a free download, complimentary consultation, or some kind of goodie. He started to recognize the marketing-speak and skimmed past those.

Several appeared to be from professors at the university. Who knew consultations were scheduled and assignments handed out via email? Her friend Laura was apparently also a study partner. There were a couple of threads where they went back and forth over some of the classwork.

He switched to the Sent Mail folder. The last time Jenny had initiated or replied to a message was the morning she disappeared. She had responded to a couple of the freebie offers, and there was a note to an Emily, a name he remembered from her phone contacts. The two were going back and forth about a plan to go out on Saturday night with a group of friends.

A separate message went to an Anna Wentworth, and he noticed there was an attachment. He opened the message with the subject line **Here's mine!** and read the short note: **Here's mine. What do you think? Interesting to do this**.

The attached was a Word document and he swallowed hard when he read the title of it. Me – deceased. The piece that read like an obituary, written by Jenny herself. She called it 'interesting.' He called it plain weird. He needed to find out who this Anna Wentworth was.

Back to Jenny's inbox he scanned the senders of everything received after Jenny had sent the strange document to Anna. Sure enough, there was a reply.

Chapter 13

Now

I needed to see Linda Arnold again. On the face of it, her report to the police had seemed complete and honest. Now that I'd begun digging into Jenny's and Ricky's past, I was thinking there had been a lot left unsaid by Linda. Surely the police had dug deeper, discovered some of the same things I was learning now. And they had pretty much concluded that Jenny and Ricky had run off together. Or that Ricky had enticed her away and maybe harmed her.

Linda was the only link between then and now, and I had no idea how much longer she would be clear-headed and able to help. Those cancer drugs were strong and it might get tricky to catch her in the mood to talk.

I meandered from my office to the upstairs bathroom and checked myself in the mirror. My shirt looked a bit slept-in, as did my hair. I rounded up a hairbrush from my purse and found a ponytail band in my desk drawer. Applying those, brushing my teeth, and washing my face made a big improvement. I smoothed my t-shirt and took Freckles outside for her morning duties. Back in the kitchen, we broke into the office stash of dog food (a necessity, I'd discovered years ago, because I spent too many late nights at work). She seemed happy with that, but I knew coffee alone wasn't going to quite get me through. I made an executive decision to hit the Lotaburger on Rio Grande before going by Linda's house.

This New Mexico chain began with burgers and fries, which are still tops on my list, but I have to say, the breakfast burritos are unsurpassed. Huge and well-filled with eggs, bacon, potatoes and green chile, it's heaven in a foil-wrapped packet, which you can eat sitting at a stool and watching the world drive by or feast on in the car.

I chose the latter, as I wanted time to look back through the emailed reports, which I had forwarded from Ron's account to my own sometime in the wee morning hours. I scrolled through them on my phone as I munched happily, and by the time I tossed my burrito wrapper in the trash barrel and started the Jeep again, I was feeling much more human.

Linda's trim little house looked fresh and bright in the morning sunlight when I pulled up at the curb. Cassie stood there, directing a water hose at the flowers in narrow beds that ran along the front of the porch. She stared curiously at the vehicle until she recognized me. I parked under the shade of an overhanging sycamore and rolled windows down a generous amount for Freckles, who had her paws up on the backseat window edge and was wagging her whole body at the teen across the lawn.

"Hey, Cassie, how's it going?" I stuffed my phone into the side pocket on my purse and grabbed its shoulder strap as I got out of the car.

She set the hose in one of the beds and crossed toward me. "Hi, Charlie. Is there some news?"

I shook my head. "Sorry, nothing concrete yet. But I've been searching a lot."

"Did you try Instagram and Snapchat?" She seemed eager to offer ideas. "I tried them but didn't have much luck. Too many people with the same names."

I chuckled a little. "Yeah, I noticed that too. But we have some other things to try." Before she could pin me for details, I switched subjects a bit. "Listen, is this a good time for me to see your grandmother?"

"Sure. She's had her breakfast and is probably in the den. Go on in—I need to move this hose before too much water runs toward the street."

Conscientious kid. It's amazing how many people flout the city's laws on landscape water usage and just allow their sprinklers and hoses to run water for blocks down the street. Well, there's a fine for that. I was glad to see Cassie exhibiting responsibility concerning her family's expenses.

I walked up the steps to the porch and opened the screen door, calling out to Linda as I walked inside.

"In here. I'm in the den." Her voice sounded thinner than I remembered from a few days ago.

I walked in to find her on the sofa, her back against one of the padded arms with a big pillow behind her, her legs stretched out and covered with an afghan. She wore a bright turquoise top and her hair had been freshly washed, possibly also Cassie's doing. She caught me admiring that fact.

"I got lucky with my chemo," she said. "Didn't lose

much of my hair at all. Of course when some of the numbers came back not so great, I decided I wasn't going to spend a whole lot more time on that route. Why spend my last few months traipsing to doctors, when it's not going to make a different outcome, right? Cassie and I got in a couple of fun road trips this summer, and that's a lot better, to my way of thinking, than keeping a bunch of sterile old appointments."

She shifted, lowering her legs to sit upright and setting her book aside. "But that's not what you came to talk about."

A get-right-to-it kind of lady. I liked that. I dropped my purse to the floor beside one of the armchairs and sat facing her.

"Well, I just wanted to give a little update on what I've been doing and maybe pick your brain a little, hoping you can fill in some gaps for me."

"Bottom line—any luck yet?"

Another aspect of her no-nonsense attitude. "I haven't located her, if that's what you mean. So, no."

She nodded, eyes lowered to the coffee table in front of her. "I understand."

"I've accessed several databases, things the credit companies use when verifying a person's employment history, their credit status, and such. It can give us a good picture of how they've moved about, how much they earn and spend—well, you know."

"That's a good idea! So, has Jenny's name come up.?

I took a breath. "Prior to her disappearance, yes. I found her, the record that she was attending UNM, her driver's license and credit card information."

"But … since then?"

I shook my head. "Sorry, nothing yet. Now—that's not to say that she might be using a different name now. She could have remarried. I should let you know that I also ran some background checks on Ricky Blake."

Did I imagine that her expression hardened a little?

"I'll be frank. Ricky's name showed up more often than Jenny's. He apparently worked sporadically, although there's nothing on his employment record in recent times. He also has an arrest record." I paused a moment to let that sink in. "Drugs. Minor charges, but still enough that they didn't get dismissed. He was sent to drug rehab centers twice. And, no, I haven't yet been able to contact those places. The rules are so strict these days about releasing any patient information at all. I may not be able to learn many details."

She chewed at a dry spot on her lower lip, waiting for me to continue.

"Anyway, I know from the report that the police believed Jenny most likely took off with Ricky, went along with his lifestyle of her own free will. At this point, I don't think the facts bear that out. At the very least she would have renewed her driver's license—"

"If they stayed in New Mexico. Otherwise, she might have gotten a new one somewhere else."

"Very true. But her employment history would have shown jobs in other states. That would at least give me a starting point in tracking down a new home address or something."

"So that's it, then? You're out of leads?"

"Not at all. I still have a big list of people to talk to, people she might have kept in touch with ..." My voice trailed off as I realized the one person on the planet Jenny would have kept in touch with was sitting right here.

Mother and daughter had been close—as far as I knew.

Linda read my thoughts and nodded. "We were close. And I swear to you, there had been no argument or split that would cause her to willingly cut me—and Cassie!—off for all these years."

"I know. I got that sense, right from the beginning." Again, I let the moment of silence stretch out, in case there was more she wanted to say. When she didn't speak, I continued. "All I can be fairly certain about right now is that either Jenny didn't leave with Ricky, or if the two were together they were living under the radar, working in the underground economy—which wouldn't be unheard of for a musician like Ricky. I plan on doing some more checking on that aspect, but it's tough. When people can't be found by the IRS, they most likely can't be found by me, either."

She smiled a little at that. "But still, there are ways for someone living that way to keep in touch with family. I know my Jenny. She would have contacted me. She would have found a way to come back for Cassie."

Probably. Maybe. I had to bring up the part no one wanted to hear.

"I've mentioned that I have more sources, more people I can speak with, including the two cops who worked the case at the time. But—" This was the hard part. "But, we also need to be prepared that it could turn out Jenny isn't alive, that she didn't even survive beyond that awful day." I couldn't believe I'd uttered that possibility, and to a dying mother at that.

Surprisingly, Linda's face appeared even more calm. She nodded. "I know."

"Linda? I'm wondering … I, um, kind of get the sense

that you believed this all along. Is that true?"

She let out a long sigh that seemed to bring forth a pain deep within her. I felt it fill the space between us, but I couldn't be sure if this was an aspect of her condition or if the pain was purely emotional. Either would make sense.

Finally, she gave a slight nod and her words came out as barely a whisper. "When the years went by … yes, I had to resign myself."

"But—" I glanced toward the front door and could still hear the outdoor water running. "But Cassie? Did you keep the hope about her mother alive for her? Or did she come to me despite the conversations you and she must have had over the years?"

"The latter. I never could bring myself to say to her, outright, that her mother was probably dead. Because there was always the possibility that one day she might come back to us. It's the horror any family faces when someone is missing. There's no proof they've died, but there's no proof they are alive either. I had to leave that little ray of hope open, for both of us."

I nodded silently and willed the tears not to spill over. It was true—I had nothing to compare with their experience. When my parents died, at least it was known as a fact. Everyone had to come to grips and deal with it, and eventually we all did. This poor woman … the poor girl outside … I couldn't begin to imagine their pain.

"Charlie? Thank you for trying. I will tell Cassie what you've told me, and I will try to both break it to her gently and to let her see the finality of it. She's old enough now. It's time to be truthful."

I wanted to say she's *not* old enough now. A person is *never* old enough for this news. But Linda had to handle it in the best way she knew. She would not be here much longer either, and she needed to prepare Cassie for the idea of spending a few years with the uncle and aunt she barely knew and then to make her own way in the adult world. It was simply the way things went. But as the thoughts ran through my head, the tears escaped and trailed down my cheeks.

Linda reached to the end table at her side and passed me the tissue box. I dabbed at my eyes and she dabbed hers, and we let those words be the decree on her decision. When I stood a moment later, I stepped over and gave her a long hug, promising to return the unused portion of the money she had paid. She seemed to be wrapped in her own thoughts entirely.

I picked up my purse, wished Linda well, and headed toward the front door. I was in the foyer, barely out of sight of the den door, when a hand reached out and grabbed my arm.

Cassie, her firm grip never wavering, put a finger to her lips and led me outside and down the sidewalk.

"I heard everything. Charlie, please don't quit."

Her urgently whispered plea, the near-panic on her face—well, I couldn't just ignore the girl who'd gone to such lengths to get me started on this case. And darn if I didn't still relate to her. It had taken me many years to learn the full truth of my own parents' deaths. She would not rest until she knew what had happened to her mother, and I couldn't blame her a bit. She shouldn't have to wait until she was thirty to know the truth.

"Okay," I said. "I'll keep looking."

Chapter 14

Our plan was to meet again briefly before I started back to work on the case. Cassie told me she had been searching the house and found a box of mementos her grandmother had kept of Jenny's. I wasn't sure whether she meant things like old birthday cards and plaster molds with kid-sized handprints, or if there could be something pertinent to finding Jenny now. But I figured it was worth sitting down together and taking a look.

Cassie would smuggle the box out to Linda's car as soon as she drifted into a nap, and then she would drive over to my office. I spotted the older Toyota minivan from my upstairs bay window, even before Freckles sounded the alert. For a moment, as Cassie climbed out and retrieved a cardboard box from the back seat, I could imagine this same van filled with kids as Linda acted as chauffeur to the soccer team or the Girl Scouts or whatever activities had consumed Cassie's childhood days.

I reached the front door at the same time as my client.

"Hey, can I help you with that?" The box looked heavy.

"It's okay. I got it," she said.

We headed directly for the conference room table and she set the box there with a mild thud. I must admit to curiosity—almost the feeling of wondering what's in that great big Christmas present in the corner. Unfortunately, this would not be a very happy occasion. I watched as the girl unfolded the tucked-in cardboard flaps to reveal the contents.

"I assume you've already gone through this?" I asked.

"A little. There are some papers and photos. Mostly what caught my eye were the clothes. It's a peek into a different time, you know? There's a fancy dress that must have been a prom dress or something."

She lifted out the package, which had been set carefully on top of the heavier items to avoid crushing it. Folding back the layers of tissue paper, she revealed a gown of midnight blue satin and held it up. It was floor-length, with a V neckline, high waist, and flowing skirt. A button-sized rhinestone ornament at the point where bodice met skirt in front was the only ornamentation, and it was exactly enough. Jenny Blake had classic good taste.

"Look—she and I are nearly the same size!" She lifted the dress by the shoulder straps and held it against her body. I had to agree, it would probably be a perfect fit for Jenny's daughter. "There's a picture of her in this dress." Cassie reached into the box. "I'll bet this is her and my dad going to their senior prom."

I studied the photo she handed me, betting she was

right about the occasion. The couple were posed in front of a deep red curtain with some kind of shimmery threads woven into it, Jenny in this blue dress, Ricky in a rented tuxedo. She had a corsage of blue and white flowers on a band around her wrist.

It was my first look at Ricky Blake and I took in the details: average height, slender build (although it's so hard to tell about men in formal wear), blonde hair, a jaunty smile with slightly crooked teeth, the kind of smile that exudes youthful we'll-conquer-the-world confidence. His bowtie was deep blue, his eyes matching it. He stood with Jenny in the protective curve of his shoulder.

Cute couple. So young, shining with the prospect of a wonderful life ahead, nothing to suggest either of their lives would come to anything but perfection. I'm afraid I gave a sigh as I handed the picture back to Cassie. She draped the dress over the back of a chair and turned back to the box.

Next layer down revealed a couple of purses and a wallet. I got a strange feeling as I held them in my hands. The light weight of the two purses indicated that they were empty, cleared of the day-to-day things Jenny had probably carried. Both were in good condition, although not expensive brands. Just decent leather shoulder bags that Linda had probably had a hard time giving away. As with the formal gown, the purses probably evoked images of the daughter who never came home.

The wallet had enough bulk to suggest it still contained something. "Do you mind if I look?" I asked Cassie.

"Go for it." Her attention had returned to the box. "I love the things in here," she said, pulling out a small jewelry box and opening the lid.

I gave a glance, spotting a tangle of earrings and other glittery things, but my real interest was on gathering information. I sat down and unsnapped the clasp on the wallet.

The police had been through this. It was evident from the way the driver's license, credit card, and the few dollars in cash were jammed back into various slots that a woman had not organized this wallet. Plus, okay, I admit that I remembered seeing part of the police report which listed the personal possessions of the missing woman.

Other than verifying most of what I'd learned from my online searches, the wallet didn't contain anything new or earthshaking. I set it aside and picked up one of the shoulder bags. The pocket on the front was a little stretched out of shape, making me think this was probably accessed often, most likely where Jenny would drop her cell phone or car keys inside for quick access. But none of those items were here now.

Unzipping the top, I found the inner compartments equally empty but I turned it upside down and gave a shake, to be sure. A tiny inner section was zipped closed so I opened that to reveal a little space that might hold a credit card or matchbook, nothing much bigger. At first glance it appeared empty but I ran an index finger inside it and felt a slip of paper.

What came out appeared to be a clipping from a classified newspaper ad. I hadn't seen one of these in years. I brought it out to the light and unfolded it. One side showed a partial photo, maybe part of an advertisement. The other was the printed classified.

Need help? Nar-Anon meetings every evening.

There was an address on Lomas Boulevard, which I

thought corresponded to a church. I'd have to check. Or not. Obviously, this clipping was old. So, what did it mean? Jenny's having it tucked into a hidden spot in her purse suggested maybe it was something she was thinking about but had not acted upon. Or maybe she meant to give the clipping to someone. Ricky?

No, wait. Wasn't Narcotics Anonymous for drug users? Nar-Anon, like Al-Anon, was for families of addicts. Maybe Jenny herself had attended.

Cassie was watching me. She reached for the scrap of newspaper and read what I'd just been looking at.

"My grandmother said my dad had gotten messed up in some bad stuff," she said quietly. "Do you think this was it?"

I had to be frank with her. "Yes. I didn't really want to tell you this until I learned more about what was going on back then. But I found background information that showed your dad spent some time in rehab. Twice, actually."

She nodded slowly.

"That was years after he left, even after your mother disappeared."

She let out a ragged breath. "So it looks like she knew about his drug use, maybe was looking for a way to help him."

"Could be." I gave her what I hoped passed for a smile. "In fact, I'll bet you're right. Maybe all their problems came from this, and he didn't just leave because of what everyone said."

"That he was useless and didn't want to be a father." It wasn't a question. Poor kid had probably heard talk about it all her life.

"I'm not the best person to give advice, Cassie, but

we might consider the idea that your mom asked him to leave, for this very reason. If she'd stuck with him, she might have gotten pulled into the same set of problems. Maybe you've been better off all along because of the fact he wasn't in your life."

"I know. Grandma says the same thing. I mean, she has always tried to be fair and not to criticize, but it comes out, you know. She blames him for Mom being gone, no matter what was behind it." She set the little jewelry box aside. "I've even wondered if Mom left to get away from him, to hide out or something."

I know the skepticism showed on my face. "But never to contact your grandmother, *never* to try and see you again? It just doesn't seem very logical." I couldn't bring myself to say the reason for that could only be that Jenny was dead. Cassie had already overheard me talking with Linda this morning. She didn't need it repeated.

For the next ten minutes she busied herself with the contents of the box and wouldn't make eye contact.

Chapter 15

Then

Ricky crouched beside a dumpster behind a bakery on Fourth Street, thinking about the cops who'd been at the house. A hundred thoughts flitted through his head, and it was frustrating that he couldn't seem to keep them straight.

He'd seen the guy standing at Jenny's car. Where was she? What were the men there for? *What had they found?*

He pictured the loose board under the bed. Had Jenny discovered it and reported him?

Why was he *here*? He stared at his surroundings. Oh yeah. He'd hitched a ride with a guy he barely knew. *I need to see my baby girl,* he'd told the truck driver who delivered sodas to the convenience stores in Espanola. It sounded better than *I gotta score some blow.* And he kind of remembered the guy asking him questions about the wife and kid, and him making up a bunch of shit to help fill the ninety-minute drive. Maybe he'd started to believe his own story, that seeing his baby was the real reason for this driving need to get inside that house.

He gripped the sides of his head, which was pounding now. The dumpster stank, and the smell churned his stomach. He wanted to get away but couldn't think where he would go. Wherever he'd spent the last few nights—one of the guys in the band he played with on Saturday nights had let him crash in a spare room, but said it was temporary. Something told him he'd better get back there before the guy decided to hock his guitar and throw out the pack containing his two changes of clothes. All the important stuff was with him, a small wad of cash and the baggie of white powder he was here to sell. Except he needed a hit of it himself.

He took a deep breath, nearly retched, and decided he had to get away from the dumpster. They said your sense of smell was dulled when you used coke, but not today. He stood up and walked out of the alley, but when he hit the street the November wind nearly took his breath away. He gripped the edges of his leather jacket and zipped it closed, but it offered no protection against the forty-degree air and the twenty-mile-an-hour wind. Shit!

At least the cold cleared his head a little. Okay, can't go by the house, can't open the baggie here on the street. He needed to sell the baggie and get himself a ride back to Espanola before El Tiburon realized he was gone. Those thugs of his wouldn't let a couple thousand dollars slide.

The Fourth Street bus rolled up to a bus stop at the next corner. That would get him downtown. He ran to catch it.

There were only three other people on the bus, all near the front. He ambled to the back where he could be alone. At least he was out of the wind. He leaned his head against the side window and let the warmth lull him into a doze. How had he gotten here—not *here*, today, here in life?

Everybody warned him—his mom who worked double shifts waitressing, a couple of buddies from school, and then Jenny—the musician's lifestyle wasn't an easy one. Booze and drugs nearly always came into it. Late nights, sleeping away the days, impossible to hold any kind of 'normal' job and do your music at night. And at first, it was all about the music. He played in a couple of garage bands in high school, learned the popular songs, could duplicate some complex licks, got in with a better band, lied about his age so he could play in casinos.

These guys were big time—or so he thought—and one of their routines was to snort a few lines right before they went on stage. Ricky hesitated. He had a wife at home. He didn't do this stuff. Until he did. And then, man oh man, could he play! Life on stage was so much better, so enhanced, and his riffs were something else.

Each night a different guy brought the goody. And then, the fourth time they did it, somebody said, "Your turn to bring the stuff tomorrow night." *What? Where did you buy the stuff?* It took him less than ten minutes to find someone to sell him a baggie. Which took all the cash he'd earned for the weekend. And that took some explaining at home when he showed up, having worked a solid week and had no money to pay the rent. He and Jenny fought.

Everything escalated. His habit, her complaining. She was about to have a baby any day now, she nagged, as if the sight of that huge belly wasn't reminder enough. He left her home every night now, not just when the band was playing.

The bus was stopping every couple of blocks, so he kept an eye out for a likely cross street that would get him into the center of downtown without having to walk very far.

He'd never been good with money—Jenny handled the rent and the groceries and all that—but now it positively melted away. Where, he didn't know, but he never had any cash. He started asking around. Hey, man, a guy told him. El Tiburon, out of Espanola, he's always looking for dealers. You can make a fortune, and you can stay with the band.

Something about Espanola rang a bell. Rio Arriba County was connected, part of the pipeline from Mexico to all parts north ... something like that. It felt dangerous, but it was also exhilarating the first time he drove his pickup truck up there and met with two heavyweights in the Chaco Cartel. He'd never felt quite so blonde-haired and blue eyed. They teased him a little and said that was good—he could blend in better with Anglos and bring in a lot of new business.

Oh, okay. It sounded feasible, and why not?

By that evening he had a disposable cell phone and all the coke he could buy with what cash he'd had on him. So, first stop was to meet up with the band and show how good he could treat them. He'd make his money back the next morning, outside one of the high schools. That's what the Chaco guys had told him would work best. Pick a school in a good neighborhood, where the kids had more money than they knew what to do with.

That lasted a week, until some girl saw her boyfriend

talking to him and figured it out. Next day, the narcs were on his tail and he barely escaped. He shook off that image. No way was he wasting yet another twenty-eight days in some stupid program. Or worse—the judge wouldn't give him rehab next time. It was the old three-strikes-you're-out rule. He shook off those thoughts. He'd gotten away and he was doing just fine, thank you very much.

Right now, he needed to catch up with a guy he knew who always spent money. He'd sell the baggie in his pocket and then try to get back to the house where more waited under the floorboard. All he needed to do was get Jenny on the phone and sweet-talk her into believing he missed her and the baby. With luck she would invite him to dinner and he'd figure out a way to get at his stash.

He held on to that thought until he was off the bus and standing in the protected doorway of a pawn shop on Central. But Jenny's phone went straight to voicemail. Hmm. It had worked last week and she had actually come to meet him for coffee.

Oh well, he thought. He would do his deal and then try her again. She'd jabbered on last time about being in school. That's probably where she was now.

Chapter 16

Now

Two days went by, during which I felt my investigation was taking one step forward and two steps back. While trying to make some sense of the items Cassie had brought in the box from Linda's house, I thought maybe the larger perspective might come from speaking with the police officers who had handled the case from the beginning.

I started with a call to APD and asked for the Missing Persons division. I know, maybe I could have tried Kent Taylor, the cop Ron works with sometimes, but Kent deals better with Ron. I guess that's because I've gotten on the wrong side of him a few times. More importantly, Kent is a homicide detective and most likely wouldn't have had much to do with the Jenny Blake case back then. I'd be lucky to find anyone who remembered it at all.

So, anyway, I began by asking whether I might speak with either Ernie DeAngelo or Alan Curtis, the two names I had spotted in the file.

"Detective DeAngelo retired some years ago, I believe," said the female voice who picked up when my call was transferred. "He was already gone when I came into this division."

"How about Alan Curtis?"

There was a silence space on the line. "I will need to check. That name isn't familiar at all."

I got up from my dining room table, using the time to walk to the kitchen to see if the coffee was still warm, then to let Freckles outside. By the time the dog came in, I was still on hold, but the woman came back on the line before I had quite poured myself a second cup.

"It seems Detective Curtis was only with APD for four years and then he took a job with another department. The last anyone remembers is that it was in Indianapolis."

I thanked her and hung up. Now that Curtis was so much further along the career path would he remember anything from this one unsolved case that went way too far back in time? It was worth a shot, I supposed, so I looked up the number for Indianapolis PD and made the call. Surprisingly, Alan Curtis picked up quickly after the call was transferred. I went into a recap, explaining my role in the case and asking whether he remembered the Jenny Blake disappearance.

"My first unsolved missing person case. Of course I remember."

The smooth, cultured voice didn't match how I'd imagined Alan Curtis to be. I'd had a picture of two crusty old cops, talking to the parties involved but hardened to the reality that so many people go missing because they want to. Based on the conclusions written in the angular handwriting of Ernie DeAngelo, I assumed both cops were treating Jenny's case as just one of many such.

"I'm not sure how many details I can give you," he continued, "but I remember her photo. I remember the distraught mother and the little baby. A girl, wasn't it?"

"Wow, you *are* good with the details."

"Like I said, my first case after I made detective. What can I do for you now? I assume Ms. Blake hasn't turned up. We never hear about those."

"No, sadly, she hasn't. It's her daughter, actually, who hired us to keep working on it. The girl is sixteen now. Her grandmother raised a pretty sharp cookie."

There was a moment's silence, and I realized I hadn't gotten to the point—what he could do for me now.

"Sorry. I know you're busy. What I'm wondering now, and I know this is a longshot, is whether you remember anything about the case that wasn't documented. Your own impressions, maybe something you learned after you stopped actively working on it. I don't know ... but I imagine there are things that come to an officer, maybe even a few years later. Was there any angle that wasn't worked at the time, something I might be able to follow up?"

A long exhale at the other end of the line. "Let me think ... Problem is, I left Albuquerque less than a year after we worked the Blake case. Maybe six months after we felt we'd exhausted our leads and the file got stuck away as a cold case. In the meantime, dozens more cases come across the desk. *Some*body is reported missing nearly every day."

"Wow."

"If you read the stats, you already know that a lot of them turn up, safe and well. Kids that head out partying and don't tell their parents, spouses who fight and later make up. Rebellious teens—those often don't turn out well because they end up on the streets. And then sometimes a person just feels they need to get away, but they don't tell anyone. Head off to a cabin somewhere for a week or so, and they're stunned to learn their family has called the police. We got a lot of that."

"I imagine that's one reason the ones who stay missing, especially under odd circumstances, can stick in your mind."

"True."

"And Jenny Blake?"

"It looked like we ruled out a fight with a family member, a deep unhappiness, or anything like that. As I recall, she was a student, doing well in college, looking forward to her mid-term exams. I do remember it was late fall at the time. I never seemed to take a heavy enough coat on the days we hiked around door-to-door to question people. Believe me, now that I'm in the Midwest, I have an appreciation for winter weather." A slight chuckle. "No, I can't think of any new evidence that jumped out at us later."

"I thought I'd talk with your partner, Ernie DeAngelo. You wouldn't happen to remember if he expressed any other thoughts, something he didn't write in his notes?"

"Afraid not. We worked okay together, DeAngelo and me, but we never did get really close. He was inches away from retirement, and any personal chitchat went that direction. How much the wife wanted them to retire to

Phoenix, and how much he was looking forward to it. Thought he'd take up golf, although I don't remember him ever saying he played the game. Me, I was new enough that I felt the pressure of the older guy critiquing everything I did. Don't get me wrong. DeAngelo was a good cop, a seasoned detective, and I learned a lot. He just wasn't the chummy type."

"So, he must have retired before you left? Or shortly after?"

"Yeah. Shortly after. I came out here and never did hear whether he and the wife got their retirement wish or not. We didn't keep in touch."

Although the information was practically non-existent, I thanked Detective Curtis and gave him my number. Just in case. I was just starting an online search for Ernie DeAngelo, whose age I guessed would be about eighty now, in the Phoenix area, when my phone rang.

Elsa's voice sounded agitated. "Charlie, I need some help."

When someone in her nineties issues that statement, you don't question. You go. I closed my laptop's cover and ran for the back door.

Chapter 17

This is the big emergency?" I asked. I had bypassed Dottie in the kitchen and found Elsa standing in front of her closet.

"I never said it was an emergency," she reminded. "Only that I needed some help."

True enough. I accepted the mild chastisement with a nod.

"I can't decide what to wear to the wedding," she said, staring at the row of dresses on hangers. "Maybe I need to go shopping for something new."

To wear to a wedding that probably wouldn't last as long as the shopping trip? I wasn't volunteering for that one. I've clothes-shopped with Elsa before. She tries on a hundred things—at the pace of a tortoise—before choosing. I didn't say any of this out loud.

"Let's see, Gram. There must be something appropriate here." I stepped forward and began poking into the cluttered mass. Realistically, any of her church dresses would work perfectly well for a summer afternoon wedding in a park.

"I saw Iris's dress yesterday," she told me as I pulled out a couple of choices. "She's going all out with white chiffon. Or it might be pink lace. She's narrowed it down to two."

I couldn't begin to imagine either on Iris, but I didn't comment. "Well, you don't need to outshine the bride, you know. How about this one?"

I held up a lavender dress with matching jacket that had small tucks on the front, which I knew to be one of her favorites. She was reaching for a bright turquoise one— the dress was tasteful (probably more so than Iris's white chiffon, if the truth be told), but it was an older one.

"It's nice. You'll want to try it on to be sure it still fits well."

She tossed that one on the bed and studied the closet again. I could see this going on a while, just like the department store visits.

"Let's pick one more, then you try on all three, and we'll know which is the winner." I reached for a flowered print—pink and white—and its coordinating pink jacket. "This one's nice."

She shook her head. "I'm thinking bolder colors."

There was no point in reminding her that pastels suited her coloring better. I reached for a vivid blue that brought out the color in her eyes, holding it up and doing a little pose with it.

"Okay. I'll try on these three," she said.

I quickly shut the closet door so we could remain

undistracted. "Need some help?"

"No, no. You go check on Dottie and I'll come out when I have the first one on."

"Good plan," I said, pulling the bedroom door closed behind me.

"Having fun yet?" Dottie teased when I walked into the dining room where she was setting the table for their early supper.

"Don't tell me she tried to talk you into shopping for something new."

"Oh, she try. But I been that route once, last Christmas. Ain't doing that again. But nothin I pick from the closet catch her fancy. That's when she called you. Sorry."

"It's okay, really. We've done this routine a lot of times over the years, believe me. In the beginning she was the one standing at my closet door, trying to get me to wear something the least bit feminine to a school dance. I would've gone in jeans if I'd had my way." I glanced down at my current pair, which were showing some wear. "I have to say she was right."

Fifteen minutes later, Elsa emerged wearing the bright turquoise dress, which, as I'd feared, was baggy in the shoulders and snug in the waist. Dottie and I both gave it a head shake and suggested she try the next. Within an hour—during which time Dottie convinced me to try a few of the peanut butter cookies she'd baked this morning—we'd settled on the vivid blue one and everyone was happy, mostly me because I was raring to get back to my work on the case.

In a metro area of 4.5 million people, there are bound to be more than one or two DeAngelos, but I persevered until I found an Ernest DeAngelo who seemed to be in the correct age range and was a retired police officer (this discovered, interestingly enough, on Facebook where a daughter loved to post things about her elderly parents). By the time I unearthed all this juicy stuff, it was after seven p.m., which seemed an ideal time to place a call, and luckily Names and Numbers gave me the means to do that.

"Carefree Manor," came a chipper voice over the line.

"Oh. I thought I was calling the number of Ernest DeAngelo," I said, momentarily flummoxed.

"That's right. I will connect you."

Why hadn't the Facebooking daughter thought to mention that he lived in a facility? As the phone rang, I wondered if the place was truly carefree or a manor. I suspected it would prove to be neither. When a female voice answered, I asked again to speak to Mr. DeAngelo.

"Who's calling? He doesn't accept sales calls." The voice carried a certain proprietary tone.

"Are you his daughter?" Before she could answer I rushed on. "I'm calling from Albuquerque, and one of Detective DeAngelo's former partners on the police force told me where to reach him." Okay, so that statement was only about twenty-five percent true …

"Oh! What did you say your name was?"

"Charlie Parker. I'm with RJP Investigations. We're looking into one of his old cases, and I hoped I might speak with him about it. Maybe just a few minutes?"

"Charlie, you said? Hi, yes, I am his daughter, Janeen. Mother passed away last year so I'm here with Dad nearly every day. Listen," she lowered her voice slightly, "I'm afraid he doesn't remember much these days. Too many changes in the past few years. He can't keep it all straight. And his hearing is terrible. Stubborn man, he won't wear hearing aids. Phone conversations are nearly impossible for him."

"Oh, sorry to hear that. I'd hoped this case might have stuck in his mind. His partner, Alan Curtis, still remembered it."

"How long ago was this? You know, amazingly, his memories from a long time ago are much better than his memories of recent events. Some days he thinks I'm Mom, if I'm in his little kitchenette making coffee or something."

I gave her a few little facts, that the case was fifteen years ago and was probably one of the last ones he worked before he retired.

"I don't know, Charlie. You might actually have some luck with him. If you were to stop by while I'm here. I can maybe help get past the hearing impediment."

Stop by. Well, why not? I could probably get a last-minute seat on a Southwest flight—there were probably a dozen a day between our two cities. I told her to plan on my being there day after tomorrow, and I got her cell number so we could connect once I reached the city.

In the background, I could hear a ragged male voice. "Who's on the phone, Janeen?"

"Dad, good news—you're going to have a visitor!"

I had to hold my phone away from my ear; she evidently didn't realize how loudly she had to speak to him. I told her I would let her know once I had a flight booked, and we said a quick goodbye. Less than a minute later I was on the airline website, looking at my options.

It would be crappy of me to visit the city without touching base with my other brother, Paul, and his family. We're not nearly as close as I am with Ron, but still. To call in advance, or just get there and then see if a meal or something could be worked out?

Plans with Paul's group tend to get complicated. Dinner can't be arranged until softball is done, and that's never a preset time because games can go long or short. And Lorraine now has a new career, so her hours are unpredictable. Truthfully, all of that was fine with me—a cup of coffee with Paul would be ideal. But if I announced my visit, they would come up with something that could very well send me driving all over the huge metropolis and barely meeting up. Yeah, I'd wait and call when I got there.

I chose flights that would get me there late tomorrow evening and out the next day. I got a hotel room near the airport and a rental car with GPS. That should meet nearly all my needs. No one, including Paul, could talk me into staying longer because I had the wedding obligation on Saturday. I texted Janeen my flight info, suggesting she choose anytime Thursday after midmorning for our meeting.

All set. And with that bit of business done, I realized I'd better be prepared with questions for the retired detective so I sat back down with the file.

Chapter 18

By midnight I had been through the police file completely, and my eyes were burning with dryness. All I wanted was my bed. And then I slept until 9:30, so what had been the point of staying up so late? I showered and dressed, finding a change of clothes to take to Phoenix, remembering it would be a thousand degrees hot there. Remind me again—why had I decided this trip would be a good idea?

Never mind that. Freckles and I walked out to the back yard and went through the hedge over to Elsa's, where I needed to ask a favor.

"You bet," said Dottie. "Little Freckle-sweetie can stay with us anytime."

"It's only tonight," I promised. "I'll be back home tomorrow late afternoon."

Dottie bent over to tickle the top of the dog's head, while Freckles urgently sniffed at the pockets of the caregiver's apron. When she got a whiff of the ever-present doggie treat inside, she plopped her bottom on the ground and stared up expectantly. Dottie laughed and handed over the biscuit.

"See? We get along jus fine."

"I'll bring her crate and food over in a little while," I promised.

Back at home, I stacked the dog's overnight gear beside the kitchen door. Crate, bedding, bowls for food and water, baggie with two days' supply of food, extra treats, leash, a couple of toys … this was way more stuff than I was taking with me, and the dog was only traveling as far as the house next door. Sheesh!

Next up was to gather the items I wanted to have along for the Blake case. I'd already decided I would take the police file. Seeing the report and the notes in his own writing might spur memories for Detective DeAngelo—at least I hoped they would.

Something else might work to bring back a memory. I called Cassie and asked if I might borrow a couple of the items we'd looked at from the box of her mother's things. She agreed and said she could drop them off at my office when she left for work. We were still being a little clandestine about my working the case after Linda had semi-fired me.

I needed to scramble to get there in time, but at least things at home felt fairly organized. Freckles trailed me anxiously as I picked up the tote bag filled with her gear in one hand, the handle of the crate in the other, and we walked over to Elsa's. I quickly set up the crate in the living room and handed Dottie the rest of the things.

"She gonna do fine, don't you worry about nothin,'" she told me.

"I know she will. Just got anxious-mama feelings."

She patted my shoulder and then pulled me in for one of her famed Dottie hugs. Nobody can feel anxious after receiving one of those. I left the dog in Elsa's kitchen, staring up at the bag of treats on the counter. Dottie was right—my little girl would be just fine.

I had ten minutes to meet Cassie at the office, so I basically raced through my house, locking the back door, grabbing my purse and keys, and heading out. I steered into the driveway of the Victorian at the same moment she pulled up to the curb in her grandmother's minivan. We both stopped and met on the front lawn.

"Here are the purse and wallet," she said, handing them over. "That's all you wanted?"

"Yeah, that's it." I had told her about my quick Phoenix trip. "Most likely these are the items the detective saw and handled. I'm hoping to spark his memories of the case."

She nodded, understanding. "I know it's been a long time. Hopefully he'll remember something that helps."

She got back in the van and drove away, and I pulled around to my usual parking spot and went in the back door. Sally's vehicle was here. I'd forgotten this was one of her half-days, so I walked directly to the reception desk, planning to fill her in on the new case.

"Messages I took off the answering machine," she said, handing me a stack of pink slips. No matter how modern technology gets in certain areas, some things were still done old-school, especially in this office. "Most of them are for Ron, but I thought you'd want to take a look."

I flipped through them, recognizing the names of several regular clients. I held onto the ones that would likely be about billing or some other office procedure, and handed the others back.

"Would you mind giving each of these a call, let them know Ron's away and when he'll be back? If anyone still needs to talk to someone, I can call them back day after tomorrow."

Most of Ron's regular clients would be surprised to hear that he'd taken an actual vacation, but I was betting their business could wait until he got back.

"Sure, no problem. And what's with 'day after tomorrow'? Going somewhere yourself?"

"Actually, yes." I laughed and gave a quick explanation. "Just shows you never know how a case will unfold."

Sally picked up the phone and started making the calls while I went upstairs, feeling as though something was missing because there was no furry ball of brown and white at my heels, no clicking of doggie toenails on the wooden floors. Things are simply too quiet when there's no dog around. A little pang went through me—I'm such a softy about pets.

The calls I'd agreed to return took another hour of my time, by the time I looked up billing statements for a couple of people and researched the files for requested information.

Back to the Blake case. Last night, in my reading through the police reports, it occurred to me it might be smart to talk with some of the same witnesses the detectives had interviewed. Not that I expected any of them would have had a sudden flash of insight about Jenny and what had happened to her, but simply to see if someone might provide me a spark of an idea I could question DeAngelo about.

Laura Jaramillo, the school friend Jenny sometimes carpooled with, seemed impatient when I identified myself and told her why I was calling.

"I don't know why everyone kept calling me about this," she said. "Okay, I understand why Jenny's mother called. It's what we moms do. But the police? I had already said I hadn't talked to Jenny in a couple of days. I didn't know anything about it then, and I still don't."

All I could do was thank her for her time and click off the call.

From the detective's notes I had gotten a phone number for Emily Banji, with whom Jenny had spoken on the morning she disappeared. I was amazed when the number actually still belonged to the same young woman.

"Wow, that name's a blast from the past. Jenny Blake," she said, sounding a little breathless. "Sorry, I'm on the treadmill at the gym. Too hot to run outdoors unless I go at five a.m. and, sorry, I'm not doing *that*."

"I'm sure the police talked to you at the time Jenny disappeared," I said, knowing full well that they had. "They say you talked to her that morning."

"Yeah, I guess I did. We talked a lot." Puff, puff. "Friends since high school."

"That day, do you remember what you talked about?"

"Ooh, not specifically. Too long ago. Most likely making plans to go out. Whenever she could, Jenny would get her mom to babysit. We'd go hit one of the clubs. You know, we all just turned twenty-one, so that was the fun thing." Emily drew a deep breath.

All of that agreed with what the detective had written

in his notes.

"So, I'm curious—have you thought of anything else in the meantime? Any little thing she said that gave a clue about what happened later?"

"Hang on," she said. "I'm putting this thing on cool-down mode."

I heard quick electronic beeps in the background and the steady, whirring sound changed tone. Emily's breathing was still huffing.

"Now ... what was I thinking about ..."

"Clues? Anything about Jenny and that day?"

"You know, it was nothing special. I think we talked about whether we might be on for that Saturday night, girl's night out. There were five or six of us back then, and the group changed up, depending on who was available. I was usually the one who either sent out a text or called around to put it together."

"And Jenny was up for it, planning to go that week?"

"Yeah, as I recall, she was. I think I told that to the police officer."

She had. DeAngelo put it in his notes, but I'd wanted to verify.

"What about afterward, when you learned she'd gone missing? Did you speak with her mother or anyone else?"

"Oh, yeah, that's right. Mrs. Arnold called me, and I guess a few of the others, too. I basically told her the same thing I've told you. She did ask whether Jenny had been in touch with her ex. God, Ricky Blake—that guy was a case."

"In what way?"

"So full of himself. You know, he had hit on every one of Jenny's friends. She was clueless, of course, and none of us would *think* of telling her. When he bailed, none of us were surprised and none of us were sad about it."

"He was a musician with a band, right?"

"That's what he *said*. But then Ricky said a lot of things that were pure bull. You never knew what to believe. Except for poor Jenny. She believed it all."

Interesting. Linda hadn't brought out this aspect of her former son-in-law, and I'd found nothing along these lines in the police notes.

"Do you think Ricky might have been back in touch with Jenny right before her disappearance?"

The treadmill sound in the background whirred to a stop. "If he did, she never said anything to me. If I had to guess, I'd say no."

I got the sense Emily was finished with her workout and antsy to get on with other things, so I glanced down at my notes.

"One last thing," I said. "Was Anna Wentworth part of your group who went out together?"

"Anna Wentworth … no, I don't recognize the name."

"Okay, thanks. I'll let you go." I clicked off the call and quickly jotted down a few facts and additional questions.

Anna Wentworth, the next name on my list, was someone Jenny had apparently sent an obituary she'd written about herself.

Chapter 19

For a twenty-one year old, writing one's own obituary seemed like a bizarre thing to do. I couldn't wait to see if Anna Wentworth remembered receiving Jenny's, and how she might explain it.

"Jennifer Blake … Jenny Blake … I don't recall anyone …" The woman at the other end sounded as if she really was giving my request some serious thought.

"She wrote her own obituary and emailed it to you. This was about fifteen years ago."

Somehow that clicked. "Oh my gosh, yes. I remember now." A hearty laugh. "What a silly thing that was."

"Jenny Blake disappeared less than a day after she sent that message. Her family has heard nothing from her since then."

Two beats of complete silence. "Oh god, I never knew."

I believed her. "Anna, how did you know Jenny? Longtime friends, or what?"

"No, not at all. Casual acquaintances, at the most."

"Can you tell me more?"

"Yeah, well, sure. I would see her around, usually at the library at UNM. We seemed to choose similar study hours, and we'd recognize each other and smile or say hi. I was hustling for my master's at the time. She was a lot younger, and I seem to remember she was majoring in business admin ... no, but it was something like that. Anyway, this one day I was into the newspaper archives for some reason and I had flipped to the obituaries at the back of the *Journal*. I read a couple of them, and I must have shaken my head or made some kind of a sound. This girl across the table looked up at me. I think I apologized for disturbing her ... she said it was okay, she was at a frustration level at working on the tax code. That's right! Accounting was her major."

I was jotting notes, mainly doodling.

"So we whispered back and forth a little and she asked what I was reading in the paper. I commented that it was the obituaries, and how dry they all were written. So-and-so died, survived by blah-blah number of children and grandchildren. It's like there was a formula for the notices but they gave no picture of the person, their life, their interests."

I knew what she meant and hoped I wouldn't ever need to provide the data for someone I knew. But that brought an image of Elsa into my head, so I forced my thoughts to shut up and went back to listening.

"We got to joking around about it, playing with some of the listings in the paper, guessing. Was that guy a stunt pilot? Had this elderly woman been a spy during the war?

What was *interesting* about them, the thing that didn't make it into the bland listings? And Jenny said, 'People should write their own, before they die. I bet I could come up with a good one for myself.' And that idea kind of took hold. I told her I'd write mine if she would write hers, and we could share them if we wanted to."

"And that was it? A lark?"

"Sure, why not? She must have gone home and done hers right away. I think it came in my email within a day or two. I kept thinking I should get around to doing mine. But things got crazy and I never did."

"You received hers though?"

"Yeah, I'm sure I did. In fact, I kind of recall that she listed some things that would have been her dream career—fame and glory kind of stuff that all young girls think about—not accounting and learning the tax code, for sure. I meant to tease her about it the next time I saw her …" There was a long, thoughtful pause. "But then I never did. See her. It never occurred to me until just now. I got so busy with midterm finals and the fact I would be getting my degree at the end of the semester. Dammit, it never entered my mind that I never did see this girl again. How could I have been so thoughtless?"

Anna seemed genuinely upset. I found myself trying to reassure her. "Well, UNM is a huge campus. Not an easy place to run into someone unless you're in the same classes."

"True. But still."

"There was an investigation into her disappearance. Didn't the police contact you?"

"No—now that, I would definitely remember."

A glance at the clock told me I was running late, so

I thanked Anna Wentworth for her time and gave one final reassurance that her losing track of Jenny Blake was understandable. I was stuffing things into my purse as I said goodbye.

Back home, I organized a briefcase with the paperwork I would carry. I was forgetting something, I knew it. Halfway to the airport it hit me. Drake! I'd never even told my husband I was about to hop on a plane.

I parked my Jeep, wheeled my bag into the terminal, and poked numbers into the little kiosk thingy until it spat out a boarding pass for me. The security line was insane, but I made it through and down to gate A-12, naturally the one at the very end of the line. I'm not complaining—the Albuquerque airport is still one of the easiest in the country in which to negotiate one's way around.

My boarding group was already filing into the jetway and I joined them, finding that inside the plane there were only middle seats remaining. I received an impatient look from the aisle guy who had to stand up to let me get through, but I figured if he didn't want someone stepping over his toes, he could have taken the middle seat himself. He didn't seem thrilled that I immediately pulled out my phone and made a call, hoping to hear Drake's voice before the announcement came that we had to turn off our electronics.

No Drake, but that made sense. In the late afternoons they would normally do a final pre-dark recon of the fire area. I left him a quick message to let him know about this sudden shift in plans. Not that he couldn't reach me just as easily in Phoenix as at home, but if the worst happened and the plane went down, it was only polite to let him know so he wouldn't be shocked when he got that dreaded airline call. Okay, I'm putting those thoughts *right* out of my head. It won't happen.

And it didn't. The flight was fine, other than the normal bumpiness arriving into the Phoenix area because of the waves of heat coming off the earth. I handled the terminal crowds and the rental desk and stepped out to the curb where a van would take me to the lot to get my car. That's when the temperature nearly knocked me off my feet—I know it's like this, but the blast always takes me by surprise.

Picture heating your oven to four hundred degrees, opening the door, and stepping right inside. It's kind of like that. Even at dusk the air temperature was well over a hundred degrees—actually 118, according to the app on my phone, which I opened while I rode the van to pick up my rental. Okay, that was information I probably didn't want to know.

The cars were under covered parking, and some blessed concierge soul had come out and started mine, running the AC a few minutes. I tipped heavily, got in, and programmed the address of my hotel into the GPS. Getting out of this massive airport is an adventure in itself, as even the locals will attest, but I managed it with the helpful directions delivered in a soothing female voice that never once got ruffled.

During the flight I had debated once again about calling my brother Paul to see about meeting up this evening for a drink or something, but the day (and now the heat) were beginning to wear on me. I opted instead to get settled in my room and call him from there. A plan was soon in place to meet for breakfast, just the two of us.

A quick call to Janeen DeAngelo, and we had a date for mid-morning at Carefree Manor.

I slept well and awoke refreshed—love how hotels near airports are built to such soundproof standards. By eight-thirty I had showered and dressed and braced myself to go outdoors. Paul had graciously offered to drive to my part of the city and meet near the hotel.

The restaurant was next door, less than a block away. I debated—walk or drive—and decided it was ridiculous to drive such a short distance. I'd had no exercise at all yesterday. I would walk.

Distances can be deceiving, especially when you are physically miserable. The good thing was that it had cooled off from last night. The early morning air was a balmy 104, but I could do this. And yes, I was feeling a little broiled by the time I stepped inside, enough that I didn't immediately notice that the inside of the Village Inn was air-conditioned down to what felt like 37 degrees after I'd been in there ten minutes. It's another thing the locals know, which I had forgotten—take a coat with you everywhere unless your body can easily adapt to major temperature changes.

Paul waved at me from a corner booth (wearing a sport coat, I noted).

"Hey little sis!" He stood and greeted me with a hug. His whole family are a huggy bunch.

We ordered—pancakes for him, a veggie omelet for me—and ran through our usual topics of conversation while we had coffee and waited for our food. How were Lorraine and the kids? Fine. How was Drake? Fine, busy. How's Gram these days? I gave the rundown of what I knew: she's still going strong, and has invited me to attend a wedding tomorrow as her plus-one. Dropping in the fact of a social obligation the next day automatically saved me from having to explain why I wasn't staying long.

The waitress came along with a laden tray just as I was telling Paul what time my flight would leave this afternoon. We ate, contented that we had exhausted all the social obligations between us. Don't get me wrong—I love my brother dearly. I can take or leave the rest of his family. They're all nice people. We just have nothing in common.

He politely asked about the case I'd told him was the reason for my trip, but his eyes glazed over a bit the moment I went into any detail. His pancakes had his full attention. With Ron, I can spend a whole day talking business or socializing with Victoria. This one is just a different type of relationship. And that's fine.

We split the check, hugged again at the exit door, and headed our separate ways.

Chapter 20

Since it's impossible to guess how long it might take to get from point A to point B in this city, traffic being a real bear, I arrived at Carefree Manor thirty minutes before my appointed time with Detective Ernie DeAngelo and his daughter Janeen. I used the time to sit in my air-conditioned car and glance back through his notes to formulate my questions. That is, *if* the man was actually astute enough to comprehend and could bring up memories from his working years. Janeen had been cautious and promised nothing in that regard.

One of the detective's notes that intrigued me was a mention of their finding a packet of cocaine inside the Sixth Street house. There was a notation in DeAngelo's writing: *the husband???* I hoped he could tell me whether anything ever came of that. It could be that Ricky Blake had been doing prison time all these years, which would account for his having no work history or credit history. Maybe.

Depending on what I might learn here, I would need to sit down and compare the dates from the various sources and see if anything matched. When the dashboard clocked ticked over to five minutes before our appointment time, I set the notes back inside my briefcase and went into the building marked Office.

Carefree Manor consisted of four buildings. Three of them were three-story stucco and tile apartments that formed a horseshoe shape around a center courtyard. The smaller building, where the office was located, contained the complex's common areas. I signed in at a reception desk, where a lady in business attire reached for a phone, to announce me. Janeen DeAngelo approached within a couple of minutes. She was a little older than I, probably mid-forties, wearing a cherry-red skort, red and white top with geometric designs, and white canvas slip-on shoes. Her dark hair was pulled up into a messy bun on top of her head.

She smiled and shook my hand. "Hi, Charlie. Good to meet you. I've told Dad he was having a visitor this morning and he'd get to talk shop."

She led the way past a library on the right, decorated in desert hues of tan, turquoise and coral. I could see several tables set up with jigsaw puzzles in progress and comfortable looking wingback chairs, most of them occupied with chattering older women. On the left was the dining room. The doors were closed now and a signboard on an easel announced it would reopen for lunch at 11:30. A couple of smaller meeting rooms lined the wide corridor on the right, and there was a small room with a half-door. The sign above called it the Activity Center, where apparently the residents could book little excursions to the museums, grocery store, or doctor appointments.

We walked out a rear door and crossed an open area filled with shuffleboard and bocce ball courts, attractive plantings, and a swimming pool surrounded by lounge chairs. Surprisingly, given the oppressive heat, there was quite a bit of activity.

"He got very excited when I mentioned you were investigating one of his old cases," Janeen said as we approached an elevator and stepped inside.

"Does he remember a lot from those days?" I asked.

She pressed the button for the third floor, then waggled her hand in a sometimes-yes, sometimes-no motion. "The past is easier for him than the present. You know, he and Mom had such great plans when they moved here. She loved having their own apartment but with the convenience of someone else doing all the cooking and cleaning. She really got into the social life of the various ladies' clubs here in the complex—book club, knitting … she was even taking up watercolors. Dad was going to play golf every single day. They'd brought their own car and could go anywhere they wanted, so they were out to my house a lot to do things with the kids."

The elevator stopped and she indicated we would turn left at the hallway intersection. Her pace slowed. "Then things changed. Mom's cancer, only a year after they came here. Dad never did get around to playing much golf; he just lost interest. And my kids grew up. Ten and twelve when the grandparents arrived, they were soon in high school and had no time for family. Now they're both finishing college and living in other cities. I feel bad for older people who make their own life plans based on their grandchildren. Life begins to move along too fast for them to keep up."

She stopped in front of a tan door marked 321. "At least that's what happened to Dad." Her smile brightened once again as she opened the door and ushered me inside. There was a short entryway with a little kitchenette on my left, a living room straight ahead with sliding glass door leading to a balcony with a padded lounge chair and a bunch of potted plants on it. One doorway, on my right, must lead to the bedroom.

"Dad, your company's here," she announced, a bit loudly. My reminder—the old cop had diminished hearing.

The man who strode out of the bedroom certainly didn't appear frail or senile. He walked confidently and greeted me with a pleasant expression, not exuberant but certainly friendly. He wore cotton khaki slacks, a short sleeved button-down shirt in a tropical print that revealed age spots dotted all over his arms, and sturdy brown lace-up shoes (the only kind a respectable street cop would wear, I suspected). His hair had gone gray, with streaks to remind me that it had once been dark, and his dark eyes seemed focused.

We shook hands, then he turned to Janeen. "Who's this again?"

"Her name is Charlie Parker. She's a private investigator from Albuquerque."

I automatically started to correct the part about my being a licensed investigator, but what was the point? She'd told him fifteen minutes ago that he had a visitor coming and already needed to repeat the information. I wondered if the whole trip would be a waste of time. But I wasn't going into this without my positive attitude in place.

"I understand you were with APD for a lot of years," I said.

"I was, indeed. Went to the police academy right out of high school. Patrol officer for fifteen years before I made detective, and then I was in Missing Persons for the rest of my career."

Janeen, standing behind him, nodded. Apparently, he had all those facts firmly stored, even if other parts of his memory were slipping.

"Would you two like something to drink while you talk?" she asked, slipping past me into the kitchenette. "I've made iced tea and there's lemonade."

"I want the lemon stuff," DeAngelo said.

I nodded that I would take the same. While Janeen got busy with glasses and ice, her father ushered me toward the sofa.

"I brought some things from the case I'm working on," I told him. "A young woman was reported missing by her mother. The frightening thing was that she had been home alone with her one-year-old baby, and when the mother arrived the baby was alone in the house. The missing woman was Jennifer Blake."

He sat in an armchair across from me and leaned forward with elbows on knees, nodding. I held out the photo of Jenny and Cassie and he took it. After studying the faces for a long minute, he said, "The house was in the north valley somewhere. Yeah, we talked to the neighbors."

"Yes—on Sixth Street. It was you and your partner at the time, Alan Curtis."

More nodding. "Curtis. New guy. Wasn't with me very long."

"According to your notes …" I reached into the

briefcase I had set on the sofa beside me and pulled out his old notebook pages, "... the main suspect was Jenny Blake's ex-husband, a musician named Ricky Blake. I've spoken with the girl's mother and she says a lot of people thought Ricky may have come back and Jenny decided to leave with him. She—Linda Arnold, the mother—didn't believe that to be the case. She has felt, all along, that Jenny was abducted by an intruder."

DeAngelo held his hand out for the handwritten notes I held.

He silently read through a few of the small sheets from the spiral notebook, his forehead wrinkling in concentration.

Janeen came in with two glasses of lemonade, which she set on coasters on the coffee table. She pointed over her shoulder toward the bedroom, indicating she would be nearby if needed. While the detective stared at his notes, I took a sip. The beverage was freshly made and wonderful, reminding me how much citrus is grown locally in Arizona.

"Boy, does this take me back," he said, running his thumb over the lines written in his own hand. "I wonder how many of these little notebooks I filled up over the years. I'd get big packs of them from Costco. Probably used one or two of them on each case, sometimes more."

I smiled when he looked up at me. So far, the memories were coming to him—I hoped he could get more specific. I pointed to one of the small sheets I had read at least a dozen times.

"Jenny and Ricky—the possibility that they might have run off together. It looks like you took the idea seriously. You have some notes about trying to locate the ex."

He nodded and reread the note I indicated. But then

he shook his head.

"Did you ever have any luck with that? Finding him? I couldn't find anything much about him in the file."

"No, never did actually make contact."

"Linda Arnold and a few of Jenny's friends have told me Ricky was a musician, that he played in a band, but someone raised a doubt about that. One friend told me Ricky had lied about a lot of things."

DeAngelo flipped a couple of pages in the notes and read some more. I sipped my lemonade and gave him time.

"This," he said at last. "This note, 'mud and blood.' That was the name of the only band I could find associated with him."

Interesting. I'd seen *mud and blood* written there, and assumed it referred to some physical evidence. It was something I had intended to ask about. So now I had the answer.

"I've never heard of them. Were they popular?" I could pretty much guess they weren't exactly famous. After all, I was in the right age group at the time to know a little something about the music of my generation.

A smile turned up one corner of the detective's mouth. "Nah. I found an old website someone had set up for them. Pretty rudimentary by today's standards. Their schedule of appearances included some high school dances and one music festival in a park somewhere. The last of those gigs was well before the timeframe of this case. I assumed they split up after that. It's what bands do."

"Excellent memory you have for this kind of thing."

He stared down at the papers in his hand. "Don't let me fool you. Things from the past, these notes bring it all back. I can't tell you what I had for breakfast this morning."

His admission was heartfelt, and so sad. I wasn't sure what to say, but reminded myself that I was here for a reason. I needed to take advantage of his clarity while he had it. I pulled Jenny's purse from my briefcase and handed it over to him.

"Does this bring back any other memories of the case?"

He picked up the purse and ran his fingers through the zippered pockets. "A cell phone. There was a phone in here. Oh, and we took a laptop from the house. Check those. It's how we got numbers for some friends of the victim."

I made a mental note to see if I could get hold of those items. All Cassie got access to were the written records. They might reveal something more than what I already knew, although I had a feeling the detectives' notes were fairly thorough.

"I'll check them out. Do you recall any other physical evidence that might help with my search?"

His eyes narrowed, as though he was manually willing them to focus. "Drugs. We confiscated a half-kilo of cocaine from the house."

"From Jenny Blake's house on Sixth?" Wow. I'd picked up rumors of Ricky and some possible drug use, but assumed it was small-time stuff. A pound of cocaine was a lot. "Did Jenny—?"

"We didn't think the female subject was involved. We almost didn't find the stash. We were nearly done searching the house when I noticed scrapes where the bed in the main bedroom had been scooted across the wood floor several times. The scratches looked old, but we pushed it out and looked. There was a loose floorboard and when I pried it up, there was the bag of coke."

He looked down again at his notes, refreshing his memory. "It looked like the stuff had been there awhile. The floor was dusty, the bag of coke was dusty. I figured the ex had skipped out so quick he forgot it."

"I came up with some hints about drugs, but never imagined that much."

"The Rio Arriba cartel was big in northern New Mexico, probably still is, for all I know. We suspected a connection, based on a rumor that Ricky was in a new band based in Espanola. Hard to imagine an Anglo kid fitting in, but who knows."

"You never did actually locate him then?"

Something in the man's eyes shifted and I had a feeling I was losing him.

"Ernie? Ricky Blake—no leads?"

He shook his head and cleared up again. "No. We never located him. Can't say that we tried too hard. Our job was to find Jennifer."

He handed the notes back to me, picked up his lemonade and sipped a little of it. When I showed him Jenny's wallet and the items inside, I could tell his attention was fading. I gave it another ten minutes to see if he would snap to with more information, but the interview was fairly much over. I gathered the pages and items I'd brought and packed them away.

Janeen must have had an ear to the conversation because she seemed to know the exact moment to reappear. I thanked Ernie DeAngelo for his help, wished him well, and started for the door. His daughter walked me out.

"That's the sharpest I've seen him in a very long time," she said, turning to face me when we reached the elevator.

"He seemed to perk up when he saw his own handwriting on the notes. I was amazed at the amount of detail he recalled."

She shrugged. "As I said, he's a lot better with the past than the present. And much better with good memories than bad ones. I can't get him to talk about Mom's death at all, but you saw how he lit up when he got on the topic of his career."

I nodded.

"He loved being a cop, Charlie. Too bad he can't go back to it now. But that's the way it is."

I squeezed her hand and stepped into the open elevator.

Chapter 21

Then

Curtis looked up from the open door of the blue Celica when DeAngelo called out to him. He closed the door and joined his partner on the front porch. "Wind's picking up—I didn't hear what you said. Let's get inside."

"I was asking what you found in the car." The senior detective glanced at the Luminol bottle and special flashlight in his partner's hands. "You spray down the whole thing?"

"Seats, dash, steering wheel, door handles. Nada."

Well, at least there hadn't been a bloody crime or removal of a body in Jenny Blake's vehicle. "Let's check a few places in the house, just see if anything pops up, although I have my doubts. Ms. Arnold said she left the house as she found it, other than taking the baby and her gear home with her."

"I sure didn't see any sign of a struggle," Curtis commented as they walked indoors to get out of the wind.

"Doesn't make sense that somebody would abduct the young woman, then come back and straighten up the house, especially if there's a screaming baby inside to alert anyone passing by. Still, it's better if we can tell the chief we covered our bases."

"Right." Curtis began by spritzing the blood-detecting chemical on the front doorknob and frame. When he shined the blacklight on the fluid, nothing showed up. If blood were present, any droplets would glow pinkish purple.

"I'm going to walk through the place one more time," DeAngelo said. "Have fun."

"Ha. Ha." Curtis said with a grimace. It was probably the most irreverent thing he'd ever said, the closest thing to a joke, around his superior.

DeAngelo parked himself on the living room sofa and stared at the open laptop he'd left on the cheap coffee table. "Ever hear of someone writing their own obituary?"

Curtis had sprayed the Luminol on the floor near the front door and was shining his light on it. "For real or as a joke?"

"Either."

"My aunt told me she was going to write her own." He moved toward the kitchen door and spritzed the doorjamb on both sides. "Said she could do a better job than some newspaper employee who knew nothing about her."

"Did she write it and then share it with friends?"

The younger detective shrugged. "No idea. She didn't send it to me, is all I know."

"Okay. Maybe it's a thing with the younger crowd. I've

got the email address of the person Ms. Blake sent hers to. I think I'll look her up and see if I can find out what it's all about." He shut down the computer and put it back in its case, tagging it as evidence and placing the case near the box of other items they'd collected.

He meandered back into the bedroom, switching on the overhead light, looking for anything he might have missed before. A picture on the wall seemed crooked. He lifted a corner of it and peered behind. Nothing. He even took it down and examined the back. Still nothing. Get a grip, he told himself. It was crooked because nobody was particular enough to straighten it, probably had hung that way for weeks.

He'd already been through the dresser drawers. Now he picked up each of the many pillows on the bed, shaking them and tossing them aside. A cardigan sweater had been tucked under one of them, and he imagined Jenny Blake slipping it on to warm her arms when she read in bed on chilly nights. At least that's what his own wife did. He'd even teased her about it. He lifted the comforter, blanket, and sheet but found nothing that didn't look a hundred percent like a bed that had been slept in.

Kneeling, he raised the bed skirt and peered under. No storage boxes or junk. Amazing. This was the place his wife stashed all kinds of extra stuff that she'd probably never use. The hardwood floor was dusty, but that was about it. Then the light hit some marks in the wood. He pulled his small flashlight from his pocket and took a closer look.

There were definitely scratches on the wood floor, and when he checked the other three legs of the bed he discovered the same. The bed had been pushed across the floor, several times, if he had to guess. Not that it would be unusual, but something about this one was setting off his cop-radar.

"Hey, Curtis, give me a hand real quick, would you?"

When his partner arrived, he explained. "I want to move the bed away from the wall over there, but need to do it without disturbing much. Maybe if we lift slightly as we pull?"

Once the bed was out of the way, he spotted the thing that had triggered his senses. Near the wall he could tell one of the floorboards was loose. Before approaching it, he pulled out his camera and took shots of the bed, floor, and surrounding area. As he'd gathered from his sideways glance earlier, the floor was thick with dust that obviously hadn't been disturbed in a while. He took out his pocket knife and used the screwdriver attachment to get at the loose board, prying it upward until he could see the space beneath. A plastic bag filled with something white, the whole thing about the size and shape of a brick. He knew instantly what it was.

Somebody who had lived in this house was into cocaine. Not just using. Dealing.

Every bit of his police training had taught him never to jump to conclusions, but at this moment if he had to bet money … he'd say Ricky Blake had left behind one very important item when he'd moved away. Unfortunately, this item could have put Jenny Blake in grave danger, especially if she didn't even realize she possessed it. And if she did know it was there—if this was her doing—she was likely in trouble with some very bad dudes.

Curtis let out a low whistle when DeAngelo pulled the brick from its hiding spot.

"Get me an evidence bag. We'll get this plastic dusted

for prints when we get to the station."

During the short drive back downtown they discussed potential loose ends.

"Fill me in," DeAngelo said. "What was in the Celica?"

"Not much. The usual paperwork, insurance card, a baby car seat. The mother must have a second one in her own vehicle, since she took the kid but not the car seat. I ran the plate and the victim's driver's license. No wants or warrants, no traffic tickets. I gave the credit card info to Conroy. She'll find out if there's been recent activity on the card."

"So, impound the car, or not—what do you say?"

"Your call, boss. I sprayed Luminol around inside, didn't pick up a thing. Didn't find any evidence of a crime."

"Okay, so no. There're enough vehicles in the impound lot as it is, and those guys are swamped." He glanced over at his partner. "Other than that brick under the bedroom floor, we don't even know that we have a crime yet."

"So, any bets we're just spinning our wheels?"

The senior cop didn't hesitate. "I didn't say that. Just sayin' we need to dig some more. It's early days. We still got the rest of her computer, her cell phone, and now this *package* from under the floor. Now that's a bet I will take— gotta be coke."

He had no sooner pulled off the street, into the department's employee parking area, than his phone rang. He stared at the screen for a moment before he recognized the number.

"Oh great, it's Linda Arnold."

Chapter 22

Now

The weather gods cooperated on the day of the wedding. A cool front had moved through during the night, with a brisk wind to carry away some of the oppressive heat we'd endured for the past six weeks (although after my visit to Phoenix I would never again complain about heat in Albuquerque). The high for the day was predicted to be a pleasant eighty-five at two o'clock, the time set forth on the invitation.

Despite our fashion consultation a few days ago, Elsa had changed her mind about what to wear. With Dottie's assistance, she was dressed in the lavender outfit. The large purple hat, I suspected, had come from Dottie's own collection. But it was a fun look, and Gram seemed quite pleased with herself. She chattered nonstop in the car as

I drove east on Lomas, watching for the turn to the park.

Two blocks off the busy six-lane boulevard, we found the place, and it was no problem at all to figure out which of the picnic areas was the wedding venue. I heard a sharp intake of breath from Gram's side of the car as we took in the swagged yards and yards of diaphanous white fabric that hung from the rafters and edges of the covered palapa. Gigantic bundles of pink silk flowers marked the top of each swag, and the support poles were wound with garlands of something in green and pink. From each corner of the four-sided structure there soared a massive bouquet of pink balloons. I felt my eyes go wide. Who decorated this place—a fourteen year old with a streak of gypsy in her?

I parked at the curb about twenty yards from the … okay, I wasn't sure what to call it at this point. As we got out, Gram spotted Iris across the way. She gave a shout and waved, but it didn't seem that her friend heard her. I took her elbow and we started across the grass.

The crowd—I guessed about fifty people at this point—seemed to consist of people in Iris's age range and people under forty. Bride's side, groom's side. Fairly easy to figure out. Except here I was, firmly sticking by Elsa for the duration.

Iris spotted us just then and she came rushing toward us with her creampuff of a dress fluttering as she moved and a veil threatening to leave its tiara anchor if the breeze caught it just right.

"Elsa! I'm so happy you came. And Charlie, thanks for coming along too." The bride reached out and took each of our hands, giving a little squeeze.

Elsa beamed, although I picked up a hint that she was

a little taken aback by the frou-frou and all the fuss. When she had told me about the wedding plans, she had the distinct impression that Iris's white wedding outfit would be a tailored suit and the ceremony in the park considerably simpler than this.

"I want you to meet Jeffrey Lougan," Iris said, turning to point toward a tall, good-looking man who was chatting with a group of the younger people in the shade. "Oh, sweetheart! Jeffrey! Come meet my friends."

He put on a bright smile when she waved him over, and he stood attentively as Iris gushed over how long she had known Elsa.

"Ah, the beautiful Miss Elsa," he said, taking her hand in a courtly gesture and bowing over it. "I have heard many good things."

He didn't quite say he had heard good things about me, but he was gracious enough in taking my hand too.

"Jeffrey's sister planned the decorations and got all her cousins to set everything up this morning," Iris said, beaming at the garish setup.

"Nice." I hoped my smile wasn't too revealing.

"Here she is, our budding designer," Iris said, waving over a twenty-something with dark hair in long curls and a form-fitting hot-pink dress that left nothing to the imagination, "and one of my maids of honor. This is Celeste."

As I acknowledged the introduction, I spotted three other girls in the same attire.

"Iris, pastor Mike is ready any time," Celeste said, tilting her head toward the decorated structure.

"Oh. Oh! So excited!"

"This is it, my love," Jeffrey said, his eyes on Iris. He

extended an arm and she looped hers through it.

"Let me get your bouquet," Celeste said, dashing off.

"We'd better take our seats," Elsa told me.

"Oh, yes, you're next to Aunt Reyna. We've saved you two seats on the very front row," Jeffrey said. "One of the ushers will show you."

A young man met us at the entrance, a guy who looked so much like Jeffrey he must be a relative. In fact, as I looked at the faces we passed on the way to our chairs, I figured out that nearly everyone other than the old folks in Elsa's crowd had to be related. It looked like Iris was marrying into a great big happy family.

The minister was a surprise—thirty-ish, with a shaved head and tattooed arms, wearing a white robe that seemed vaguely Hindu—but he read his lines and got the others to repeat theirs, and the deed was done in under ten minutes.

While the bride and groom scurried off to the side to sign their license and make it all legal, the four bridesmaids and six groomsmen led the way toward the open bar at the back. By the increased noise level, I guessed a few of them had already been at the punch. The aunt who had sat next to Elsa stood, stretched a little, and stepped aside so we could pass. She glanced toward the groom, a satisfied look on her face. I caught myself watching the group dynamic and didn't realize Elsa was having a bit of an issue with her purse, which had become lodged between the legs of her chair and mine.

"Go on ahead, Reyna," I said. "We might be a minute."

I reached for the tangled purse strap, thinking all the while that Reyna must be Celeste's mother; they looked so much alike. Then again, every dark-haired person in the place looked very much alike. I looped Elsa's purse over her arm, noticing tables of food near the bar.

"Can I bring you something?" I asked.

But she'd spotted another friend from her church and was already heading toward the white-haired woman. Good. She wouldn't go too far and she had company. I decided I would see what the food offerings were and fill a couple of plates. Already, several of the young men had begun rearranging the rows of folding chairs into groupings, and small tables appeared. Informal, quick dining at its best. A short queue had formed in front of the food, which appeared to consist of hot hors d'oeuvres over Sterno heat and plates of fruits and veggies.

As I moved forward, I spotted Iris and Jeffrey at a table away from the wedding palapa, along with a dark-suited man I didn't recognize. Aunt Reyna was standing there, pointing at a sheaf of papers on the table. This looked like more than a signing of the license. I remembered asking if Iris was making sure they had a prenup—but that would have been signed before the wedding, not today. Hmm. Well, maybe I would get a chance to discreetly ask her about it later. Or maybe I would just butt out and not interfere.

Two more of Elsa's church lady friends had joined the conversation by the time I arrived with the food, which I set on one of the small tables.

"Here, you ladies start on this," I suggested, "and I'll bring more."

They all smiled and seemed glad to get off their feet. This time as I stood in the food line I noticed the foursome at the other table had disappeared. I looked for Iris and saw her, smiling and clinging to Jeffrey's hand as they walked into the shade to join their guests. Her eyes were on the tiered wedding cake, which sat on its own table. His eyes drifted toward another table that held a few wrapped presents and a large box earmarked for cash gifts. I'd begun this day with mild distrust of the man, and now I felt it growing steadily.

"Charlie?"

I turned to see Aunt Reyna standing next to me. Had my face given away my feelings? I rearranged my smile accordingly.

"Very nice party," I said. "And just look at the happy couple."

Her expression softened. "Yes, I am so happy to see my nephew together with his true love."

"So, it's his first marriage, then?"

"There was a girl, several years ago. Such a tragedy. They were to be married in the spring, but there was a terrible accident. He never recovered—would not look at another woman. Well, not until he met Iris. We are all so happy for him."

"Yes, well, they both seem very … happy." Happy, happy, happy—it seemed the most anyone could say about the couple and the day.

I reached the stack of plates and reached for a large one. "For Elsa and three of her friends," I said with a nod toward the chatty table in the corner. *Come on*, why was I explaining myself to the aunt?

But Reyna had turned her attention elsewhere, back to Jeffrey and Iris. I noticed nearly everyone in the groom's family had their eyes on the couple. What was that about?

I loaded the plate with meatballs and sausages, some shrimp and cocktail sauce, a big pile of nachos, and topped it with carrot and celery sticks. If this didn't give all the old ladies indigestion, nothing would. I nabbed one of the meatballs for myself with a small wooden skewer and turned back to view the crowd. This time I couldn't tell that anyone was necessarily staring at the bride and groom. Was I just becoming a little crazy and making stuff up in my head?

I joined Elsa and her friends, pulling up another chair, listening to their chitchat about their church activities, wishing I was home working on the Blake case or, better yet, that Drake and I were home together. This summer was dragging on far too long; we could be up at our tiny-house cabin in the mountains and—

Ding-ding-ding came the universal signal for attention, a fork being tapped against the side of a champagne glass. The same young men came around with glasses of champagne on trays—maybe they were paid waitstaff rather than cousins, after all? Who knew? Who cared? I took one, as did each of my table companions. Toasts were made, champagne drunk, the cake was cut and handed out. By the time the dance music began throbbing through unseen speakers somewhere, I could tell Elsa's energy was lagging.

We were standing up, ready to make our excuses and leave, when I saw Iris and Jeffrey approaching. Well, we'd better at least congratulate the couple and wish them well. I'd heard they planned a cruise for their honeymoon trip.

Iris was radiant, Jeffrey beaming. We said all the right things.

When Jeffrey turned aside to say something to another man about his age (and yes, I guessed a relative), Iris took Elsa by the arm.

"Isn't he wonderful? I can't believe what a sweet and thoughtful man I've married. And *so* good looking. Do you know, we've started a tradition of having a cup of tea together at bedtime. Jeffrey makes it and delivers my cup to me in bed. So romantic. We sip our tea and talk about the day. I am so incredibly lucky."

"He sounds like a prize," Elsa told her.

Jeffrey stepped back up to us. "Iris, what do you think?" He tilted his head toward the man he'd been talking to.

"Oh, yes. Elsa, Jeffrey wanted to introduce you to his friend, Mark." Iris took a step sideways to let Mark approach, and Jeffrey formally made the introductions.

"*Enchanté*, madam," Mark said, bending over Elsa's hand and kissing it.

She blushed and pulled her hand back.

"I apologize," Mark said. "if that was somewhat forward of me. I admit that I share my cousin's love for mature women. You are ravishing in that purple hat. What can I say?"

"You can say goodbye," I inserted. "We were just leaving. It was nice to meet all of you."

And to Iris, I added, "Enjoy the dancing, and give us a report on your cruise when you return."

Elsa had shaken off her fluster over the younger man's attention, and it seemed all was well. I took her home and saw her safely into the care of Dottie, who promised to get her into her comfy robe and see that she got some rest.

It didn't take me five minutes after I got inside my own house to change from my summer dress into shorts and a t-shirt, pour a glass of iced tea, and start a computer search on the Lougan family. I'd never picked up such hinky vibes from so many people in one place, especially the aunt and Jeffrey, but cousin Mark was definitely up there on my list.

I found a Facebook profile on Jeffrey Lougan, which

actually kind of surprised me. If he was the entrepreneur and successful businessman Iris described, I would have thought he'd more likely gravitate to LinkedIn. But there he was, smiling face and sketchy background. The profile had only been set up six months ago, and nearly all the Friends seemed to be family members. I didn't, however, spot either Reyna or Mark among them.

So, okay, maybe they weren't into this stuff. I have to admit, I'm not much into it myself. I tried general searches for his name, then tacked CEO to the end of it, hoping to figure out what kind of business he was in. No luck. I thought of other ways to learn more, but without the deeper searches available on Ron's software at the office, I couldn't go a lot further.

At this point all I could do would be to strongly caution Elsa about having any involvement with Jeffrey's friend Mark. Friend. Cousin. Whatever the relationship was. They were a little too similar for my comfort level when it came to my Gram.

Chapter 23

Then

Curtis walked on ahead with the box of evidence from the Blake house while DeAngelo took the call from Linda Arnold.

"Did you find any evidence of who took my daughter?" she asked, not bothering with any niceties first.

"We have just this minute walked back into the squad room after searching the house, Ms. Arnold. We'll need some time to go through everything and analyze it. It's only been a couple of days."

"Two days with my daughter in the hands of someone dangerous!"

"We don't know that for certain, ma'am. We have to be open to any possibility at this point."

"What about the cigarette butt outside the front door?

You took that for testing. Did you learn anything from that?"

"Ma'am, DNA results take a little time. Yes, the testing methods are better now, but it's not an instant thing. I've asked that it be given top priority in the lab."

Then she brought up what he already knew—no one in the family smoked; it had to be a stranger. And for whatever reason she believed it, this smoker was someone with evil intent. He brought up the idea that there could be any number of explanations—a sales person, friend, anybody.

"If DNA is recovered from the cigarette, and *if* it's a match to anyone in our law enforcement databases, please be assured that we will check it out. Right now, I need to get busy with my partner and others in the department so we can begin looking at everything. We will be in touch."

Linda Arnold seemed dismayed that he didn't have immediate answers. He reminded himself that all families reacted this way, wanted answers and became agitated when the police couldn't solve the crime right away. They all watched too much TV and thought real life arrests happened just as fast.

Curtis had set the evidence box on a worktable in the middle of the room, and DeAngelo placed Jenny Blake's computer case next to it. Now, the real work began.

Felice Conroy looked up from her desk when she saw him enter the room. She picked up a scrap of note paper and walked toward them, a tall black woman who wore her hair in about a million long braids. DeAngelo couldn't for the life of him figure out how she did them and how they always looked smooth and neat. His granddaughter sometimes wore her hair in braids but strands were always poking out of them well before the end of the day.

Conroy waved the slip of paper in the air. "Checked out the credit and debit cards for you."

"Want to start an incident wall?" Curtis asked. He had already erased some previous scribbles from the large whiteboard that covered part of one wall in the room.

"Sure. Let's see what we got," DeAngelo said.

He always began with a photo of the victim, so he pulled out the picture he'd been carrying around to show to potential witnesses. He stuck it in the center of the board with a little piece of clear tape.

"Conroy, whatcha got?"

Felice stepped forward with her notes and began writing on the board. "Jenny Blake carried one debit card and one credit card, right?"

"That's all we found in her wallet, except for a few bucks in cash."

"So, I did a credit check on those," she said, "and I found squat. The credit card was used earlier this month at the Walmart on Carlisle. She spent $47.83. Don't know how she gets out for so little—I can't leave that store without spending a hundred, easy." She flashed her brilliant smile with the perfect teeth.

Curtis chuckled. DeAngelo merely waited.

"Okay, the debit card was used more often. Groceries for one adult and one baby don't amount to much. Her one splurge seemed to be a daily visit to the convenience store in the neighborhood where the amount of the purchase would indicate a coffee or soda or something. It's a couple bucks a day, and she used the debit card to buy it."

"When was—"

"The last time she purchased her coffee was the day

before she vanished."

"And nothing since?"

"Nothing at all since."

"I'd like to read more into that," DeAngelo said, "but it makes sense. She walked out without her purse, debit and credit cards were inside the purse … couldn't very well use them."

"Maybe she'd had more cash in the house and she took that with her," Conroy suggested.

DeAngelo didn't mention the drugs. Not yet. The packet they found was too dusty to have recently been placed there or accessed. He didn't see that as the source of Jenny's cash anyway. He started writing other evidence on the wall. In black marker he put: Cigarette butt (being processed for DNA); purse and wallet—he drew a blue line between the word wallet and Conroy's notes about recent spending on the cards. Beside Jenny Blake's picture he wrote her mother's name, her ex-husband's name, and the baby's name.

Below the picture he jotted the list of people they had spoken to—the nosy neighbor across the street, the owner of the convenience store, the kid who'd claimed to be home sick, a couple of others—and a brief note about what each had told them. He also noted that Curtis had examined the victim's car and sprayed it with Luminol, which revealed nothing. When he stepped back from the board, he realized they basically knew squat about Jenny and her movements of that morning.

"We don't have much, do we?" Conroy stated the obvious.

Curtis was pawing through the evidence box, and he added a few notes. He transferred the pictures from his camera to a nearby printer, and as they rolled off, he taped a few of them to the board as well, shots of the exterior and interior of the house.

"Let's talk this out a little," DeAngelo suggested. "We got the mother stating that she and the daughter had made plans for her to stop by and take the baby to the doctor, and Jenny would be leaving soon for her classes. Mom gets to the house, baby's alone. So, who would come to the door who had Jenny's trust enough that she would step outside with them and leave her baby alone?"

As the only woman in the group, Conroy spoke up. "Well, stepping outside is one thing, maybe to answer a question or chat for a few minutes with someone she knew … yeah, maybe. But to go away with that person, to get in a car, leaving the door unlocked and the baby alone, nuh-uh. No mom's doing that."

"You'd say she didn't go willingly."

"Damn right, I'm saying that."

"But there was no sign of a struggle inside the house," Curtis said, pointing at the interior photos.

"So she stepped outside, for whatever reason." Conroy shrugged. "There was a noise, a person outside the windows, a kitty cat, a puppy dog, a knock on the door by someone she knew …"

"And she thought it would only a take a minute …" DeAngelo said.

"Right. So, her purse and coat were there 'cause she was going right back inside." Conroy seemed happy with her logic.

"But, she didn't go right back inside—she never went back inside—and she was gone by the time her mother came by … what … within an hour? A half hour?"

"Thereabouts. Linda Arnold said they had talked on the phone less than an hour before she got there." Curtis had Jenny's cell phone in his gloved hand. He tapped a couple of icons on it. "And that seems right. Here in her list of recent calls, there's Ms. Arnold's number, the most recent on the list."

"We'll need to check out all the calls on the phone, going back at least three days before she disappeared. Conroy, if you've got the time?"

"I'm making the time. This missing-mommy, abandoned-baby situation has my attention."

"Find out who the numbers belong to and follow up."

"Got it." She took the cell phone and went back to her desk.

"Meanwhile, think," DeAngelo said to Curtis and two other officers who'd paused to stare at the board. "Who could have talked Jenny into walking out of the house without her purse, leaving her baby behind, and getting into their car? It had to be someone she knew and trusted. C'mon, we all know the stats. Murders by random strangers are rare." He held up a cautionary hand. "Yes, I know we're only talking about an abduction at this point, but still. Ninety-seven percent of victims are killed or harmed by someone they know, and often it's someone they once loved."

"The ex," Curtis offered.

"Think about it. Ricky seems the most likely. Maybe she spotted him from the window, went out to talk with him, got in the car because it was chilly out and she didn't have her coat, but then he drives away …"

"It's a logical scenario. But what would he want? Why would he have come by?" Conroy piped up from across the room.

The brick. But DeAngelo didn't say it. "That's what we have to figure out. We gotta locate this guy. Let me know immediately if one of those phone numbers ties in to him."

"Meanwhile," he said, turning back to Curtis and picking up the evidence box. "Let's get this stuff down to the lab for prints and whatever other trace evidence they can find."

Chapter 24

Then

The deal had gone well. Better than that—great. The guy had bought the baggie Ricky brought with him, and he'd even offered a hit from it. Ricky's downer mood instantly soared. Now, all he had to do was reach Jenny and talk his way into the house. He wondered if those two cops were gone by now. And why had they been there, anyway?

If he could just get her on the phone, he'd play like he was all concerned and get her to talk to him. That was always the secret with Jenny—flash her a smile, compliment her hair or her clothes or something, run his fingertip across her cheek—she'd melt. Just like she always did. He'd get into the house, maybe get lucky and get her into bed. It'd been too long since the last band gig and the groupies that hung around for a little fun afterward.

He stood at the end of an alley off Third Street and pulled his phone from his pocket. A strange male voice answered and Ricky immediately hung up. What the hell? But the thought died the moment a dark shadow crossed in front of him.

"Ricky Blake ... hey hombre." The guttural voice was unmistakable. Serpiente—the snake. His real name was Raul, but that was almost as scary.

Ricky shoved the phone into his pocket and put on a smile but he felt it waver.

"Man, you owe the boss something." The wiry guy, who was rumored to be able to kill a person with a two-finger pinch, stepped in closer. "You know what I'm talkin' about."

"Sure."

"Payment for product—he trusted you. Tiburon extended you credit. The loan came due a long time ago." Another step closer. Ricky found himself edging backward but he was already against a cinderblock wall.

"Yeah, sure, man. Got part of it right here." He patted his pocket but didn't reach for the cash.

"Ah, hombre, you see? Part of it ... that isn't good enough. Tiburon wants it all. He's—what would you say?—calling in the loan."

"I, uh, well, see that's the thing. I don't exactly have it with me."

His mind raced. He pictured the alley behind him. Could he outrun the whippy little guy? But before he could think of a way to glance over his shoulder subtly, he heard a sound behind him. A footstep. He spun to look and nearly crashed into a human wall. El Toro, the silent but deadly muscle Tiburon sent after someone who needed to learn a lesson. Oh shit.

Double shit. A black SUV with dark-tinted windows screeched to a halt at the curb, less than ten feet away. Ricky wanted to run, make a dash for the open street, but his legs had turned to water. Before he knew it, the two thugs had shoved him into the back seat of the dark vehicle and they were on the move.

* * *

When he came to, the light was fading and he was freezing cold. Images muddled in his brain—brass knuckles smashing into his face, shouted threats, muttering between the two men in Spanish. He rolled over, nearly screaming at the pain in his ribs, reaching with a grimy hand to touch his face, which was swollen beyond recognition. He managed to open one eye enough to see that he was in a large open space, a warehouse of some kind. In the distance he heard low conversation in Spanish. They weren't finished with him yet.

He thought of getting up, willed his body to try, but it was too much effort and he drifted back into a half-conscious haze.

Jenny. He was meeting her for coffee, asking to talk things over with her. But that was a week ago, maybe more. He couldn't remember. He focused on what the cartel thugs wanted, the brick of coke he'd foolishly left behind when he packed up his stuff after the big blowout fight with Jenny. Stupid, stupid, stupid.

The coffee shop. He drifted back to that day, how he'd tried so hard not to appear desperate when he asked his wife to take him back. How about a visit, he'd wheedled. I miss you and the baby … For the first time ever she hadn't fallen for his winsome smile and flirty talk.

"I had the locks changed when you left, Ricky. You're into a bad lifestyle now and I'm not having Cassie exposed to that." Damn, her voice had been firm.

"I'm giving all that up," he promised. "We'll go on the road, just you and me. I'll find another band. If I can get to Branson, I'll join up with a Christian rock band. They won't be into the bad stuff, the drinking and drugs, like the musicians around here."

She hadn't even dignified that with an answer. "I don't trust you, Ricky. You've lied to me so often. I can't believe anything you say anymore."

The cold began to seep into his muscles and his consciousness again, and the memory of their encounter at the coffee shop faded away. A garage door opened somewhere—he heard the whir of the opener—and a vehicle drove in. For a moment he felt warmth from its engine, but the voices in Spanish became louder, coming closer. In his head, Jenny's sweet face blended with what was going on now.

Had she seen something she shouldn't have? Witnessed the cartel thugs talking to him at some point? Maybe she'd found the brick under the floor and reported it, and that's why the cops were at the house. And maybe El Tiburon suspected that he, Ricky, had given them up, ratted out their operation. If he could only convince them …

A sharp kick in the ribs sent fire throughout his body. He heard himself scream, and the scream echoed through the cavernous space.

"*Gringo*! You little *pendejo*—wake up!" It was the voice of Raul, the serpent.

Then a deeper voice, a smoother one, a scarier one.

"You say you still have the product I consigned to you? Where is it? What is the address?"

Someone grabbed his left hand and he dimly realized they would smash his ability to make chords on the guitar. A heavy boot on the fingers and his hand went numb. But the electric pain from his core overrode everything else right now. He began to babble, to beg for mercy until everything became a blur of noise and pain.

In one moment of clarity, Ricky realized you don't walk away from the cartel, and you don't cross them. The moment they got the brick he was dead meat. As for Jenny and the baby, he may have just signed their death warrants too.

Chapter 25

Now

I had intended to go back through the police file and compare it with my notes from my Phoenix trip and the visit with Detective DeAngelo, but I ended up happily sidetracked when Drake called to say he was getting an extra two days off. The helicopter had to go in for scheduled maintenance—those hundred-hour inspections don't get delayed just because there's a fire somewhere—so he would fly it to the airport and we could have some time together while the mechanics did their thing.

With no more than a small pang of guilt, I dropped the case, let the house stay dusty, and turned off my cell phone while the two of us drove up to our tiny cabin on the east side of the Sandia mountains. Other than nibbling on the picnic foods I'd packed and occasionally emerging into sunlight to take the dog outside, we spent two glorious days in bed. It was exactly the break we needed. No matter how busy I get when he's away, our time together is sacred and I couldn't believe how much I'd missed my husband.

On the third day we took a long hike through the foothills at dawn, tidied the cabin, and made our way home. A stop in the small artist's colony of Madrid, some lunch at a favorite café in Tijeras, and we were on the way straight through the city to drop Drake off at the westside airport. He had to be back on the fire contract by dark.

Freckles and I watched him go through his preflight checklist and rev up the turbine engine, watching wistfully as the aircraft lifted skyward. Back at home I spent the afternoon putting away our picnic gear and doing laundry, but I could feel the Blake case beginning to tug at me again. It was time for me to get back to work.

I pulled out the police file, plus my own notes from my meeting with Detective DeAngelo. The old man had been surprisingly lucid about many details, but something was nagging at me. His memory began to fail once he got onto the subject of the drug cartel up north. Why was that? I poured a glass of iced tea and paced the length of my living room, thinking back to the conversation.

Logically, there could be any number of reasons why a cop from the Missing Persons detail in Albuquerque wouldn't know much about the doings of a group of drug runners a hundred miles away—jurisdiction being one of them. If this Chaco Cartel was well known (and I had no idea if they were) they would likely be on the radar of the feds, DEA, ATF, other departments well outside the purview of DeAngelo's department. Still, he'd made a connection between these dudes and Ricky Blake.

"Why didn't you put more of it in writing?" I mused aloud as I stood over the table and stared at his handwritten notes.

I set my glass down and flipped back through the various interviews. None of the neighbors mentioned drugs at all—fine, most likely they wouldn't. Even the young couple's friends wouldn't talk about that aspect, I suspected. People on the margins of a drug user's life are either oblivious to the clues, in denial that there are clues, or they're involved too. None of those people would admit anything to a cop who comes around asking questions. So, okay. That was most likely a dead end.

Other cops—I could see if I could find someone who would look up old records for me. I needed someone who was around at the time when DeAngelo and Curtis worked the case. It took two phone calls. Twenty minutes later I was speaking with a Felice Conroy and explaining how RJP Investigations had been hired to take a look at the old Blake case. I gave a few little details in hopes it would refresh her memory.

"Oh my gosh, that was the young mother who went missing and left her baby alone in the house," she immediately said.

"You do remember the case."

"Like it was last week. That poor girl, that poor little baby. It was the situation. My own kids were still little then, and I couldn't imagine what it would take for me to walk out of the house and leave them alone."

"It really struck a chord with you."

"Absolutely."

"I wonder if we could meet and talk? I don't want to interfere with your current work, but a half hour of your time would be—"

"I get off work in thirty minutes. How about the coffee shop at Central and Girard? It's on my way home."

And not far from me. "Perfect. Will you be in uniform?"

"Oh heavens no. I'm strictly a desk jockey, computer programmer. I've got on a bright yellow jacket today."

"Great, see you soon."

I spotted Conroy the moment I walked in to The Coffee Place, a tall black woman in bright yellow, sitting at a corner table and staring at a phone screen and tapping it with her thumbs. She appeared to be in her mid-forties, attractive, with her hair in a chin-length bob. She looked up and put the phone away when I approached. We did quick introductions and I offered to buy her a coffee. Turned out she'd already ordered an iced latte, and I asked the waitress for the same.

"I've always wondered what happened to that little baby. It seems there was a grandmother or some other family in the picture," she said as soon as our beverages came. "Cute little thing—it would have killed me to see her go into the system."

"I can report that she's grown up to be a pretty impressive teenager. In fact, she's the one who hired me to look into her mother's disappearance."

"You don't say. Wow." She sipped her latte and set the glass mug back down. "I'm so glad to hear it."

I had brought the copy of the police file with me. "I didn't see your name in here, only Curtis and DeAngelo, so I hadn't realized there was another officer on the case."

"Like I said, I'm strictly computer research. On this case I looked into the financial records of the missing girl, helped the detectives make some connections ... well, basically talked things through with them a little. My name probably isn't in the file because I never gave a sworn statement or filed any reports. I just tell what I find, they write it up."

"I spoke with each of them, actually traveled to Phoenix a few days ago to meet DeAngelo in person."

"Oh yeah? How's he doing?"

I filled her in, keeping it basic. "His daughter has been looking out for him ever since his wife died. I gathered she's the only family member he has."

Felice nodded slowly. "He talked very little about his family. I was aware of a wife and two kids, and he talked a little about the daughter. Never about the son. Don't know what the story was there. Of course, I never knew him socially at all. Could be that he just liked to keep his family life private. Lot of cops do. It's their way of feeling that they are protecting the family from the bad influences of the job. Can't say if that works or not."

I had been flipping through the folder, looking for the things Felice mentioned. "I don't see a whole lot about Jenny Blake's financial records here."

"Wasn't much to it, as I recall. You'll want to see what notes the detectives made. I seem to remember she only carried one or two banking cards—she was pretty young—and she hadn't used them at any time after the disappearance was reported. That's the kind of thing we're normally looking for. Someone's gone, but if they're okay they still gotta be spending some money, right?"

I nodded. It made sense.

"So, if they're not spending on their cards, they've got some cash stashed away, someone else starts footing the bills, or …" Deep breath. "Or they're not okay."

By her pained expression I could see that she was thinking specifically of Jenny.

"Following the timeline here in the case reports, it seems DeAngelo and Curtis worked the case pretty actively for a week or two, then the notes get skimpier, and within a couple months they kind of gave up. Do you recall them saying anything more, months later?"

She shook her head. "Every once in awhile I'd ask about that missing mom, but there wasn't anything. They seemed to think the ex-husband was somehow involved, but I don't think they ever caught up with him. There was one conversation … and this was maybe a week or two after the reported disappearance. The guys were talking about the grandmother—well, Jenny's mother—and one of them said the woman seemed resigned to the idea her daughter was dead. Seemed strange to me at the time because family members will always hold out hope. I've seen missing persons cases go *years*, and there's always the family member who'll swear that their loved one is alive and well someplace."

"Maybe Linda Arnold just wasn't one of those."

A shrug. "Maybe. I mean, I have to admit that some are more realistic. If they've had no word after a long time, they'll begin to accept that the person isn't coming back, that they've probably died."

"DNA testing has come a long way," I surmised, thinking back to another recent investigation of mine. "I'd imagine whenever an unidentified body is found they can match it up with a missing person?"

"It's getting better and more accurate," she agreed. "For a long time now, it's standard protocol to collect personal items—hairbrushes, toothbrushes, and such—and start a record on any missing person."

Conroy glanced at her phone and noticed the time. "Look, I gotta get going. Family's going to be screamin for their dinner, you know what I mean."

I smiled and thanked her for the information, although a little disappointed there hadn't been a firm clue to point me in a set direction. But every little bit helped fill in the picture. I handed her one of my cards, in case she thought of anything more, and I insisted on grabbing the check.

She walked out to a white Ford in the parking lot and I spent a couple more minutes glancing over the notes I'd quickly made. Something stood out, and I knew Janeen DeAngelo could help me. But the call shouldn't happen in a public place. I left money on the table and hurried out to my Jeep.

Chapter 26

The late afternoon air was beginning to cool so I rolled down all my windows to get a breeze to come through. Janeen answered on the second ring and we did a moment of how's-it-going chitchat.

"I've got a personal question," I said.

"Okay, sure."

"Someone said your dad mentioned having a son."

There was a definite pause in her breathing. Finally, "Yeah, I had a brother. Ernie."

"I'm sorry, it's too personal. If he died …"

"No, it's okay. Years ago and much water under the bridge. Gosh, I don't know that I've heard his name spoken aloud in years."

"Maybe I misunderstood. Was there a rift of some kind?"

"No, you were right the first time. Ernie died. Drugs. He was eighteen and I was fourteen. It's the kind of thing that can rip a family apart, create anger, blame, and distrust."

"I can't even imagine. I'm so sorry."

"My dad felt all those things. He had to lash out. This was his namesake child, the boy on whom he'd pinned so many hopes. My mother went into mouse mode, scurrying around the house doing a thousand little chores to keep busy, ducking out of sight whenever Dad went on a rant. I hid out in my room a lot, luckily immersed in books. Reading helped me get through a lot."

"And yet your parents stayed together. This kind of thing often breaks couples apart."

"Yeah, amazingly they did. Mainly because Mom just wasn't a fighter—wouldn't argue, wouldn't defend. In mouse mode, she just huddled in the corners while he got it all out. And eventually, he calmed down. Either the anger and frustration was spent or he just lost himself in his work. It was good that he had such an immersive job. Didn't give him a lot of time and space to dwell, you know."

"It must have been *so* difficult for you."

"For all of us. But once Dad's anger settled down, it was as if Ernie had never lived there. They converted his bedroom into a pretty guest room—seldom used, and none of the family ever needed to go in there much so it could be ignored. Dad never spoke Ernie's name. Mom and I quickly learned not to. I guess we just fell into the same pattern. We couldn't bring my brother back by talking about him, so we just didn't."

"And he still handles it this way? Not bringing up your brother at all?"

"To this day. I imagine he'll keep it up to the end of his life."

"So sad. For what it's worth, Janeen, you have my sympathies."

Her voice sounded a little thick as she said she needed to go. I hung up, disturbed. I definitely took my own family way too much for granted. I started the Jeep and drove home in a pensive mood.

Freckles greeted me, wagging her stubby tail enthusiastically, reminding me that certain family members are completely devoted. Either that or she knew it was past time for her dinner. I'd no sooner scooped kibble into her bowl than my phone rang. Drake reported that he'd arrived safely at the fire base camp and was settling in for the night. Again, I thanked all the powers that be for the closeness we share.

My conversations with Felice Conroy and Janeen DeAngelo went in circles in my head. It felt as if I were missing something vital, but I had no idea what. I snacked on cold cuts and cheese, carrying a plate with me to the sofa and opening the case file on my lap.

The one thing I hadn't noticed, nor had I thought to ask about, was whether the detectives had questioned Ricky Blake's family. I knew they had talked to Jenny's, but what about his? If they truly believed, as the older cop's notes seemed to indicate, that Jenny and Ricky had gone away together, surely they would have looked up his family and asked a bunch of questions. Maybe I'd just missed it.

Nibbling a piece of cheddar, I started once again at the back of the file folder and ran my index finger down each line of text in the reports and notes, pausing each time I came to Ricky Blake's name. Ricky and Jenny, Jenny and

Linda, Ricky and his band. No other Blakes showed up until near the end of the investigation. On small notebook pages similar to DeAngelo's were a small batch initialed AC—Alan Curtis. And there was where I found a notation about a phone call to a Paula Blake in Clovis.

The small town is on the eastern plains of New Mexico, almost on the Texas border, ranching country. My most vivid memory of traveling through there was the smell from a rendering plant somewhere along the highway. Otherwise, I knew little about the place. I read through Curtis's notes but couldn't tell if he had actually visited any Blakes there.

He had, however, written down the phone number so, on a whim, I dialed it. The problem with such a whim is that I wasn't prepared with questions when the phone was answered. A deep female voice that sounded like too many cigarettes and too much booze gave a brusque hello.

"Paula Blake?"

There may have been a grunt in response—canned laughter from a TV sitcom in the background sort of drowned it out.

"I'm calling from Albuquerque. My name is Charlie Parker—"

"You with the cops?"

"Um, no, I'm—"

"'Cause it seem like ever call I get from Albuquerque somehow involves the cops."

Hmm, interesting. "Recently? I mean, have you heard from the Albuquerque cops recently?"

A laugh that turned into a nasty-sounding cough. "Nah, I suppose that was a long time ago."

"I'm trying to locate your son Ricky. Do you happen to

have an address or phone number for him?"

"You people still on *that*? I told the guy the last time he called. Ricky and me, we ain't been in touch. My gosh—hang on a second, will ya?" The television sounds had risen to a crescendo that even Paula couldn't ignore. Suddenly, the sound level dropped dramatically. "Okay, I'm back. I swear … now what was I sayin?"

"Ricky? How I might contact him."

"No idea. He went off with, I don't know, some band of his. Claimed they was gonna make it big. Prob'ly did. Never saw fit to tell his mother about it. We don't talk no more."

"And when—"

"Thank the lord my other kids ain't like that one. My Lisa, sweetest thing. She sent me the prettiest Mother's Day card last week."

I was too busy reaching for a pen to jot down information to remind her that Mother's Day had been two months ago. Maybe Lisa had actually sent the card only last week.

"Maybe Lisa could help me," I suggested. "Can you give me her number?"

"Hang on, I don't remember numbers. She programmed it for me into some speed-dial thing here … just a second."

There was an odd series of noises—clatters and pings and electronic beeps—during which I was fairly certain we would get disconnected. Amazingly, she came back on the line about thirty seconds later and read off a quick series of numbers. I jotted frantically and then read them back to her.

"Thanks, I'll check with her about Ricky. I also wanted to ask you about his family—Jenny and Cassie. Did you ever have any contact with them, either before Ricky left or afterward?" Since my real purpose was to locate Jenny, even though it seemed farfetched I couldn't discount the idea that Jenny had reached out to her in-laws.

That hope was dashed when Paula came back with, "Who?"

"Ricky's wife and baby daughter. Did you ever have contact with them?"

There was nearly a minute of silence and I almost called out to see if she was still there.

"No. Not a bit. Now I gotta get back to my shows."

Strange reaction, and I could think of a half-dozen ways to interpret it. But Paula was done with me. The call went dead. I could almost believe that Paula didn't know about Ricky's marriage or the baby. But more likely, the passing years had simply erased any memory of the people who had only been in her son's life for a short while. I had no idea, and I couldn't judge what might have gone on in this woman's life.

All I knew was that she'd been a dead-end clue in my search. I dialed the number she'd given me, but it went to voicemail. I hung up. An in-person visit would be best, if I could get an address for Ricky Blake's sister.

At my computer I performed a reverse look-up on the phone number. I got a full name: Lisa Hardy. Her address was in the northeast heights near the fairgrounds. It was a little past the dinner hour for most people but not too late to pay a call, especially since we would have daylight until nearly nine p.m. I left a disappointed puppy behind and went out to my Jeep.

Chapter 27

Lisa Hardy was lifting bags of groceries from the trunk of her white Chevy sedan when I pulled up in front of her house. It was a typical older home in this part of the city that had developed in the 1950s, with white stucco, flat roof, small covered porch, and one-car garage. Lisa paused and watched me a little warily as I got out of my vehicle and started toward her. I noted a slightly stocky woman in her mid-forties, blonde with her hair up in a clip that left wispy bits hanging out at all angles. She wore denim shorts, brown sandals, and a tunic top in bright orange.

She further stiffened when I called her by name. She had me pegged as some kind of sales person and was trying to figure out what list her name had appeared on.

I introduced myself and held out a business card. "Your mother gave me your contact information."

None of that warmed her up at all. She had set the grocery bags down and stood with her arms crossed, barely giving my card a glance.

"We're investigating an old case. Fifteen years ago Ricky Blake's wife disappeared, and her family is still looking for answers."

"You think Ricky had something to do with her being gone? I can tell you, that's not what happened."

"Do you know what did happen? It would help me a lot, a *whole lot*, if I could just find her."

She shook her head, relaxing a bit now that she knew I wasn't selling something or hitting her up for a donation.

"Sorry, I really don't know anything about ... what was her name? Jeri?"

"Jenny. So you two weren't close?"

Lisa glanced toward the grocery bags. "Look, I got stuff in here that's melting. Come on inside."

I picked up a couple of the bags and followed her inside. The front door opened directly into the living room, which was tidy despite its worn carpeting and outdated furniture. A teen girl with earbuds poked her head out of a doorway as we walked toward the kitchen. She gave a curious glance my way and Lisa gave her a smile.

"Where's your brother?" she asked the girl.

"Next door."

"Okay."

The teen disappeared into her girl-cave again and I followed Lisa into a tiny kitchen where we set the bags on the countertop. She tilted her head toward a tall stool in one corner. "Have a seat if you want while I put this stuff away."

She worked quickly, separating the frozen foods and

getting them immediately into the fridge's upper-half freezer section.

"You're busy, so I'll be quick," I told her. "You sort of indicated you and Jenny weren't close? How about you and Ricky?"

She carried a bag of tomatoes and one of lettuce to the fridge and set them in the crisper before turning back to me with a sigh. "There were three of us. I'm the oldest, Tommy's two years younger. Ricky was the baby, kind of an afterthought, I suppose. By the time he came along Mom and Dad were tired of parenting, so they just didn't do much of it with him. He had these charming good looks and got away with anything he wanted to. Being the oldest and a girl, I got the responsibility. 'Lisa, look after your brothers.' 'Lisa clean up that spilled oatmeal.' 'Lisa, Lisa, Lisa.' And you know what—I couldn't wait to get out of there."

She wadded up an empty shopping bag and started on the next, pulling out two boxes of cereal.

"I met Sam Hardy when I got my first office job, an insurance company. He was manager of the Clovis branch, but told me he was going to grab the first promotion that would bring him to Albuquerque. I knew that's what I wanted—out of the small town life and away from my family."

"You never kept in touch?"

"Oh sure, I still have that burden of being the oldest daughter. I've helped Mom out with money, made the arrangements for Dad's funeral when that happened. Still check in with her now and then. She's a feisty one and we're just very different personalities, so I wouldn't say we're close." She stacked four cans of green beans in an overhead cupboard. "Tommy turned out fine—he's a mechanic for the Dodge dealer over on Lomas. Married, three kids. We're fairly close but not right in each other's faces, you know?"

"Ricky got married young, didn't he?"

"Oh yeah. I always thought he'd got that girl pregnant, but it was at least a year or so before the baby came along. They were a cute couple, but the whole thing fell apart—his doing, *all* his doing."

"From talking to some others, it seems he couldn't let go of the idea of being a career musician, making the big time with a band."

"That was it. All he'd talk about. By then I'm settled in with Sam, and my kids were just babies, so I got my hands full. I still remember this one time—we got a babysitter and went to one of Ricky's *shows*. Ha, it was a noisy bar where I could hardly hear myself think. The band was …" She rolled her eyes. "Horrible. I'm a country-western girl, so that rock stuff just doesn't do it for me. Ricky's up there, all jammin' on the guitar while two other guys are screaming out nonsense lyrics. Sam and I couldn't wait to get out of there."

She made a dismissive gesture with one hand and turned back to her groceries.

"Anyway, I loosely kept tabs and I heard the band members were into drugs. Didn't surprise me, with that racket they produced. It'd take a druggie to stay in the same room with it. I cut no slack at all for that stuff, especially not around my kids. Ricky came around once, obviously high, brought little junk presents for the kids, and I wouldn't let him see them. Told him not to *ever* come back to my home until he dropped that habit."

"When was this? Recently?"

"Oh no, way back then. I think his wife had left him … or he left her … I don't know. Never quite got the whole story. Heard rumors that the band had headed off somewhere back east—Nashville? No, maybe it was New York. You know, I really didn't care. There'd been too many of his little antics, too many bridges burned. I meant what I said when I told him not to come back unless he was clean and sober. And he never did."

"To this day?"

"To this day, I haven't seen my younger brother." A faintly wistful expression crossed her face, but it was gone in a flash. "I figure he's made his own life somewhere else. Either stayed in music and went down a path I wouldn't like, or who knows—maybe he got some other girl pregnant, straightened up his act and is living happily ever after with her people."

"So you have no idea where I can reach Ricky?"

She shook her head as she bunched up the last of the plastic shopping bags. "Don't know, don't care."

I felt a pang of sorrow for her. Whatever she said about not caring, the reddening tip of her nose said there was an emotional connection.

"One last thing and then I'm getting out of your hair. Do you think Tommy has ever heard anything from Ricky?"

"I seriously doubt it, but you can sure ask him." She ripped a page from a scratch pad and jotted down a number and address. "Go for it."

The sun was setting behind the volcanos on the west side when I got back out to the Jeep. Tommy Blake's address was less than a mile from here, so I figured I might as well try to connect with him now, rather than driving back to this part of town on another day. I pulled away from Lisa's house—it was an easy bet she would be at the window, watching me—and drove to the next corner before stopping to make the call.

The male voice chuckled when I identified myself. "Lisa said you'd be calling. Come on over."

I found the place with no trouble. Tommy's house was so similar to Lisa's, the brother and sister might have gone real estate shopping together. A red pickup truck sat outside the tan stucco house, along with a midsize sedan and an older, slightly battered white truck. A teenage boy lifted his head from under the hood when I parked and walked up the sidewalk.

The man who met me at the door was clearly Lisa's brother—similar facial features, sandy hair with a receding hairline, although his spare weight had gone to his middle whereas hers had settled in the hips. When he smiled I saw the definite resemblance. I also got a hint of the winning smile Ricky must have had, the way it could be turned into the flirtatious grin that had won Jenny over.

"The wife's got some iced tea made, if you want some."

I walked inside, declined the tea, and promised I wouldn't stay long. I didn't need Tommy to go into the family history, so I cut to my real questions.

"Did Lisa fill you in on what I'm here for, that I'm trying to locate Ricky's ex-wife and hoping if I find him, he might know something?"

He nodded.

"Lisa told me she hasn't been in touch or seen Ricky in years. So, I'm wondering if it's the same for you? Brothers often have a whole different kind of relationship."

"You mean Lisa wasn't at all tolerant toward Ricky's

music and the drugs … and I might be."

"Oh—no! I wasn't implying—"

A dark-haired woman wandered into the living room where we'd settled on a pair of recliner chairs. She handed Tommy his iced tea and then settled a hip on the arm of the overstuffed chair. He introduced her as Cathy.

"This one," Cathy said, "he'd forgive his little brother almost anything. Offered to help out, get Ricky into rehab. Even paid for it the first time, and we didn't have a lot to spare in those days."

He patted his wife's knee. "I'd just hoped it would work. Couldn't let him crash and burn and not make a move to help."

She smiled lovingly at him; obviously they'd settled this between them a long time ago.

"Second time, I told Ricky it was on him. He could get assistance, but he had to apply for it and get himself there. He went, but that time it didn't *take* either. I did my bit, but I agreed with Lisa after that."

"It sounds like you're the kind of brother he might have come back to, once he did get his life straight."

"I would have thought so, but nope. Not a word in all these years."

"You and Lisa have talked about it? About what might have happened with him?"

"Endlessly," Cathy said with an eye roll.

"For a *while*," Tommy amended. "A few years went by, no word. We figure he'd have ID on him, so if something bad happened the cops would have been in touch with the family. If Mama got word, she'd have been on the phone to Lisa right away."

Cathy shrugged. "So, we figure he's gone off somewhere, made his own way. Or not. But he doesn't care enough to stay in touch."

"This case I'm investigating actually involves the disappearance of Ricky's ex-wife. They had been divorced about a year, but there was some speculation that he convinced her to get back together and go away with him. Some think he might have lured her into thinking the band was about to hit fame and fortune, and she could be part of that rather than staying home with a baby. Any thoughts on that?"

"We barely knew Jenny. She was real tight with her mother and had her hands full with the baby, and ... wasn't she going to college or something?"

I nodded.

"Yeah, so we hardly saw her at all, and never, really, after she and Ricky split. The baby was a cutie, but by then we had two of our own and we got together a lot with Lisa and her kids. It wasn't as if that kid got much of our attention, sorry to say. I always supposed Jenny remarried and made a good home for her kid, one she didn't need the Blake family for."

"You didn't hear about it when Jenny disappeared?"

He shrugged. "Heard about it, yeah. Somebody might have come around asking if I knew where to find my brother. Wouldn't be the first—usually they were bill collectors though. I probably just said I had no idea what he was up to, 'cause that would have been after his second time in rehab and I was getting pretty fed up. When nobody followed up with more questions, I just assumed she came back and took up her life again."

That statement left me a little stunned. But, then again, what actually happens in people's minds after they hear someone has gone missing? Unless it becomes a big deal in the media, with a police search and an ending—good or bad—most people probably assume it turned out okay. Those flyers stapled to telephone poles or put up on community bulletin boards eventually become tattered or get replaced with newer ones. And the missing just fade away unless family members like Cassie and Linda push for answers.

And that's when I had come into the picture. I barely remembered thanking the Blakes for their time and walking back to my car. But determination took over as soon as I started the engine. I had to follow this through and figure out what went on back then. I couldn't let Jenny become a face on another of those tattered flyers that no one looks at anymore.

I pulled into my driveway, saw Dottie's car at Elsa's and lights on inside. At least some things in life were normal.

Chapter 28

Then

The problem with the brick of cocaine was the sheer number of prints all over the plastic bag. At least three or four people had handled it, according to the lab technician who dusted it.

"I can tell with my naked eyes there are that many," she told DeAngelo. "I'll lift what I can and get them into the computer. Then we'll see what matches."

"Meanwhile, can you tell me if there are traces of the cocaine on any of the other pieces of evidence?" Not that he *needed* to know whether it was Ricky or Jenny who handled the drugs, but it could send the case off in a different direction if Jenny was the one.

"Yeah, I did that right away, before I started handling anything. And no, no traces of the coke on the purse or its contents, nothing on anything you brought in."

He wasn't surprised. From all appearances the brick had most likely been in that same spot under the floor since before Ricky Blake had moved out of that house. He asked the lab tech to call him the moment she was able to identify any of the prints, then he went back upstairs to see how Conroy was coming along with the cell phone.

"Bunch of calls," Felice said as he approached her desk, "but not that many unique numbers. Her mother, three or four friends. I found one that showed on her caller ID as 'unknown' and I was just about to check out the number to see who the carrier is."

Her eyes shifted toward her computer screen. "And here we go … It's an Espanola prefix, a block assigned to CellsRUs, which is one of those pay-as-you-go plans where people buy minutes as they need them. They're handy for lower income folks and seniors, a way to make and receive calls, but includes no fancies like data."

"Seniors, poor people, and drug dealers," he observed. "Sorry if that's not politically correct."

"No, you're right. Not only drug dealers—people wanting to conduct illegitimate business get them all the time. The phone isn't registered to an account of any type. This particular block of numbers was sold through the Walmart store in Espanola. Guy walks in, buys a cheap phone with a SIM card, buys another card for a certain dollar amount worth of minutes—he's set to go."

Neither of them needed the reminder that this particular small town was the hub for the Chaco Cartel. Nor did they need reminding that El Tiburon, the head of the cartel, had a nasty reputation. If Ricky Blake got himself involved with them, he'd likely stepped into something way deeper than he could handle.

"Want me to call over to Narcotics and see if I can find any connections?" Conroy asked.

"No, just stick with the financials and records on Jenny Blake. She's our priority right now. I know a guy over there. I'll give him a call as soon as I check out this other lead." DeAngelo had an uneasy feeling in the pit of his stomach.

Curtis called to him from across the room. He'd tacked a new photo to the incident board. "One of the bands Ricky Blake played in. Been a few months, but I've got their names. Shall we follow up?"

"Let's go."

As it turned out, it took more than three days to locate the band. The core members were still together, and they'd gotten a series of gigs on the Indian casino circuit, playing as the opening act for bigger-name bands. Curtis's lead, which said The Purple Marauders were playing Sandia Casino, turned out to be old. With Thanksgiving weekend coming up, they were busy and on the move. After driving out to the far northern reaches of the city, only to find out the group had played Sandia last weekend, they started calling around.

The Downs—no. Isleta—no. Route 66—no.

The cops branched out a bit farther away. Santa Ana, no luck there. Finally found out the Marauders would be playing at Black Mesa that night. The smaller casino was partway to Santa Fe, but at least it was a lead. They hopped in the department's Taurus and headed that way, Curtis at the wheel this time. A little way past Bernalillo, DeAngelo's cell phone rang and he recognized his wife's phone number.

His daughter's voice surprised him. "Daddy ... there's trouble. We need you."

"I'm on the road, middle of a case, Janeen. What is it?"

"Ernie's in the hospital. Mom's with him."

Janeen hadn't called him daddy since she was twelve. He didn't want to ask. Knew better, somehow. "Okay, I'll get there as soon as I can, but it's going to be at least an hour."

"Problem?" Curtis asked as he stuck the phone back in his pocket.

He wasn't about to discuss his family's darkest secret. "There's the casino, next exit."

Curtis sent him a pointed stare but DeAngelo just looked away, watching the dried out chamisa-covered hills roll past them at seventy miles an hour. The car slowed, took the exit, and Curtis cruised the parking lot. Outside one of the side doors he spotted an older, beat up looking RV with a magnetic stick-on sign: The Purple Marauders. He pointed at it and DeAngelo nodded. They pulled to a stop crosswise in front of it.

A guy with dark, wavy hair to his shoulders stepped out before the two detectives had climbed out of the car. The cops exchanged a look that meant, you never know what's inside a vehicle like this—play it cool.

"Hey, man, how's it going? We're looking for Ricky Blake," Curtis called out, casual as could be.

The guy had stepped off the RV step onto the pavement. "Haven't seen him in awhile. Like, months."

"He played with the band, right?"

"Yeah, we gave him a try."

"Just a try?"

"Well, you know. Guys come and go in bands like ours. He came. He went."

Curtis nodded. DeAngelo glanced around, trying to

appear as casual and nonthreatening as possible.

"So, it sounds like he *went* some time ago," Curtis said. "Any idea where he went? Playing with another band in town?"

A second man appeared in the doorway, same long hair, lots of facial scruff. He seemed more curious than anything. At Curtis's question he spoke up. "Last I heard, he was still looking for work. Nobody serious about their music is gonna hire that guy. He's a flake."

Curtis looked toward the first guy, who said, "Yeah. Totally."

"Any thoughts on where to find him?" DeAngelo asked.

"Can't say as I've thought of him at all, frankly," said the dark-haired one, the man who seemed to be the band leader. "We're in this to play our music, earn some money, get discovered. Guy like that's just gonna bring us down. Sorry, but I got to the point where I just don't care."

Both cops nodded, and the guy turned to go back inside the RV.

"Well, that was a waste," Curtis said as he pulled away. "Want to check out anything else while we're out this way?"

"Based on what? Without a lead, Blake could be anywhere at all by now. I gotta get back."

"Right. The call from home."

But DeAngelo wasn't planning to elaborate. He needed to get his personal vehicle and get to the hospital to find out what the hell was going on with his son.

Chapter 29

Now

I had to admit I was running out of ideas on my case. Jenny's family knew nothing. Ricky's family knew nothing. It could turn out that the police were right; the couple could have run off together and started a whole new life. But that didn't feel right either, not from what I'd heard about Jenny's feelings toward her daughter.

I was smearing some peanut butter on bread when I heard a tap at the kitchen door. Elsa was peering through the glass.

"Hey, I thought you and Dottie were all settled in for the night," I said, holding up the sandwich, offering to make her one.

She waved off the food. "We ate early. I just came by to see if you have any of that diarrhea medicine."

"Um, probably somewhere around here. What happened? Dottie's cooking not agreeing with you?"

"Oh, it's not for me. Iris came back from her honeymoon cruise not feeling so great."

"Oh, that's too bad. It's no fun to get sick when you're traveling, especially if *that's* the problem," I said, wiggling my fingers in front of my lower abdomen.

"I don't know for sure if it is," she said, taking a seat at the kitchen table and indicating I should go ahead and eat my sandwich. "I just wanted to be able to offer her something for her ailment."

I couldn't imagine that Iris wouldn't have already gone to the pharmacy herself, or sent the handsome new husband, if she needed medication. But I didn't say this to Elsa. She just wanted to help, and this was her go-to solution. I remember, from my teen years. If anything at all is making you feel bad, it has to be intestinal.

"So, did Iris say if they had a good time?"

"Well, we had plans for the day. She was going to pick me up for lunch and then we thought we'd check out the new exhibit at the museum. She never showed."

"What? No word, nothing."

"Until I called her to ask what the heck. She sounded awful. She apologized for forgetting our date, and that's when she said she hadn't been feeling well. I told her to go to the doctor, but you know Iris. She insisted she'll be fine, that it's just some kind of bug she picked up on the cruise."

"Could be," I said between sticky bites of PB and J.

"Actually, by the end of the conversation I think she was perking up. She told me how they walked a lot, going around the various decks on the ship on the days they weren't in port somewhere. Said one night they were out at the rail,

staring at the stars and how romantic that was. Guess she
got so carried away, trying to spot the Big Dipper, that she
nearly toppled overboard. A crew member who happened
to come out the door at that moment helped Jeffrey pull
her back. They had a big laugh over her clumsiness, and
she decided she'd had a little too much wine with dinner
that night." Gram was smiling at the memory of the story.
"Maybe that's what's got her feeling bad now. Too much
of a good time."

"Maybe so." But alarm bells were going off in my
brain. I didn't want to say anything yet, but found a packet
of Imodium for Gram to take with her.

I watched her walk back through the break in the hedge
and saw her back porchlight go off before I raced to my
computer. I hadn't liked the looks of this Jeffrey fellow,
right from the start. Now my suspicions were running on
high.

Delving into Ron's special databases works great if you
know a little something about the person you're researching.
Unfortunately, I knew next to nothing about Jeffrey or
any of his family. I started by entering the one thing I did
know, his name. The date of birth, social security number,
and address fields must have been pretty important—a box
came up on the screen saying "Insufficient data to locate
results."

So, okay. I decided to mine the depths of social media
once again. I had found a skimpy Facebook profile on
Jeffrey, but since the wedding I had a little more data.
Celeste, his sister, was there, but all of her posts seemed
to be about hair, makeup, and lunches with a bunch of
ladies. I didn't see much of anything about family events,
not even a post about her brother's wedding so recently.

No birthdays, not even a kid party or anything where I could ferret out clues. I tried Reyna's name but, as before, nothing showed up.

Drumrolling my fingertips lightly over the keys, I started thinking of names from the wedding. How many of the cousins had I actually been introduced to? Not many. But I entered whatever names came to mind, along with the surname Lougan, in hopes someone from that side of Jeffrey's family would pop up. Nothing. Rats.

I don't like doing this, and normally wouldn't, but I picked up the phone and called Ron. Hey, he'd gotten more than a week of vacation, unpestered by his little sis. He could take one call, and I hoped he'd be willing to make a call. I further justified the interruption by telling myself he would be coming home soon anyway and might as well get back into the swing of working. Right?

He sounded relaxed and happy when he answered. Good. I led with the soft questions—were they having fun, how was the weather (I know, it's Hawaii, the weather is always the same)—and then filled him in on how I'd taken Gram to her friend's wedding, and oh by the way, how would he like to contact his buddy Kent Taylor at APD and ask if he could run some fingerprints through the system?

"What prints?" he asked.

"Um, I'm just not trusting this Jeffrey guy that Iris married, and now he's trying to fix up Gram with a friend of his."

"No way you're letting that happen, are you?"

As if I could actually control my gram. "Doing my best to stop it."

When I related what Gram had told me about Iris's

new illness and the cruise ship mishap, he suddenly began to take notice.

"I'll make the call to Kent. He kind of owes me a favor from a couple months ago. When can you take the prints by?"

Oops. I hadn't quite worked it out that far. "Um, I'll get them tomorrow."

"I'll call him in the morning."

Good. Done. Except for the part about obtaining fingerprints from someone I barely knew. I clicked off the call and then spent the next fifteen minutes pacing the floor, trying to come up with a way to solve this within the next twenty-four hours. I could invite them all to dinner and when it came time to clear the table, I could keep Jeffrey's glass and silverware separate from the others, and take those to Kent Taylor.

But racing through the actual logistics of that brilliant idea, dinner plans take time to put together. Maybe Iris was feeling so poorly she wouldn't want to come over; Jeffrey could come up with any little excuse and shoot down my plan; I don't actually love cooking for a crowd. Scratch the dinner party.

Okay ... but what if I took the visit to them? I only needed one cohort to make this work. Well, and a lot of other little pieces had to fall into place perfectly. But we'd deal with that as the situation dictated. Dang, I should have studied improv.

Chapter 30

Then

DeAngelo parked in a slot marked "Official Use Only," slapped his APD placard onto the dash of his private car, and walked into the UNM Hospital ER. He hated these places—the smells, the people who either seemed resigned to waiting forever for treatment or frantic because a loved one was in pain or bleeding, the overall sadness. At least this wasn't a Saturday night, he told himself. It could be worse.

He gave his name to a woman behind a glass wall that had a little speaker built into it. "My son was brought in."

She tapped something on her computer keyboard and then fiddled with a stack of paper folders for what seemed like a half hour but was probably three or four minutes. "I'm checking … be right back," she murmured, getting her wide ass out of the chair.

Before she'd made it out of her cubicle, he spotted Janeen on the other side of another glass wall. He tapped on the glass to get the receptionist's attention. "There's my daughter. If you'll let me through, she can take me to him."

An obnoxious buzzer sounded and the latch on a heavy door to his right clicked. He pushed through and Janeen rushed into his arms.

"Daddy, we've been so scared. Mom brought Ernie in and gave me her phone to call you."

"Shush, shh, it'll be okay." He held her at arm's length, trying to read her expression. *Would* it be okay? "Is he—?"

She nodded. "For now. Mom's with him. He's hooked up to machines—" Her voice broke.

His greatest fear, all of their greatest fear, was that one of these times it wouldn't turn out all right. He had to face the fact that his son was an addict. They'd been finding drugs in his room since he was eleven, and each time it was something harder and more dangerous. They'd hauled him to rehab, committed him to programs that, twenty-eight days later, he would walk out of, saying all the right things before he went right back to his old ways. Twenty-some years later, it was amazing Ernie was alive.

He put an arm around Janeen's shoulder and they walked down a hall surrounded by curtained bays and glassed-in rooms filled with patients and families. He realized which room his son was in when he saw the uniformed cop standing outside. DeAngelo sent Janeen inside while he revealed the badge on his belt and introduced himself to the officer.

"What's this about?"

"Sorry sir, I've got orders to be here."

"Whose orders? Why?"

"Head of Narcotics Division. I'm afraid I don't know much more than that." The young officer gave him a name and let DeAngelo pass into the room.

Janeen and his wife sat on opposite sides of the bed, where Ernie lay. His son was sweating profusely, twitching, and muttering nonsense. His arms and legs were in restraints, and DeAngelo suspected those were as much to protect him from harming himself as to keep him in the bed and prevent escape.

He gave his wife a long hug before suggesting she and Janeen go get something to eat.

"I can't leave his side. I'm not hungry." Her face was both frantic and weary at the same time, the very things that made him detest the whole ER scenario.

"Janeen, take your mother to the cafeteria. Now." His tone was gentle but the words allowed no room for argument. What he didn't say was, *I need to be alone with my son*, but Janeen picked up on it.

As the women walked out, he stepped to the bedside. Ernie's eyes went in and out of focus, but for a moment DeAngelo knew the young man recognized him. He gripped the flailing arm.

"Son, you know what this does to your mother. You know what it's doing to you. One of these days you won't—" He dropped his hold and turned away. Damn. Damn!

He looked up to see a doctor standing in the doorway, a tablet computer in hand. The man stepped inside, took a look at the vital signs flashing across a monitor at the head of the bed, and tapped a few things onto the tablet.

"Can we talk outside?" DeAngelo asked.

They'd walked a few feet down the corridor when DeAngelo recognized another man walking toward them. He couldn't immediately bring up the name but the face was that of the head of APD's Narcotics Division. It seemed Ernie's little misstep wasn't going to go away this time. He couldn't say he was unhappy about that. Maybe it was time his son paid a higher price than simply being sent to yet another rehab joint. But hard time was tough, and scary. And dangerous. Nobody wanted that for their kid.

"Doctor."

"Detective."

The greetings were terse, but DeAngelo just wanted to get to the bottom line. What was going to happen next?

The doctor turned to him first. "We believe your son is out of the woods now. We would keep him sedated until the drugs get out of his system, but frankly, he doesn't need more of anything pumped into his system right now. To some extent he's just going to have to ride it out."

DeAngelo nodded. He turned to the other detective. "And I suppose there's an arrest pending?"

The man who'd introduced himself as Arthur (DeAngelo assumed that was the last name), tilted his head in acknowledgement. "We're still tracking information as to who did this to him. And then, yes, we're hoping to get high enough in the organization to make a meaningful arrest."

"Wait, what? What am I missing?"

The doctor spoke up. "We hadn't gotten a chance to speak," he said to the other cop. "We're fairly certain your son's drug intake was not self-inflicted. Because of where the injection is located, we think someone else gave him this dose. And it could have very easily been a fatal dose."

"What—someone tried to murder him?"

"Most likely to shut him up," Arthur said. "The Chaco Cartel is a nasty bunch. No loyalty among them."

DeAngelo gave the doctor a look and the man quickly excused himself and said he would be available for any other questions. But he couldn't seem to leave quickly enough. "Let's step outside," DeAngelo said to Detective Arthur.

The wind channeling down the side of the building nearly took his breath away, so they walked down the sidewalk and around a corner to a sunny spot.

"Are you saying my son was *dealing*? For the Chaco Cartel?"

"It's not what any parent wants to hear—"

"And no one in Narcotics thought to tell me? As a courtesy to a fellow officer?"

"Sir, your son isn't a minor. He's a grown man making a man's choices. We're under no obliga—"

"I know." DeAngelo felt the fire go out of him.

"I'm sorry. We've been tailing Ernie, tracking cartel movement for a while but we hadn't actually gotten around to doing enough of a background check to know he was the son of a cop. If I'd known that—well, frankly, I still don't know if I could have said anything that would have made a difference. What happened today … it might have happened anyway."

Arthur shook his hand and headed toward the parking lot, leaving DeAngelo standing in the sunshine and wondering what the hell he should do next. Obviously, he couldn't get his son off drugs—he'd tried every route he knew already, and he knew it was true what they all said. The first step is for the addict to acknowledge he has a problem. That might happen, but it might not.

No, all he could actually *do* would be to stand by his wife and to do nothing to draw cartel attention to the rest of the family.

Chapter 31

Now

I had a somewhat brilliant thought in the middle of the night. Well, it went along with my idea after talking to Ron, that if I wanted fingerprints from Jeffrey Lougan I needed to get into their home to do it.

So, as soon as it was daylight, I headed toward Elsa's, where I could hear laughter beyond the hedge. Freckles trailed along and we found the two women in the garden, filling a basket with tomatoes from the loaded vines.

"You're just in time," Dottie said. "We still got beans and zucchini to pick and it's gettin' hotter out here by the minute."

I pitched in and pulled a few of the ripe squash from the nearest vine while I told Gram about my idea that the two of us visit Iris and take a little get-well gift.

"That's perfect!" she said. "We made some chicken noodle soup yesterday and there's plenty left to share. And we can take her a few of these zucchini."

"We'll stop at a store on the way and get a card."

"And we can take her a few of these zucchini." Elsa's eyes were bright and hopeful, her voice a little stronger the second time she suggested it.

I hated to remind her how overloaded *everyone* gets with zucchini every summer, but at least it looked like we had a plan. Now, I would have to think of a way to be sure Jeffrey was there. Either that or be ready to steal something I could be very certain he had touched. But that led my thoughts off on all sorts of icky tangents—nah, I'd better hope to catch him with a beer in his hand or something easy.

After calling ahead to say we'd love to pop by to see the newlywed couple, we grabbed flowers and a card. Dottie had packed the soup and garden bounty into a pretty wicker basket and tied on a fluffy bow, so we had a nice little combo welcome-home and get-well gift. I drove and Elsa gave directions.

Iris lived in Tanoan, an upscale country club neighborhood in the far northeast heights. Her home was a classic Tudor with touches of Swiss chalet—unusual in New Mexico, which was the reason it stood out among the stucco and tile bunch and the occasional boxy modern one. Easy to see why Jeffrey 'gave in' and moved in with her. Nearly any man would grab the chance to move up the social scale to this degree and play golf every day, even if he did have to abandon what had probably been a cramped bachelor pad to do so. Sorry—my skepticism showing through.

The devoted husband answered the door (yay—score my primary wish for the visit!). He showed us through a long foyer decorated with a combination of Asian tapestries and English antiques, and we emerged in a sunny living room. Floor-to-ceiling windows revealed the Sandia mountains in such a way that you'd never guess there were several hundred houses in the community, not to mention thousands more between here and the city limits. I had to admit, the architect had designed the home to fit its location superbly.

Iris was reclining on an elegant settee covered in aqua silk damask, wearing a loose caftan in a tropical print. A novel lay open on her lap, but her eyes were closed when we entered the room. At Jeffrey's "Darling, we have company" she immediately put on a smile and sat straighter, even before she saw who it was.

"Oh, Elsa, flowers! And Charlie. It's good to see you again." The smile and the greeting both came from beneath a layer of malaise, although she hid it fairly well.

"We won't stay long," I promised. "Elsa made soup, and I can testify that it cures *everything*."

"I'm happy to see you, and I'll have the soup for lunch later." She looked up at Jeffrey, practically batting her eyes. "Darling, can you put the food in the kitchen and find a vase for the flowers? They're in the cabinet above the fridge."

He snapped to and took the food basket in one hand, the flowers in the other. I watched until he was nearly at the kitchen door. "Oh, let me help with that. I'll bet most men don't know a whole lot about arranging flowers." As if I did.

He gave a grateful smile.

"If you'll just do the reaching and get the vase?" I took the food basket and set it on the countertop.

He opened the high cupboard and started to reach for a cut-glass crystal piece.

"Oh, I don't think that one's quite tall enough," I said, struck suddenly by inspiration. "That next one to the right, the tall clear one—it looks more suitable."

Clear and smooth, and much more suitable for getting prints. If I managed this right, I wouldn't have to steal any drinking glasses and then figure out how to gracefully return them.

"Thanks. Now you go on back to whatever you were doing. I'll get the flowers in here in a jiffy and I'll put the food in the fridge." I made little scurrying motions with my hands. I've never seen a man yet who didn't mind being run out of the kitchen.

My purse was still hanging from its shoulder strap, which was a good thing. I wouldn't need to rummage through the kitchen in hopes that Iris had cornstarch. I peered around the pillar that separated the two rooms and saw that Elsa was chatting away. Iris still had sort of a pale, clammy look about her. Jeffrey's voice came from somewhere farther away, the sounds of a phone call in progress, so I went to work.

I found white notepaper on a pad stuck to the side of the fridge, the kind everyone has for their shopping lists. I ripped a clean sheet from the middle of the pad. Now, tape. Everybody has tape. As quietly as possible I opened and closed a few drawers until I found the one. Scotch tape, duct tape or packaging tape. I took the packaging tape—clearest and stickiest. From my purse I pulled my tiny round blusher compact and the little fluffy brush that came with it. Ready.

Rechecking the positions of everyone in the house, I quickly fluffed out the brush and lightly dabbed it over the places on the vase where Jeffrey had touched it. Voila. A beautiful set of prints stood out. Blowing off the excess powder I twirled the brush a little more to settle powder in the whorls of each print, then carefully lifted each one with a piece of the tape.

"Everything okay in there?" Iris called out.

"Just fine! I was looking for shears to trim the flower stems. Found them. So I'll just be another couple minutes."

All this while I carefully stuck the tape to the bright white paper. Sure enough, I had a set of blush-bronze prints. I could only hope there was enough contrast for the police scanner to pick them up. I really didn't want to come back and do this again.

I slipped the prints into an old envelope in my purse, then rinsed and dried the vase before quickly clipping the flower stems and stuffing them into water specially mixed with the small packet of keep-fresh stuff that came with them. When I emerged into the living room, Iris exclaimed over them.

"Sorry it took so long. The vase seemed to have some fingerprints on it."

Iris waved to a spot on a side table. "So I can look at them while I sit here and read," she said.

"Elsa, I think Iris is looking a little tired," I said. "Maybe we should be going."

Iris waved off the suggestion. "Whatever this bug is, it comes and goes. So strange. I sleep like a log, really, and then I'm fairly energetic first thing in the morning. But the last few days, I've just gotten *so* lazy after breakfast. I rest a little and perk up, then by lunchtime I'm wanting another nap."

"Have you seen a doctor?"

"Only the one on the ship. He gave me some seasick medication that helped with the nausea but made my tiredness even worse. I really do think I just picked up some ailment from the tropics or the food or something."

Elsa pulled the packet of Imodium from her purse, but Iris shook her head. "Thank you. I'll try it. Actually, although there's been stomach upset and all that, today I'm feeling more of a general tiredness. *So tired.*"

Jeffrey appeared from the foyer, nudging Elsa a little with the idea of getting together with his friend Mark. Really, I thought that whole plan had been put to rest. I caught Elsa's eye and gave the *let's go* signal.

"Iris, I want you to see a doctor," I said. "You've always been so energetic, so something's not right. If you can't drive yourself, I'll be happy to take you."

"Oh, Charlie, that's very sweet. But Jeffrey can take me. That's no problem."

I hoped it wouldn't be.

Chapter 32

My phone rang shortly after I'd pulled into the driveway at home and escorted Elsa back to her place. Ron's name appeared on the screen.

"Okay," he said, without much preamble, "Taylor agreed. He'll process the prints for you. Just drop them by his desk whenever you have them."

"Got 'em now. I'll run right down there."

"He said to warn you it might take a few days. Depends on whether your suspect is in the system locally or if he has to go into the nationwide databases."

My suspect. I hadn't thought of Jeffrey Lougan that way, but maybe he was. Okay, he definitely is a suspect if Iris's maladies are being inflicted upon her. And based on the drastic change I'd seen since the wedding day, I couldn't delay.

"How's your other case coming along?" he asked.

"What? Bored with your tropical vacation?"

"Tease all you want. We're having a great time, but I'm ready to get back to food I understand and a climate that doesn't make me sweat like a pig all day."

I had to laugh. It's true, when you're accustomed to dry air, the humidity takes some getting used to, and vice versa. Drake had commented on it a lot when he first moved back to the mainland after his stint there.

"So, the Blake case is coming along." I didn't want to admit I was at the point where I have a lot of data but haven't yet put it together.

"Fill me in."

Geez, he wasn't going to let this go, so I went through what I had so far—Jenny's disappearance, no one in the neighborhood admitting to remembering a thing, the likelihood that her ex was somehow involved and had probably gotten tangled up in the drug scene.

"Going back to the neighborhood," he said, "have you talked to the landlord? You said she was renting the place, right? Landlords keep records, often remember things about specific tenants, and this one might have stuck in his or her mind."

"You think so?"

"It's worth asking. Jenny might have taken off but then got in financial straights, called to ask for her deposit back or something like that."

"I don't know ... she'd call the landlord but not her own mother?"

"There could be reasons. Judgement from mom, having to listen to comments which a stranger wouldn't make. She might have asked mom for money lots of times already, didn't want the hassle of explaining. Didn't want mom knowing where she was, but she'd give a landlord an address to send the money."

From what I'd seen of the relationships in the Arnold family, I was still skeptical, but figured it was worth a shot. Now I just had to find out who'd owned that rental on Sixth fifteen years ago. I was headed downtown anyway, so I'd check it out. I got back in the Jeep and drove toward police headquarters.

"What's the brownish powder?" Kent Taylor asked, staring at the sheet of fingerprints I'd just handed over.

"Um, well, it's blusher." I fidgeted slightly. "It worked—those are pretty good prints."

The homicide detective is an older guy, a bit on the chunky side, balding, but he's diligent in his job and Ron respects him a lot. So I wasn't going to get into an argument here.

"You're right, they look okay," he said. "I'll get 'em down to the lab, have the techs scan and start looking for a match. We'll let you know." He started to turn away, then paused. "You want to tell me what this is about? Do you have knowledge of a crime?"

"Just suspicions at this point. Friend of a friend married a guy I don't like the looks of, and now she's starting to get sick a lot, has had a near accident or two."

He looked at the fingerprints with a little more respect. "Look, I see the final results of domestic violence, a lot more often than I'd like. Can you suggest the friend get out of the house, go stay with someone, take a little trip or something, until we know if she's safe?"

"I don't know her that well, but I'll see what I can do." I gave Taylor a straightforward look. "Let's say these prints do turn up someone with a record, can the police step in and get the wife out of danger?"

"Depends. Without some proof that he has done something to her, probably not. And even if he has, she'd have to file a complaint. Battered wives refuse that step all the time. It's sad."

It was sad.

"Charlie, take it a step at a time. There has to be some proof. We need probable cause before we can make any kind of a move. At this point it would fall to the domestic violence division to check things out, but if need be I can make a recommendation. I'll be in touch on these prints, and you let me know if it looks like the situation is escalating."

Another thing for my to-do list, but I would gladly do what I could to keep Elsa's friend safe. I thanked Taylor for his interest and left the police station.

Next stop for me would be the county clerk's office where I hoped to follow up with Ron's suggestion and locate the owner of the property on Sixth Street. It was barely a block to the county building so I walked over.

The county treasurer's office was relatively quiet this time of year; tax bills are sent out in the fall so I saw no queues of disgruntled property owners. I found a clerk who actually wore a smile when I approached.

My request to find out the name of a property owner from fifteen years ago didn't faze her much, although she wanted me to fill out a request form and wait two weeks for an answer. That didn't sit well—I mean, she was sitting there doing nothing anyway—so I pulled out a business card, told her I'd just been in a meeting with one of APD's homicide detectives and that I was in the midst of a life-

and-death case that involved this particular property. My contact in the police department would be back in touch at any time, and I needed answers. Technically, each of those facts was true. I didn't bring up the fact that they weren't necessarily related.

The clerk's mouth bunched up in a little pinch, but she went back to her computer keyboard and asked me to repeat the address. Ten minutes later I walked out with a name. It was still up to me to find out how to contact that person now, as the clerk had helpfully informed me this was not the current owner of the property.

At least the name—Fernand McIlhaney—wasn't a common one in this town. I got a phone number right away and called it, saying I was interested in a place, and Fernand (call me Nando, everyone does) suggested I come by his office.

Once I got out of the downtown tangle, it was straight up Lomas and ten minutes later I was parking in front of Allied Properties LLC. I walked in and told a receptionist I had just spoken with Nando.

The man who stepped out of a side office was probably fifty, short and stocky, with dark hair that showed a few strands of gray. He wore thick glasses in black frames.

"You're interested in renting something?" he said, extending his hand.

"Actually, I'm interested in a property you used to own."

His jowly smile faded. Clearly I wasn't going to be signing up for anything. I handed him my business card and he invited me into his small office. He circled the cheap laminate desk and offered me one of the two vinyl covered armchairs in front of it.

"The house is on Sixth Street, the tenant was a Jennifer Blake, and this was fifteen or sixteen years ago," I said.

His mind did the backward-math to figure out what year that was.

"Ah, yeah. Back when I was doing this solo—buying and renting houses, that is. I had thirty, forty properties back then. Kept some, flipped some. Got to be a lot to handle on my own so I eventually merged with this limited partnership. We got crews now to handle all the maintenance and cleaning. It's a lot, you know. People don't realize it when they got one or two rentals and not much turnover. Build up the business and it gets a little crazy, running all over the city."

"I'm sure." I was picturing the business in his eyes, names and faces in constant motion, and began to hold little hope that he would remember Jenny.

"So, this particular one," I reminded. "You might remember it because the young couple had a baby but the husband moved out. It was just the young woman and the baby living there, and then she disappeared."

His brows were working on the memory.

"Her mother took the child into her care, and I believe she went in and cleared out their personal things at the end of the month."

"Yeah, that's kind of coming back."

"Anyway, I'm wondering if you have records going back that far, and if you can tell me whether Jennifer Blake, the tenant, ever contacted you later. Maybe asking for her deposit back, or giving a forwarding address or anything?"

His chunky fingers drummed on the desktop for a minute but he made no move to look up anything. I sighed and sat back in my chair. Eventually, he turned to the bank of file cabinets behind him and reached for a bottom drawer.

"Yep, it was before everything was on the computer. Hate those things, but the partners convinced me we needed 'em." He grunted as he leaned forward over the file folders in the drawer and ran his fingertips across the tabs. He found the one he wanted and worked it out of the tightly filled drawer.

"Okay, here we go." A deep breath to refill his lungs. "1604 Sixth Street."

I leaned forward to see what the slender file contained. Stapled to the inside of the front cover was a photo of the house I'd visited, looking very much the same as it did now. The papers in the folder seemed to be forms, but I couldn't decipher much of the tiny print.

"Yeah, I thought so. I sold this one."

"Was that right away after Jenny Blake moved out?"

"Let's check here ..." He paged through the forms. "When did you say she left?"

I gave the date of her disappearance.

He consulted a page that looked like a spreadsheet, only handwritten. Whatever. It worked.

"Looks like it sold a couple years after that." His brow wrinkled again. "Sure had a slew of tenants after Ms. Blake. She stayed more than a year. But then ... ah, yeah, I remember this time. Frustrating. Had a devil of a time keeping the place rented. People would stay a month, maybe two, and then leave. Seems like they said the place just didn't seem right. Or maybe they were saying it wasn't right for *them*. Like I said, I had a lot of rentals in those days."

"They didn't have to sign a lease?"

"I didn't do it that way then. Another thing the partners here got me started with. Leases got their good and bad points. Month by month, you can get someone out on short notice if they're trouble makers. Lease—you're stuck with 'em."

He was still running his finger down the written list. "So anyway, looks like it was a year ... no, seventeen months after Ms. Blake left that I finally got a decent, long-term tenant in that place. I remember it now. That's when I decided to unload that one, put it on the market."

I mentally filed the timeframe. "So, you have no notes about contact from Jenny Blake after she left? No forwarding address?"

"Nope. But that's not unusual. People go on with their lives, they don't contact their old landlords."

"I suppose." Since I've lived in my childhood home all my life, I really have no idea how other people do things like this.

Nando closed the folder and looked up at me, probably wishing I'd quit wasting his time. But what he said was, "Being a landlord for twenty-five plus years, I've kind of got a pretty good feel. Houses have personalities, and they have luck."

"Houses have luck?"

"Yeah, you know. It's either a lucky house or an unlucky one. That one on Sixth, I think it was just an unlucky house."

I guess my expression seemed curious.

"Well, there was the lady who went missing—her bad luck—and then my run of bad luck keeping it rented. Even when I sold it, the market was running real high back then, but I ended up taking less than the asking price because no offers had come in." He shrugged and set the folder aside. Our meeting was clearly over.

Chapter 33

Then

The Chaco Cartel. DeAngelo's blood ran cold when he realized how close his son had come to being murdered by them. Stories of retaliation and infighting within those mobs ran rampant. Ernie was under arrest and he could only hope his son could shake his addiction while in custody. For now, he could try to keep the rest of the family safe, and that meant not calling any attention to himself.

"Trying to stare a hole through that wall?" Curtis's voice broke into his partner's thoughts.

DeAngelo snapped back to the present. "Yeah, did it work?"

"Still the same old incident board, still no answers." Curtis pointed toward the short list of leads that pointed to Ricky Blake. "We haven't followed through much with the drug connection. Maybe I should make some calls."

"No! I mean, really. What are the odds the ex being a drug user has a bearing on a young woman's disappearance? And we don't have jurisdiction up north, and we don't have the manpower to pull ourselves into whatever Narcotics, DEA, and all those Fed departments have got going on. We need to move past Ricky Blake and focus our efforts on Jenny."

Curtis gave him a funny look but stuck his phone back into his pocket. "Okay, what do you suggest?"

"We made one round of calls to the hospitals, morgues, mortuaries … but it's been awhile. If Jenny ended up on the street, something could have happened in the meantime. Let's go back through the list again."

The calls were routine: Had a white female, age twenty-one, with blonde hair been admitted? It was nearly the same who-what-where-when that reporters are trained to ask. And while he was at it, Curtis called the media channels. Had they got wind of a story involving such a woman?

No, no, and no. Repeatedly.

The morgue at APD had two Jane Doe victims. Did they want to come take a look? But both were Hispanic and had the roughened look of women who'd been on the street a while. DeAngelo remembered a report from nearly two years ago that ended up matching one of them. Poor girl. And the poor family who was about to receive tragic news right before the holidays.

He thought again of retirement. He needed to get out of this career before it ate him alive.

And still, they didn't have a clue about what had happened to Jenny Blake.

Chapter 34

Now

I woke up with a start. My dream had centered around the conversation with Nando McIlhaney, a confusion of houses and renters in which I was apparently working in his office and filling out lease forms for someone. I hate dreams that mimic silly aspects of life, but very few of us have profound dreams about the meaning of the universe or any of that stuff. I guess nearly all dreams are mundane. I got up and went to the bathroom for a glass of water, wishing Drake were home. He always knows how to take my mind off silly dreams.

But as I stared into the mirror above the sink something snapped into place. Why had so many tenants rented the Sixth Street house and left right away? Because something wasn't right. What if—oh my god—what if there'd been a bad smell, something they couldn't quite identify but a thing their inner brain knew was bad. Really bad.

My stomach got a lurchy feeling, and I didn't want to think what I was thinking. I wanted to go back to bed and fall into a dream where I worked in an office and filed lease papers. Anything but this.

But the more the idea rooted itself, the harder my heart thumped and the more I felt I must be onto something. I went back in the bedroom and looked at the clock. It would be at least four hours before I could decently show up at someone's door. I put my head back on the pillow and pulled the covers up to my chin, but it was useless. No cozy little nest was helping to take the morbid thoughts away. I had to find out if there was a body buried under that house.

I sat up again, hugging my knees close to my chest. What if Jenny had been dead all this time and Ricky had stashed her body somewhere in or under the house? It could explain so much. She would have answered the door to him, would have gone outside at his request. My own look-around outside had shown a wooden cover to a crawl space on the back of the house.

Most homes in Albuquerque don't have basements, but many older ones were built with a crawl space. My own has one. It's where the furnace goes, and it makes a good spot to store extra stuff, as long as you don't mind some dust and spiders. They usually have a plain dirt floor, and the footing and foundation of the house form walls, normally three or four feet high, just enough to allow service access to the heating system and plumbing.

By the time I'd imagined all that, and the attendant possibilities, I was more than wide awake. I got up and tiptoed through the darkened house, moving around by the light of streetlamps that let small shafts of light through the drapes. Freckles was snoring away in her crate in the living room.

I brewed a cup of chamomile tea in hopes it would calm me down a bit, but that wasn't happening. By three a.m. I was still wired for action. I showered and dressed in jeans and a t-shirt and let myself quietly out to my Jeep. It was only three-thirty by now, but some people get up early for work. Okay, not usually this early. But I needed to catch the current resident of 1604 and make an unusual request.

I parked a couple of addresses down the street, not wanting to raise suspicions but, seriously, it's fairly suspicious to show up on a residential street and start watching the neighbors before four a.m. anyplace. But no police vehicles cruised by and I was fine. A light came on in the kitchen window of my target house a little after five. I'd worked out my spiel, but I didn't want to scare the resident into reporting me or, worse, pulling a gun. By five-thirty it was getting light outside and I saw tiny signs of more activity around the house. I pulled up to the front of the place, walked up to the front porch, and tapped on the screen door.

A living room curtain moved aside. I stepped back, smiled as winningly as I could, and waved. The female face withdrew, but a moment later the front door opened a crack.

"Hey, I know this is crazy early, but I wanted to catch you in case you leave early for work," I said.

"Sure. What is it?"

"We spoke a week or so ago, I don't know if you remember. I was asking about someone who lived here a long time ago …"

"Yeah?" No move to open the door beyond the security chain's length.

"May I?" I indicated the screen door on the porch. "I hate to shout this out."

I moved to open the screen door, and nobody shot at me.

"Thanks. Better," I said in a lower voice. "I wonder if it would be okay if I took a look around the back? The house has a crawl space, and I need to check under there and see if that former tenant left something behind."

I handed another of my business cards through the narrow space she allowed for me.

"Well, if the landlord said it was okay … I guess you can."

"Thanks. I'll be very quiet, and it shouldn't take long at all."

She stepped back and closed the door with a definite click of the lock. All right—I was in. Maybe.

I retrieved a couple of basic tools from the Jeep and hurried down the driveway toward the back. The small back yard was plain dirt. There was room for an extra vehicle or two, and tracks showed that someone had recently used the space for extra parking. The cover to the crawl space was a simple wooden cover laid over a sort of entrance made of cinderblocks and painted to match the house. No padlock or hasp. I imagined the landlord wouldn't want to deal with the hassle of providing a key if he had to call a maintenance person.

I lifted the plywood and swung it aside, then shone my flashlight beam around. We have black widow spiders here in the Southwest, and they love cozy, dark places. I wasn't ready for a nasty surprise bite. Clear so far.

Resting a hip on the cinderblocks, I swung my legs into the hole and paused on my knees to shine the light into the large space. Something skittered into a corner and disappeared, but not before I saw the telltale shiny black legs. The spiders were here. Okay, Charlie, don't poke around in corners and don't disturb their webs and you'll be fine. She said, bravely.

The space was the exact size of the footprint of the house, but for some reason these places always feel smaller. Something about adding the walls and rooms above makes them magically expand. A small concrete pad had been poured roughly in the center of the space, and an ancient Arco furnace stood there, quiet now during the hot months of the year.

Some cardboard boxes rested against the foundation along the north wall. Even with the heavy coating of dust I could read XMAS STUFF penned in black marker on one of them. I imagined a former tenant stashing the items out of their way, forgetting them when they moved out, and at some point wondering 'what ever happened to that old tree skirt Aunt Mary gave us?'. Rickety wooden shelves lined the wall on my right, within reach of the entrance, and I saw an assortment of jars, apparently home-canned food of some kind. No way was I touching any of that.

I duck-walked farther into the space, shining my light first at the overhead floor joists. Dangers abounded everywhere—exposed nails, spider webs, low-hanging bits of metal—and the last thing I needed was to rush off for a tetanus booster shot as a result of my investigation.

The dirt floor was fairly hard-packed between the entryway and the furnace; beyond that it became much more uneven. I aimed the light into the corners, at first seeing nothing unusual, but as the beam swung around to the south wall I felt my breath draw in sharply.

A mound of dirt stood up from the rest. Blurry footprints surrounded it and splashes of white powder lit up when the light hit them. But what grabbed my attention was what was exposed at one edge of the mounded dirt. The sole of a shoe.

Chapter 35

Yes, I beat it out of there so fast I had the spiders running from me. As soon as I hit the fresh outdoor air, I took several deep breaths before pulling out my phone and calling the police. Crap. I'd had the thought that Jenny might have been this close by, all along, but I truly didn't believe it. Despite my startling midnight insight, I truly thought I would come here, poke around, find nothing, and then have to decide what to do next. No such luck.

Then again, I had to look at this as a lucky find. A body gives many clues, and with forensics today the police could figure out how she died and maybe even who killed her. My part in solving the case for Linda and Cassie would be over; the police would handle it from here.

Cassie. My young client still held so much hope. It was going to be extremely difficult to deliver this news to her.

And I wouldn't, not until there was definitive proof. Even so, most likely the cops would take that duty because they would now have a murder case on their hands.

I couldn't sit still, but I couldn't leave either. So I paced.

The current tenant, the woman who'd answered the door, came out and got into her car and drove away. A few minutes later, Kent Taylor's car pulled to the curb out front. I met him and pointed the way to what I'd found. He wanted to know what had brought me here, I told him, he took notes. Three more vehicles arrived, including one from the office of the medical investigator. Yellow tape got strung around the driveway and perimeter of the crawlspace entrance.

The next part took hours. Since there was no life to be saved, no fresh evidence to be gathered before it deteriorated, the pace was slow and methodical. Taylor told me I could leave; he would be in touch if he needed more information from me. But I couldn't make myself simply drive away and forget it. I had to know what to say to Linda and Cassie.

I watched as the MI and two CSIs disappeared into the underground space, cameras and forensic kits at the ready. One uniformed officer told me to stand behind the yellow tape, but Kent told him I was okay.

I didn't know that I wanted to be *right* there, so I sat in my car a while, debating whether to call and give the women a little advance warning. Decided no, that wouldn't be right. I had to be sure before I said anything at all. Then I debated calling Ron to ask his advice, but it was somewhere around two a.m. in Hawaii and his answer— after he told me off for waking him—would be the same thing I was already telling myself: wait patiently, Charlie.

Not my strong suit, but I did it.

Sometime after ten o'clock I noticed more activity so I got out of my Jeep and went to find Taylor for an update. Two of the crime scene investigators were carrying a body bag toward the OMI's vehicle.

"What have they found?" I asked right away.

Kent gave me a patient look. "Well, I wasn't under there so I don't know, Charlie. But here comes Mack. We'll get a briefing."

This was apparently the State Medical Investigator. I'd never met him before. He was a tall, lanky guy (who must have been miserable crouched under the floor of the house all this time), with dark hair and a craggy face. He walked over to Taylor, pulling off his latex gloves as he approached. He glanced toward me, then back at Taylor.

"She's okay. Private investigator on a case that led her to the body."

Wow, it was more credit than Taylor had ever given me. I stood a little straighter.

"All right, well, I can't give you an ID on the victim," said Mack. "We didn't find a wallet, phone, or anything that would make the job easier."

"Can you tell us if the vic is female?" Taylor asked.

Thank you, Kent. I hadn't wanted to push my agenda here, but that was the central question for me.

Mack shook his head. "As far as I can tell, and this is before we get the scraps of clothing off and run any comprehensive exam of the remains, it's a male, most likely in his twenties. The body is almost completely decomposed—it's been here ten years or more. I'll get height and ethnicity and more ..."

His voice faded out of my consciousness for a moment.

At least it wasn't Jenny.

"… cause of death?" Kent was asking.

"There were broken ribs, fractured skull. Best guess at this point is the guy took a severe beating. Whether that caused his death, I can't say yet." He pulled off the white paper-like jumpsuit he'd donned over his own clothing and started to move away. "You'll have my full report, well, when I get to it. There are more urgent cases on the table at the moment."

We watched him climb into his vehicle and drive away. The other investigators were packing away their equipment, and the small cluster of people who'd gathered to watch the action were dispersing. It was too hot to hang around in the sun if there was nothing to see.

I debated my next move and decided I needed to say something to Taylor.

"I'm relieved to know this wasn't the woman I've been searching for. That was my fear, and now I don't have to inform her family. But I have an idea, and it might save you some time in identifying who those bones really belong to."

He was scribbling in his notebook. "I'm listening."

"Jenny Blake's ex-husband seems to have disappeared around the same time she did. I don't know if disappeared is the right word. He gave his family the impression he was heading out somewhere, either with a rock band or in hopes of joining one somewhere back east. But none of them that I've spoken to have heard from him, and it's been roughly as long as no one heard from Jenny."

"So …?"

"This," I waved toward the crawlspace, "might have been him."

He nodded but I got the sense he was thinking it might have been anyone.

"Okay, I've told you. If you want connections, I've got names and contact info for some of his family. Give me a call if you want it." I wished him well and headed for my Jeep. This day had begun way too early, with way too much intensity. I needed food and sleep.

It wasn't until I'd located the nearest McDonald's and got an Egg McMuffin into my stomach that I realized what I'd done. If Ricky Blake was dead and Jenny was missing, was it possible that I had the whole story backward, all along? What if she had killed him?

It would be the perfect reason for her to have escaped and remained hidden all this time. And I had just offered the police a way to prove it.

Chapter 36

I'll take those names now." Kent Taylor's call came only minutes after I'd arrived back home.

Well, I'd made the offer. And after all, getting the truth was more important than trying to spare the reputation of a young woman I'd never met. One thing our clients often don't realize is that what we uncover may not be what they want to hear. So, if it turned out Jenny Blake was a killer, not a victim, her family might have to live with that. I thought of Cassie, of how she'd struck a chord with me in our similarities. And I knew I would want to know the truth. I only hoped she would be okay with however this turned out.

I gave Kent the numbers. He said he would contact the Blakes and see if one of them would consent to having their DNA compared with the remains of what might be

Ricky. I suggested he start with Lisa or Tommy, the siblings. Paula Blake hadn't seemed like the cooperative type. But that was just my two-cents.

"Before you ask, I haven't forgotten your fingerprint test," he said.

He'd read my mind.

"I'll let you know if anything turns up."

Had it only been a day since we were at Iris's house? I gave Elsa a call to see if she'd checked in with her friend since then.

"I'm worried about her," she said. "Her voice sounded weaker this morning, even more than yesterday."

"Did you mention a doctor visit? I offered to drive her."

"I asked. She said she hasn't called. Doesn't like the new primary doctor they assigned her, but she can't seem to figure out how to change."

"How about if we got Iris out of the house? If an outing would be too tiring, we could invent something that involves her coming to your house. We could binge *Friends* or something."

She laughed. "I think Iris and I are more like the *Golden Girls*. But it's a good idea. But …"

"Jeffrey?"

"Yes! I feel like he's always right there, listening to our conversations, talking over me whenever I suggest anything. He's always got reasons why she shouldn't do something, and he makes it sound like all his objections are for her own good. I don't like this, Charlie. Iris is different. We used to talk and laugh. And she'd listen when friends gave advice. Now it's all about Jeffrey-this and Jeffrey-that."

About some of it, he could be right. Iris shouldn't be

overdoing if she was sick. But she wouldn't go to the doctor she didn't like. And now it sounded as though she wasn't listening to the advice of old friends. Elsa was right—I didn't like it either.

"Let me give it a try. I'll call her and see if I can figure out something."

I used the pretense of asking whether the flowers I'd arranged yesterday were still holding their shape.

"Oh, Charlie, they're beautiful! I'm lounging here on my settee and enjoying them right now."

Elsa had been right. Iris's voice seemed even shakier than before.

"And I suppose Jeffrey's waiting on you hand and foot?"

"Such a sweetheart. I couldn't imagine more attentive care. He's always running to the market, hoping to perk me up. That's where he is now, shopping for organic blueberries."

So he did leave her alone sometimes. But I didn't know how much help a trip to the grocery could be. It wasn't as if Elsa and I could race all the way across town to spend time with Iris when Jeffrey was most likely ten minutes from their house.

"Listen," I said, "Gram and I were talking about planning a girls' day out. Well, not *out,* per se, 'cause we know you aren't feeling much like shopping or dancing."

That brought a chuckle.

"We had in mind a TV marathon of chick flicks or a favorite old series, and we'd do a nice lunch. Heck, we could even do our own manicures or something." I was spouting ideas off the top of my head because truthfully an entire day of TV or manicures is totally out of character for me. But that wasn't the point.

"I don't know, Charlie. Let me check with Jeffrey when he gets home."

"Ah, Iris, come on. Elsa says you never had to check with anybody—you were the life of the party who usually came up with the plans. Let's do it—live a little."

But I could hear the tiredness in her voice when she responded, promising me she would think about it.

"Can you do one thing for me? Try to only eat things that come out of a package, not anything Jeffrey prepares for you. No food, no drinks."

"Charlie! What are you saying? He might be spiking my tea or something?" She said it with such disbelief, and in fact, I had no proof.

Was I really ready to make an accusation this serious without something to back it up?

"Never mind. I was just musing about something that's none of my business." Now I could only hope she didn't blurt out my words to dear Jeffrey the moment he came back home.

"I think I need to rest now, Charlie. I'm feeling very sleepy."

I hung up with a heavy heart. I felt for Iris, but I had nothing concrete to go on. It could very well be that she *had* caught a tropical virus of some kind. I meandered into the kitchen, not hungry but feeling a bit at loose ends.

Then an idea hit me. I dialed the office of my good friend and personal doctor, Linda Casper. The receptionist wanted to schedule me two weeks from now but I persuaded her to check with the doctor. I ended up speaking with Linda for a minute, explaining the situation and asking if we could get in soon.

"Four o'clock this afternoon. I'll make the time. Your friend's symptoms don't sound good."

We used the excuse that we were kidnapping Iris for a matinee showing of the latest Harrison Ford movie—it was the only thing in the theaters I thought would have a male lead character in the generation Iris would relate to. Jeffrey sputtered a little, but I teasingly pushed back.

"She's had her lunch and a good, long nap. We'll just get a little fresh air and an outing that doesn't take any energy. Sitting in the dark and eating popcorn can't tire anyone out too much, right?" This said as I picked up Iris's purse and Elsa led her to the door.

We were buckled into my Jeep before the new hubby could come up with anything that wouldn't make him sound like a cad.

Twenty minutes later we were in Dr. Linda Casper's office, where we were shown to an exam room immediately. Iris seemed befuddled by the sudden change of plans, although we'd explained everything in the car.

"You couldn't get in with your own doctor," I said as I guided her to the exam table while we waited for Linda. "So this is mine. I love her and I think you will too."

Luckily, my words proved true. Linda bustled in, all blonde curls and dimples, and immediately won Iris over by giving the older woman her full attention. Meanwhile, I saw what was going on. Linda was looking closely at Iris's eyes, skin and nails. She chuckled over her new patient's descriptions from the honeymoon trip, but when she turned to face me I saw alarm in her expression.

"Iris," she said in a perky voice. "I want to do a blood test, so my nurse will come in and take a little sample. Charlie?"

She tilted her head toward the door and I followed her out, crossing paths with the nurse who was already on her way in. Behind us, I could hear Iris talking with Elsa, sounding more animated than she had in days. Maybe the white-coat effect was mainly what she needed.

But Linda's expression quickly quelled my hope.

"I'm seeing distinct signs of poisoning," she said. "I'll need the blood test results to be sure, and to know what type. What are the chances of getting her into the hospital?"

"Willingly? Small."

"Because of what you told me earlier, the home situation."

"Right." My mind was racing. What could we do to keep Iris safe?

Chapter 37

Linda patted my hand, suggested we give it some thought, and hurried down the corridor. I stood there, not quite knowing what to do—go back in the exam room, follow Linda, see if they had a candy machine?

When the nurse came out, carrying a small vial of blood, it was my cue to go back inside and see where the conversation led. Elsa was sitting in a chair in the corner, and Iris was rubbing at the spot on her arm where a strip of bright pink tape secured a cotton ball to the place where the nurse had stuck her in the vein.

"So, do I get to go home now?" she asked. "The doctor didn't say there was anything wrong with me."

"Well, I think that's what the blood test is about. She's still figuring out what's making you sick."

"We could still catch that movie," Elsa suggested.

Both Iris and I sort of stared in amazement. About the time I was trying to figure out how to broach the subject, Linda bustled back into the room, all medical efficiency and authority.

"We need to get you in for treatment right away," she told Iris. "I've called ahead to Presbyterian and a team is waiting. Charlie, can you get her there right away?"

"Why on earth would I need to be in the hospital? I thought you'd just give me some pills or tell me to watch my diet. I need to ask Jeffrey about this."

"No! I mean … don't worry about that. We'll get you settled and then we can call Jeffrey," I looked up at Linda. "Yes, I'll drive her right over."

Linda put on her calmest bedside manner. "Iris, your blood tested positive for arsenic poisoning. It's very serious and needs to be treated right away. With electrolyte replacement and lots of IV fluids, I think we can get it out of your system. But this needs immediate attention. You aren't to go home first. Charlie will take you to Pres and they will take great care of you."

"But my husband—"

I stepped in and took her arm. "We'll call him just as soon as you get there. No point in worrying him until we know more."

All this time Elsa's eyes had grown wider. Our speculation about the mystery illness was suddenly becoming very real. I dashed outside and pulled the car to the front of the building and we helped Iris into the front seat.

"How on earth could I have gotten this poison?" Iris fretted as we negotiated the side streets between Linda's office and the huge hospital complex. "I just don't understand this. I'm sure they're very careful with the food on the cruise ships. I thought I just got a bad oyster or something."

"Maybe oysters can contain it," I suggested, happy to get her attention on something besides her husband. "I'll bet the doctors here can tell you more."

I pulled into the emergency entrance, as Linda had directed. The moment we walked in, a nurse in blue scrubs took over. "You're Doctor Casper's patient, right?" she said in the tone a sweet little girl would use with her grandma. "You just come with me and we'll get you started."

Meanwhile, an administrator wanted insurance information and all kinds of things I didn't personally know about Iris, so we took the liberty of doing a little wallet biopsy to see what was what. Once we'd come across the card that showed her to be a member of the hospital's health plan, that aspect of it began to flow smoothly. Copies of documents were made and I steered the woman toward Iris for any additional information they needed.

"Only thing is, do not call her husband," I said. "She'll ask for him, but *do not* do it."

The woman gave me a bland look. "Okay," was all she said.

I could only guess this wasn't the first time they'd had to keep one spouse away from the other. I was allowed behind the inner sanctum doors and made my way past a nurses' station in my search for treatment room 15. I spotted it by the fact that Elsa was parked in a stiff metal chair outside the door.

"She didn't seem to want me there while they took off her clothes and started sticking needles in." She seemed a little worn out by the morning's activities.

"Let me check in with the nurse. Then I can just run you home."

"I'm worried about her," she said, the first time today she'd shown anything less than her normal, spunky self.

"I know. Me too." I glanced around for more comfortable seating but didn't see any. "Do you know if Iris has other relatives? Children or siblings?"

She shook her head. "She had a sister who passed, a few years ago. No children that she's ever mentioned."

"Okay—I'm sure the hospital staff will get her family and medical details."

But Elsa still seemed dejected. I had a thought. "How about friends from church?"

At last she lit up. "Of course! I'll make some calls and we can put together a visitation schedule."

Really? They did those things? Anyway, planning it gave Elsa a purpose. I handed her my phone.

I peeped in the door and saw that Iris seemed to be comfortably reclining in a bed. The nurse turned at that moment and I caught her eye. Outside the door I gave her the little information I knew: Iris was possibly in danger from her husband so he shouldn't be allowed in; otherwise, the church members would like to take turns sitting at her bedside since she had no other relatives.

A doctor came toward us, about to turn into Room 15, and I gave her the same lowdown. And within fifteen minutes a pastor from the church had arrived. I was just breathing a sigh of relief that I could now take Elsa home when my phone rang.

The screen said Albuquerque Police. How do they manage to sneak up on anyone if the caller ID gives it away? I walked down the corridor and accepted the call.

Of course, it was Kent Taylor.

"I got an ID for you." Something in his tone made me think of my very early morning under the Sixth Street house.

"DNA from the bones? Already?"

"Um, no … the other one. The prints you gave me yesterday."

"Jeffrey Lougan." I dropped my voice and looked back toward the small gathering in front of Iris's room.

"Lougan, aka Jeffrey Lomas, James Lukin, Jeff Lutz …"

"Holy shit!"

The preacher down the hall looked up.

"So he has a record?"

"No kidding, Sherlock. He and his whole family are wanted on multiple counts of fraud. Typically for bilking older women out of their life savings. There are warrants out in Texas and Louisiana."

"Wow." This went beyond anything I'd imagined. I'd pictured Jeffrey in it for the easy lifestyle of the country club set, his family hanging around to get invited to the lavish parties he would convince Iris to throw.

"Kent, it's gone farther than fraud now." I followed signs to an exit and stepped outside. "His current wife, whom he married only a couple of weeks ago, is in the hospital with arsenic poisoning. You've got to pick up this guy."

I gave the Tanoan address, and Kent actually seemed excited. He even complimented me. We may have turned a corner in our shaky relationship.

Back in the ER, I spotted a lot of activity around Iris's treatment room and I rushed over to join Elsa.

"What's up?"

"Something about moving her."

"We're taking her up to ICU," the young nurse in the blue scrubs said as she and an orderly pushed the wheeled bed into the corridor. "She'll get better monitoring there."

"Is there anything—?"

"Not at the moment. Give us an hour or so to get her settled in. She won't be able to have visitors, other than family."

"No—there's a restraining order." Not quite true, but I needed them to understand the urgency. From what Kent had told me, I imagined Jeffrey doing something desperate if he figured out his plan was about to go horribly awry.

The pastor stepped forward. "I think we're talking about her church family. Thanks to Ms. Elsa, we understand the situation."

My phone pinged with an incoming text: Lougan not at address you gave. Any other place you know of?

Taylor was actually asking for my help? But I had to shake off the flattery and concentrate on the actual problem. I caught up with the rolling bed and walked along beside Iris.

"It looks like Jeffrey's not home," I said gently. "Do you know where else he might be right now?"

She smiled through the haze of her misery. "Oh, I called him. I think he's on the way here."

I tried to hide the dismay on my face as I patted her hand and asked if it would be okay for Elsa to take charge of her purse and phone. Iris nodded woozily.

"Do not let her get hold of her phone again. I'll catch up with you in the ICU waiting area." I gave Taylor the news via text. A minute later I got one in return. Will have officers there ASAP.

So, okay, maybe Jeffrey's coming here wasn't such a bad thing after all. The police should be able to catch up. In case they didn't catch him entering the complex, all I had to do was keep him away from Iris. Easy. Right. I could imagine him mad as a rattlesnake and ready to strike if he got close enough.

Chapter 38

Parking oneself in a hospital waiting room is about as interesting as watching paint dry while waiting for grass to grow. Boring upon boring, especially since this one had terrible telephone reception and no data connection. The signs on the walls advising us not to use cell phones were laughable. I ended up taking the elevator up two floors and walking to the end of a corridor to get anything at all. It was my futile hope that Kent Taylor would see fit to keep me advised. Guess we weren't all that great of friends after all.

Two hours after we landed on the ICU floor, a uniformed officer stepped out of the elevator. As I was the only one who gave him a little wave, he figured out there must be a connection and he walked toward me.

"You're in the hospital looking for Jeffrey Lougan?"

He nodded. "Four of us responded to the call but we can't post officers everywhere—this place is huge. If this is where his victim is, it's the place he'll come. That's what I figure. And since we can only spare one person—" He pointed at his own chest. I noted his name pin—R. Lopez.

I imagined Jeffrey would run the moment he spotted a uniform, and it was likely he'd spotted the original four meandering around and had skipped out fast. But if he wanted to get to Iris badly enough, he'd be back. At least I was now free of that duty.

After a quick peek in at Iris, who was now hooked up to all kinds of things that I imagined were flushing the toxin from her body, Elsa and I headed for home. Poor Gram was looking fairly tired, and I'd become impatient to get back to work.

I needed to touch base with the client who was paying me. I hadn't spoken to Cassie in more than a week, and although there was precious little to tell her, it was time to check in. I certainly wasn't bringing up the bones under the floor until I had something definite to report, but who knew how long it would take the Homicide team to get the DNA, compare it, and find a match.

Although I'd had the faint idea that it could be Ricky Blake, the truth was that it could be anyone at all.

I took a shower with some flowery-scented body wash to get the antiseptic smell of the hospital off me. Clean shorts and t-shirt felt refreshing, and Freckles was so thrilled to see me I couldn't resist carrying the old police file out to the backyard gazebo. I could re-read the notes and the dog could chase the ball I tossed out onto the lawn for her.

While that bit of entertainment was going on, I picked

up my phone and called Cassie. Hers went to voicemail, and I assumed she was at work. I left a quick call-me-back message and turned to the file on the settee beside me.

Whoever the body under the house was, the MI had said he was badly beaten. I still couldn't imagine any way Jenny Blake did that. But the involvement of the Chaco Cartel still bothered me. I knew from the notes in the file that Ricky had done drugs and the police had found a sizeable stash at that house on Sixth. Whether there was a connection to Ricky or not, there could very well be a connection between the drugs, the beating, the cartel, and a body in a shallow grave on the same property.

I just wished the police notes indicated more along that line, but they didn't. It seemed DeAngelo had been following the drug connections up to a point, then went off in another direction. Apparently his partner found that odd too. One of Curtis's notes said *Switching from cartel connection to checking the morgues for vic—no luck.*

I was pawing through the rest of his notes to see if he'd expanded on those thoughts when my phone rang.

"Hey, Charlie. It's Cassie." Her voice sounded so hopeful … I hated to dash her hopes but had to tell her I hadn't located her mom yet.

"Do you have time for a Coke or a coffee or something?" I asked. "I do have a few details I can share."

"Sure. Do you know Monica's Coffee Place on Washington?"

"I've driven by it a dozen times, never stopped. That sounds great." We agreed to meet in fifteen minutes.

I traded my running shorts for a pair of jeans, convinced Freckles to give up ball play for a little while, and went out to my Jeep. Cassie was just getting out of her car in the parking lot beside the little coffee house when I pulled up.

"They have the *best* spiced chai latte here," she said. "Yeah, I know it says coffee, but there's more."

She led the way inside and greeted the waitress familiarly. "How's your grandma?" the young woman asked. Cassie merely shrugged. We took a table beside a lace-curtained window, and I went with Cassie's suggestion for the chai.

"I was going to ask the same thing," I said while the server blended our drinks, "about how your grandmother is."

"Not great. She's fading pretty quickly. It's just hard to—" When her voice broke, I filled in with apologies for not having answers yet.

"I've covered the whole police investigation, talked to several people from back then, and there are a few things pending." I filled her in on my visit to Phoenix and that I'd tracked down some of her father's relatives.

She didn't show any more interest in them than they'd shown in her. Blood isn't everything, in fact means next to nothing if there's been a lifetime without contact. The beverages arrived just as my phone rang. It was Taylor.

I started to ignore it but Cassie waved me on. "Go ahead. It takes this a couple minutes to cool off enough to drink it anyway."

"It shouldn't take but a second." I stepped outside. I always hate those people who feel they need to share their phone calls with everyone in the room.

"Did they catch Jeffrey Lougan?" I asked before he'd hardly said hello.

"I like that, right to business." He sounded droll. "No. Actually, it's your other pending question. DNA from the remains match Ricky Blake—it's ninety-nine percent certain."

Wow, that was quick. I felt a little stunned.

"I pushed the testing through, expedited, since it's now a murder investigation for my department."

I glanced through the window at Cassie. She was staring at me. Gulp. Now I had to tell the girl her father was dead. I thanked Taylor and took a deep breath before going back inside and taking my seat.

"Cassie, I—"

"Just tell me. Is it my mom?"

"No, actually …" I fidgeted with my spoon for a second. "Not your mom. A couple days ago there was a body found under the house where she lived when you were little. It turns out the body was Ricky Blake. It's your father."

She barely blinked. "How did they identify him? I mean, is it for sure?"

"It's for sure. He had a brother and sister, and they matched the DNA."

Her lips pressed tightly for a moment before she took a deep breath and picked up her mug.

"I'm really sorry." I glanced around. "And so sorry to deliver the message like this, in a public place."

The café was nearly empty and I'd kept my voice low, but it still felt strange to handle the news this way.

"I never knew him. Never even knew there were other relatives. Mom has always felt alive for me because Grandma talked about her, told me stories, showed pictures and shared her personal things. It was enough for me."

I reached across the table and took her hand. I knew exactly how she felt. Gram had been everything to me, from my teen years and even before. We shared a moist-eyed moment before I could speak again.

"I'm still searching. I won't give up."

She nodded. "It's mainly for Grandma at this point. She always held out hope."

But I knew it was secretly Cassie who held onto hope. Linda had basically told me she'd felt for many years that Jenny had probably died. I only hoped, if and when I found the answers, it wouldn't turn out that Jenny had killed Ricky. It was the kind of tragedy that was too much for anyone to bear.

"I should talk to her again, your grandmother. It's been weighing on my mind that I'm working on finding Jenny, even though she told me not to." I gave Cassie a smile. "Yes, I know. *You* are my client and you're paying me from your inheritance money. And it's you that I want the answers for, but she deserves to know about whatever I find."

She nodded. "She does. And I feel sure you'll find the truth before she's gone."

The emotion felt thick in the air between us. This had to be the saddest tea party I'd ever attended.

Chapter 39

I watched Cassie get into the minivan and drive away. Such a good kid—Linda was lucky to have her, especially now during her illness.

As I started my Jeep my mind flicked over to my other, unofficial, case and I wondered how Iris was doing under the intensive care therapy at the hospital. A phone call probably wouldn't net me any but the blandest information, and it wasn't far out of my way to zigzag over there.

I would never imagine that an ICU hospital visit could be more uplifting than tea with a young friend, but that turned out to be the case. Iris seemed more alert already, and although the nurse cautioned me that she had a way to go before coming back to full health, the prognosis was looking a lot better.

The cop on duty had been chatting up the nurses at

their station when I walked in. He'd given me a nod and a smile. Now, as I walked past, I heard raised voices.

"You can't keep me out. She's my wife!"

I knew that voice. He must have been in the second elevator. I ran toward the sound of the argument and came upon the officer just as he was ordering Jeffrey to put his hands behind his back. The suspect made a move to run, but our young cop was quicker. He had the cuffs on in a flash and began with, "You have the right to remain silent …"

A woman stood at the elevator, jabbing repeatedly at the Down button. I knew her too. The aunt—Reyna.

"Oh, no you don't," I muttered, dashing forward and grabbing her by the wrist just as the elevator door opened.

She spun on me so fast and with so much strength it took me by surprise. "Jeffrey!" she called out, but that only served to get the cop's attention.

"Hey!" I shouted. "Over here!"

He was at my side in a flash, with his spare nylon-tie restraints out of his pocket. Reyna changed tactic and smiled up at him.

"Officer, what on earth do you think I've done wrong?"

I remembered things Kent Taylor had told me. "Well, there's conspiracy to commit murder, for starters. And then a little matter of some outstanding arrest warrants in other states."

The officer had already radioed for backup, and two hospital security men had come bounding up the stairs. I watched the whole bunch of them get into the elevator, my heart pounding.

I took the next elevator down, but I bypassed the bustle of activity near the front entrance. More police cars, the two suspects separated so they couldn't work out their story on the way to the station. It was done. Iris was safe and Elsa would be free of the unwanted attention she'd been receiving.

My Jeep just sort of drove itself home, as I was suddenly in an exhausted funk. Freckles greeted me, thrilled that I was home to feed her, but after that we just vegged in front of the TV for an hour or so and I fell into a sound sleep on the couch.

By morning I felt stiff and grubby in my previous day's clothing. It took a bit of time, a shower, and two cups of coffee before I returned to semi-normal again. There was a message on my phone. Cassie had apparently called me in the late evening and I'd slept right through the ringtone.

"Charlie, it's my grandma. Things are not so great. The doctor is talking about hospice and—" She cleared her throat. "And anyway, Grandma wants to talk to you. Um, I told her I had kept you working on the case. She's not mad or anything. I think she was kind of glad I did that. So, anyway, can you call me? I'm scared."

Poor kid. I glanced at the time. It had been more than ten hours since she called. I tapped the redial button and caught her, somewhat breathless.

"Hey, Charlie. Yeah, I'm on my way to work right now. I'm giving notice so I can be home after this, but it's the right thing to do, to give them a little heads-up."

A good kid, this one.

"You said your grandmother wants to talk with me?"

"Yes, she's anxious about something. If you could give her a call. The visiting home nurse is there now, but she'll be leaving in an hour or so. I got the impression Grandma wants to talk to you alone."

Cassie was right. Linda asked me to come at ten, right after the nurse left.

I tapped at her front door but didn't expect her to jump up to answer, so when the doorknob turned at my touch, I poked my head inside and called out to her.

"Come on in the den, Charlie. I'm not exactly running around the house these days."

Not exactly running was putting it mildly. A hospital bed had been set up in the dining room along with an assortment of the usual accessories—an adjustable height table beside it, a stand for bags of whatever intravenous fluids might come along. For now, it all looked freshly installed and unused.

"Hey, Linda," I said when I found her on the same couch where I'd last seen her. "How're you doing?"

"I suppose Cassie didn't tell you. Next step on this journey is hospice. I'm opting for it here at home, with the visiting nurses, for as long as we can handle that. But when it gets to be too much for Cassie, I'll go into a home."

"Oh, Linda … I'm so sorry."

"Sorry for what? It's the way most of us eventually will end up."

I took a seat in the chair across from her, positioning myself so she wouldn't have to crane her neck to visit. "I'm just sorry I wasn't able to find Jenny."

She nodded.

"I suppose Cassie told you the news about Ricky?"

Another nod. Her face hardened into deep lines and she suddenly looked at least twenty years older.

"I'm sorry he wasn't found alive. Who knows, he might have been ready to know Cassie now, all these years later."

"I doubt that. But I'd have given him the benefit of

the doubt." She shifted, lowering her feet to the floor and adjusting the blanket over her legs. "But that's not what I wanted to tell you. Eventually, if I don't have the courage to do it myself, I want you to tell Cassie this story. But she needs to be older. That's why I probably won't do it now."

"Okay, you've got me intrigued."

Linda plucked at the edges of her blanket, sighed deeply a couple of times. For some reason she was having to work up to this. I tried for an expression that was attentive but not to stare intrusively.

"Charlie, here's the thing. I have a confession about Jenny's disappearance." She looked up to gauge my reaction. "I did it."

"Did what? Made her disappear?"

"Yes. Exactly."

Chapter 40

Then

The weather forecasters warned of hazardous travel conditions but when it's a holiday weekend, a big one like Thanksgiving, no one listens. No one thinks anything will happen to them. And then comes a full-on blizzard.

Those thoughts went through Ismael Gutierrez's mind as the car crept eastbound along Interstate 40 at a mere thirty-five miles an hour. He couldn't see more than twenty feet ahead. He should have pulled over at Clines Corners, as dozens of others did, to wait out the storm in the coffee shop. This whole trip would be far safer by daylight, after the plows had come through.

But Santa Rosa was home and, at this point, no more than twenty miles away. He glanced at his wife in the passenger seat. Maria, his partner in life for three decades now. She looked worried. But she left the decisions to him, for better or worse. They were in this together. He dared take his right hand off the wheel long enough to squeeze her hand.

"Would you like the radio on?" she asked in her soft voice. "Maybe they'll have Christmas music."

"That would be nice." He agreed, more because it gave her something to do than because he craved sound in the car. Watching the road and surrounding traffic required all his attention. And because he was watching so carefully, he spotted the trouble in time to slowly take his foot off the gas and bring the car to a stop, well back from the chaos.

An eighteen-wheeler had jackknifed across the westbound lanes. He could see strings of lights that outlined the shape of the cab and the trailer, lights that flickered in and out of view in the blowing snow. Beyond the crosswise trailer were at least ten others, all in trouble. Several had hit the truck, others had rear-ended those, a couple had obviously panicked and hit their brakes, sliding at angles until they also became entangled.

And in the eastbound lanes, drivers had reacted poorly, slowing to stare, and several had ended up in rear-end collisions, as well.

Ismael put on his flashers and tapped his brakes multiple times, until vehicles coming up behind him began to slow.

"*Dios mio,*" Maria whispered. "People are hurt. We have to help!"

He would have loved to coast on through, to dodge the mess in the eastbound lanes and ease his way on to Santa Rosa, to his home, to a warm fireplace. But he was a doctor. He couldn't leave these people without help. And Maria—as a nurse there was no way she would abandon people in need. No emergency vehicles had arrived yet.

"Let me get us to a safe spot." He edged to the left, narrowly passing one of the crashed eastbound cars. The first few were badly mangled.

If he pulled off the highway completely, it would likely be at a downward angle and into a snowbank he couldn't steer out of, even with his SUV's all-wheel drive. Fifty feet ahead he spotted the answer, one of those crossover points with signs that stated "Official Use Only." So, let them give him a ticket.

"Bundle up," he told his wife as he brought the SUV around so it faced the interstate again. It might be hours before he could attempt to leave, but he hoped emergency personnel would arrive soon.

Maria reached into the back seat where they each kept a cold-weather emergency kit. A snowmobile suit, thick gloves, warm hats with headlamps, and heavy boots. She'd seen too many people brought into the ER at Guadalupe County Hospital with frostbite and hypothermia, people who had no idea how quickly the cold would affect them. One couple had died when their car stalled only a quarter mile from their home; they started out walking and became disoriented during a blizzard very much like this one.

They pulled on their winter gear inside the warm vehicle and stuffed their feet into the boots before opening a door. Trekking back toward the pileup, Ismael saw the problem. The first car in the eastbound side had gone out of control—probably when the driver began to stare at the truck wreck—and a dark SUV caught the bumper, spinning both vehicles sideways. From that point, he counted five other vehicles that had bashed into them, one after the other.

He couldn't open the door on the first car, but brushing

snow off the window and peering inside, it appeared the only person inside was sitting up, alert, and using his phone. Ismael gave him a thumbs-up and walked on to the next. The dark SUV didn't fare so well. With collisions from all sides, it was a mess. Through the window he could see that the driver was dead. The other passenger in the front also. The driver's side back door was crushed completely, another vehicle wedged into its side. That driver waved him on, yelling that he was okay.

Farther down the line, he could see a few people getting out of their cars, meandering, now that all traffic had come to a halt.

Maria called out, her headlight bobbing into his vision on the opposite side of the dark SUV. "This isn't good."

He looked across to see what her light revealed. The rear passenger door was open, probably sprung at the moment of impact. In the back seat he could tell that someone else had been riding there. A lightweight jacket, a paperback book—worst was the lone shoe. When the body is sent flying, shoes often come off. One shoe wasn't a good sign.

"Look around," he shouted to his wife. "Someone could be lying out in the snow."

He scrambled over the SUV's hood to join his wife.

"Here!" she shouted.

A still form lay sprawled more than fifteen feet from the roadside. They both rushed toward it.

"This girl isn't dressed for the weather at all," Maria said, removing a glove to check for a pulse. "She's alive. But very cold."

For a split second Ismael debated taking off his snowmobile suit to offer its warmth. But that would be foolish. The young woman was already cold. And her head was bleeding. He needed to keep himself warm enough to get her to safety.

"Let's get her to our car," he said.

Without waiting for Maria's agreement, he stooped to pick up the woman who weighed practically nothing. "Get my keys, run ahead," he said to his wife.

By the time he'd carried the inert form past the first bashed vehicles, his back was beginning to ache from the effort of trudging through deep snow with such a burden. But there was no way he was quitting now. Maria had reached their vehicle, started the engine, and opened a back door. Ismael set the injured woman inside, crawling in on the floor to look at her injuries. There was always the fear of doing more damage—neck or spinal—but in this case she would have frozen to death before those injuries could be dealt with anyway.

"All we can do is get her to the hospital," he told Maria as he peeled off his snowsuit and draped the warm, dry inner parts over his patient.

"I'll sit with her, you drive," she said.

He pushed it as much as he dared, but even with no other traffic moving now, they were using up the golden hour of life by the time they reached the small hospital in Santa Rosa.

Maria had phoned ahead and alerted her fellow staff in the ER, so when they pulled up to the portico outside, a gurney and team were waiting.

"The ambulances have all gone," one of the young interns told them. The hospital had only one and the volunteer fire department another two. "Everything from three counties is being sent to an accident on I-40."

"We were there. Consider her your first arrival for the night."

By the time they'd wheeled the patient indoors, she'd begun to stir restlessly. "Keep her still," Maria advised. "I think there's a broken leg in addition to the head injury. If that's all, she's lucky."

In a curtained cubicle, the young woman moaned and her eyes fluttered open. "What—what's going on?"

Ismael watched as his wife spoke gently. "Hey, sweetie, it's going to be okay. You're in the hospital. We're going to get you warmed up, and then we'll do some tests, okay?"

He stepped over to the bedside. "Can you tell us your name? Where you live?"

The woman's eyes darted back and forth in confusion. "I—I don't know."

Chapter 41

Now

I stared at Linda, not quite believing what I'd heard. "*You* made Jenny disappear?" A dozen thoughts went through my head—none of them good.

She leaned forward, planning her words. "Jenny and I did it together." At my puzzled expression, she made an impatient gesture. "Maybe I should start at the beginning."

"Maybe you should." I almost reached for a pen, but I had a feeling none of this was something I would forget. I sat back and let her talk.

"It goes back to Ricky. After he left her, nearly a year later, I suppose he began to have second thoughts about the breakup. He called Jenny a lot, wanted her to take him back. She was skeptical. He hadn't given up the idea of becoming a famous guitar player but he hadn't proven he could actually earn a living at it. And she'd begun to suspect he was drinking way too much. When he called he was often 'in a mood' she'd tell me. Sometimes high, sometimes low. But she knew she didn't want to let his unpredictability back in her life, in Cassie's life.'"

"There were drugs, too," I added.

"Yes, she eventually figured that out. And one day when he convinced her to meet him for coffee, she witnessed something."

"Uh-oh."

"Yeah. It was bad. After their meeting she saw Ricky meet up with two scary-looking men, thugs, really. The worst part was that they saw her. And she could see it in their eyes. They would use her to get to her ex. She had no idea what they wanted from him, didn't care, but she couldn't let them get to Cassie."

Linda shifted on the sofa, rearranging her blanket. "She called me in a panic and I went over to her house, where she told me all this. Of course, my first suggestion was that she and the baby just move in here. But she wouldn't do it. Said they would track her down and it would put me in danger too. She had no idea what to do, but she felt she had to do something right away. She'd seen vehicles cruising down the street, men checking out the house. So, I had the idea that she could disappear.

"We would make it look like an abduction and I would report it to the police. I figured it would make the news, and that would get these guys to believe something had happened and she was no threat to them anymore."

"So Jenny would leave the house and the baby, knowing you would be along very soon."

"Right. We had it timed almost to the minute."

"But, how did—"

"I'm getting to that. I had some friends who were planning to drive to Amarillo for the Thanksgiving weekend, so I just casually asked if they would give someone a ride. I made it sound like she was a college student who was going back to Texas for the holiday. She wouldn't have a suitcase since she had plenty of clothes at her parents' home there. She was also getting away from a boyfriend, I told them, so Jenny would want them to pull up outside the house, toot the horn, and she would dash out. She needed this 'boyfriend' not to know where she was going and not to follow."

Linda had been staring at her hands as she talked. Now she looked up at me. "I know. Looking back, it was an odd story. But my friends agreed to go along with it. In reality, we wanted it to appear she was being abducted so the cops would chase after these cartel men, rather than figure out what we were up to. Jenny had often laughed about the nosy woman across the street who watched out her windows all the time and saw *everything*. If the neighbor saw her being rushed away in an SUV, she'd tell the police what we wanted them to think. It seemed like it would work."

I was beginning to see a glimmer of logic in the plan. "Let me guess. They would take Jenny to Amarillo with them, she would hide out for awhile, or you would follow along and sneak her back …"

"Something like that. We weren't clear on the details. She suggested I move the baby and her gear to my house, then after the initial police investigation petered out, I could clear her things out of the house on Sixth. We knew she would have to stay away a few weeks, maybe a month or so, but then figured she could change her hair and do enough with her appearance to come back to Albuquerque and resume her studies at UNM."

"But she didn't come back. Something went wrong."

"There was an accident. My friends drove toward Texas, as per the plan, but the weather turned nasty and there was an accident, a horrible multi-car pileup on the interstate. The couple I was trusting with my daughter's life were both killed."

A stone sunk to the pit of my stomach. "Jenny too?"

"By the time I'd heard of the accident, I had already reported her disappearance to the police. I had planted 'evidence' at the house, in the form of a cigarette butt." She shook her head in disbelief. "I went to so much trouble with that. Used tweezers to pick a random cigarette out of a public waste bin, took it to the house, dropped it near the porch. I figured if I made a big deal about how out of place that was, they would take it seriously. And I did convince one of the investigators to take it in and test the DNA. I figured one of two things would happen—either it belonged to someone with a record, in which case the cops would follow that lead and go around in circles, or— as it turned out—the cigarette belonged to someone with no police record and it became a dead end. Either way, it would keep them busy awhile."

I remembered what I'd read in the file. "Doesn't look like it turned into a real lead for them."

"No. But by then I was dealing with worse—the accident. I searched all the reports, even called the hospitals in the area. There was no sign of Jenny. Of course she had left the house without her purse, so I had no idea if she carried any form of identification. I inquired about my friends and was told of their deaths, both gone instantly, at the scene. There were so many injuries.

"Ambulances and paramedics came from several towns. Santa Rosa was the closest, about twenty miles away but they have very limited facilities—it's a town of only about two thousand people. The other towns in the region are similar—Tucumcari, Vaughn, Fort Sumner—none of them have decent trauma centers. The worst injuries were brought to Albuquerque, and I combed the records and called everywhere, asking about anyone of her description. She would have been reported as a Jane Doe if she had died. I couldn't find any that matched."

"Oh, Linda, you must have gone through sheer hell."

"At first, yes. But my one consolation was that if I couldn't find her, neither could Ricky or those men from the drug cartel that she'd been so afraid of." Tears that had pooled in her lower lids now spilled over.

She reached for a water glass on the end table, discovered it was empty. I left my chair and went to the kitchen to refill it for her. After a long sip, she resumed.

"My only focus at that time was to keep my grand-daughter safe. After my supposed *discovery* of Cassie alone there, I grabbed up the essentials she would need and loaded her into my car. We drove a roundabout route home so I could feel sure we weren't followed." She stared at a space in the middle of the room.

"I'm sure I was just being silly. What would these drug types want with a middle-aged woman and a baby? But based on what Jenny had told me about Ricky and these guys, I couldn't be too careful. We stayed locked inside the house for at least a week. I wouldn't leave the phone, certain Jenny would call me from somewhere. And if she had survived the accident, I know she would have. That's what led me to believe, eventually, that she had died, an unidentified victim. Not being able to bring her home and bury her—that's been the worst."

"What were your feelings when Cassie hired me to find Jenny?"

"At first? That it was a waste of money. I'd tried everything, fifteen years ago. But then, I began to wonder. When someone you love is missing, you can't help but hold out *some* hope. Some tiny scrap of hope. But then I didn't want Cassie to get her hopes built up too much. You know what I mean? How cruel is it to let her keep thinking Jenny might walk through the door any day and they'll just take up together and live happily ever after?"

"She's feeling that same thread of hope you've held on to," I suggested. "Plus, she's really kind of freaked out about going to live with the aunt and uncle she barely knows."

"Ted and Myrna are good people. My brother raised two kids of his own. They'll be fine with Cassie, and even though it's not the situation everyone wants, it's only a couple of years before she'll graduate and can start college. There's enough money in my estate to cover that, and Cassie gets it all."

"So, what would you like me to do at this point?"

She sighed. "Do you think there's any chance Jenny is still alive?"

"We don't know that she died. So, yes, I'd say there's a *chance*."

"Then go for it. If you can find out where she is, even if she did die, Cassie deserves to know. Whatever happens after that ... well, I most likely won't be around to see it."

Chapter 42

My entire way of looking at the investigation had just been turned upside down, so my mind was churning with possible routes to take. I left Linda tucked in and as comfortable as I could before I headed out. That multi-car accident on I-40 would have made the news, so that would be my first stop.

With no idea how long the local newspapers have been publishing online editions, I figured my first stop should be the offices of the *Journal*. It helped that I knew the exact date of the accident, the day Jenny vanished, and was able to bring up microfiche of the news coverage.

In typical fashion, the stories at both major dailies began with the horror of it all. Blinding snowstorm, darkness coming early that time of year, so many travelers on the road heading toward their families for a long weekend of celebration. A jackknifed tractor-trailer rig headed toward Albuquerque, an SUV attempting to pass it, another car close behind slamming into it. More vehicles, sliding out of control, and then more, some going off the road to each side. Then the eastbound lanes became the scene of similar wrecks, as drivers slowed to watch and others plowed into them. In all, more than fifty vehicles had become involved.

After the horror came the heroics—brave first responders who arrived in impossible conditions to sort out the situation, perform triage, try to get help for those who could be helped. Firsthand accounts of miracles and heroes, heartrending tales of loss and those who would be affected for life.

And after that storyline of feel-good heroism exhausted itself, then came the blaming. Why hadn't snowplows kept the roadway clearer? Why hadn't state police closed the road? Drivers should receive better instruction on coping with snowy conditions, weather reports should have been updated more frequently, the state should have put up better signage—after all, this section of highway was notorious for winter accidents because of the open countryside and howling winds during storms. One reporter even suggested that the entire interstate highway system should have been planned better.

With twenty-five people dead, nearly a hundred seriously injured, someone needed to shoulder the blame.

I grew weary of the way the coverage was going after the third day of it. By the fifth day, a school shooting in Texas took over the front pages, and the crash virtually disappeared from sight.

I wasn't sure of my next move. Most likely the state police would have official records of where the victims had been taken and names of the fatalities, so I headed toward their headquarters in Santa Fe, only to be referred to the Department of Transportation, where I was told I would need to file a request for information and plan on eight to ten weeks for a response. I filled out the form, although this wasn't going to net any answers in time for Linda.

Gritting my teeth I headed home.

One thing about the hour-long drive—my mind had ample time to mull over everything and to put it in perspective. I couldn't allow myself to become lost in the tons of minutia the news reporters had dug up. I couldn't get bogged down in government paperwork. I needed to somehow get to the root of the problem and find the most likely answers my client needed right now.

It seemed Linda had done a good job of searching the news stories at the time. She'd found out that her friends died at the scene but there had been no sign of Jenny. So, what if Jenny had not been with them? What if something happened along the way, something that caused her to change her plans and not ride along?

I mulled that possibility for the last fifteen minutes of my drive, eventually coming to the conclusion that if Jenny really had avoided the accident, she would have certainly known of it and would have found a way to let her mother know she'd safely escaped. So, that little ray of hope vanished. But the good news was that I'd probably saved myself from chasing a wild lead that could go nowhere. No, Ron had always said, go with the facts you have.

Many of the accident victims had been taken to the Guadalupe County Hospital in Santa Rosa. So, I could start there. Tomorrow. Today had been eventful enough, and I needed to head into this with a plan.

I spent the evening with maps and internet research, to the point where I hoped I could negotiate my way into a small-town past. I knew I was racing against time for Linda, and this wouldn't be easy. It seemed like a good idea to enlist the help of my client, so I called her house.

Cassie answered and said Linda was already in bed for the night.

"In the morning, ask her if she knows anyone in Santa Rosa," I said. "I'm heading there tomorrow, and any little connection could prove helpful. Call me if she can provide a name."

With that possibility in the works, I made my plans. Dottie agreed to have Freckles come to their house and to stay overnight if need be. I packed a little duffle with a change of clothes and my overnight gear, just in case. Technically, since the town was only two hours away, I could drive there and back each day that I needed to investigate, but getting a room there would be simpler and a better use of my time than the extra hours on the road.

I woke up early in the morning and was out the door with my duffle bag before seven. Nine a.m. is the perfect time to arrive in a small town. I decided to grab a quick breakfast and figure out what to do next. I exited I-40 onto the famed old Route 66 and stopped at the first place I spotted. I had decided to toss out Jenny's name wherever I could, so as the waitress (Myra, by her name tag) took my order for huevos rancheros and coffee, I asked.

"She might have moved here around fifteen years ago," I suggested.

"Sorry, never heard of her, and I've worked here going on twenty years now," Myra told me. "Course I don't know all my customers by name, mostly just the regulars."

I showed her the photos. Linda had provided a better one than the original I'd begun with.

"Cute baby," Myra said after a quick glance. "But I don't think I know them."

I wanted to ask her to take a closer look, to consider that the young woman was now fifteen years older and wouldn't have the baby with her, but Myra got pulled away by another customer's coffee refill request.

Okay. All I could do was to keep going. The hospital would be the logical place to begin. They must have records, especially since so many of the victims from that fateful accident were brought here. I paid for my breakfast, went out to the Jeep, and consulted my GPS for the way to the facility.

Within minutes I was pulling up outside a neat one-story stucco building with rock trim. The grounds were landscaped in rock and natural plants, and I saw a worker blowing fallen leaves from the gutters. I parked and walked into a pristine lobby with a reception counter attended by two young women who couldn't have been more than six years old when Jenny Blake came here (assuming she did). I wasn't quite sure where to start, but began by asking to speak with the hospital administrator.

I soon found myself sitting across the desk from a gray-haired man whose business attire consisted of dark slacks, a white shirt, and bolo tie with a huge chunk of turquoise. Our initial chit-chat revealed that Mr. Baca had held his position for eight years, having transferred here from another small hospital in the same healthcare system. He vaguely remembered the horrific accident, simply because it had been on the news, but he seemed friendly and willing to help.

"Two of our physicians have been here long enough," he said. "And a few of the nurses. I might save you the trouble of speaking with everyone if we check the computer first."

He pulled a keyboard within reach and adjusted reading glasses into place. After tapping a few keys and scrolling around, he looked up.

"I don't find any records under the young woman's name."

"What about her description? She most likely didn't have any identification with her. Does white female, age twenty-one help at all?"

"That's not quite how it works, but let me check admissions for that date." When he did, his eyes widened. "Oh. It seems we had a lot of people in for treatment after the accident. The records aren't very complete. You must understand, a facility of this size, we have ER bays for four patients. It seems more than six times that many were brought in. I can only imagine, but most likely they tended to the most seriously injured, and sent many minor injuries home with a Band-Aid and an aspirin. Sorry. I don't mean to be flippant."

"I know. The staff must have been overwhelmed."

He nodded solemnly. "I'm sure they were."

"I wonder if I could meet the two doctors and those nurses who were here then. I know the chance is slim, but maybe one of them will remember Jenny Blake from her photo."

He gave a shrug and rose. "Sure. Let's see who's on duty right now."

He led the way through a set of double doors and we approached a nurses' station. Neither of the nurses sitting there—one male, one female—were possibly old enough to have been here fifteen years ago. The girl, in particular, looked fresh out of school.

Mr. Baca rattled off a few names and asked where they were.

"Lynda and Sophie are with patients, dispensing meds, I believe," said the male nurse. He glanced at the other one.

She spoke up. "Maria's somewhere ... I'm not sure. And Betty went to help out in the ER."

I had to give Baca credit for cooperativeness. He set off down a corridor of patient rooms and I trailed along. Pausing at each room and peering in, he knew who he was looking for. Outside one room we waited until the nurse with black hair and bright yellow scrubs came out. He vaguely explained what I wanted and asked if she could take a look at a photo.

She gave me a pleasant smile. "I'm Lynda. How can I help?"

I handed her the photos of Jenny—one, her high school graduation picture and the other a few years older, holding Cassie as an infant.

Lynda gave them a good long stare but finally shook her head. "Sorry. I saw so many people that night. I'll never forget it because it's the worst trauma we've ever dealt with here. We didn't have nearly enough beds, there were so many really bad injuries ..."

I nodded and took back the pictures.

She pointed at the one with Jenny alone. "She looks a little bit familiar, but ... No, I don't know her."

The fact that Jenny seemed familiar to one nurse was encouraging. Maybe one of the others would remember treating her. I held onto a thread of hope.

Baca and I resumed our trek down the hall, but the answer was the same with the two other nurses we located. Too many injuries, a tiny hospital in chaos, names and faces that just didn't stick with any of them.

"We'll check the ER," he told me, pointing toward another set of double doors at the very end of the long hallway. "Someone mentioned a cardiac patient came in a while ago, and that's Doctor Gutierrez's specialty." Then he caught sight of a woman entering one of the restrooms.

"Oh, Maria!" But she was already inside. "We'll catch her later."

We walked into the small emergency department. Here, too, a nurses' station was manned by one person who was too young to fit my criteria, a guy with a stethoscope around his neck who was staring at a computer screen.

"Doctor Gutierrez?" Baca inquired.

The nurse nodded toward one of the curtained-off bays. But when the administrator peeked in, he came back out shaking his head.

"Okay, that's strange. He must have just been here." He glanced around and made a decision. "Let's just go back to my office and have him paged."

Once again, I trailed along, looking for anyone who seemed over forty. This looked like a medical facility of very young staff, probably those right out of school who took the first job they could get to build up their time and qualify for bigger, better positions elsewhere.

An hour later, I was still twiddling my thumbs in Baca's office and getting the feeling he was more than ready to be rid of me. I ended up leaving my card and my cell number, with a request that the doctor get in touch as soon as he could.

From there, my next stop would be the police station. I found it located in a classically New Mexican old sandstone building, set in a pleasant park with grass and shady trees. On the opposite side of the street was a row of commercial buildings that looked as though they had probably sat right there, looking much the same, since the 1920s. It had taken me a whole five minutes to get here. I decided I could learn to love navigating around a small town like this.

The department consisted of a police chief, four officers, and a dispatcher who also greeted people at the front desk. I asked to speak with the chief and was escorted into a tiny office stacked to the ceiling with binders and folders. The nameplate on the desk said Chief Ramon Sanchez. The somewhat rotund man behind it indicated for me to take one of the two chairs facing him.

"I'm trying to locate a young woman who was involved in that awful accident years ago."

He remembered, shaking his head sadly. "It was a bad one. My men, all of us, were out there. The snow, it just kept coming. Even the ambulances had a hard time getting through."

I laid the two photos of Jenny Blake on his desk, facing him. He gave a quick look and kept talking, but I noticed his eyes darted back to the pictures now and then. I heard all about the logistics of the accident—how many state, county, and local law enforcement had gone out to try and restore order, how many wreckers to clear the highway, how many ambulances to transport the injured.

Eventually, I realized he wouldn't remember any one victim. For him it had all been a huge operation to get traffic moving, vehicles and people out of the frigid weather.

"Wish I could help. She does look a little bit familiar,

but I can't say that I remember her specifically from that night. If she didn't show up at the hospital, it could be that she was okay, got a ride with someone and went on to Tucumcari or someplace."

I didn't go into all the reasons I believed Jenny had not been okay. For all we knew, he could be right. I stepped outside into the bright sunshine again and looked around. Where could I turn next?

Chapter 43

I spent two hours in the newspaper office, first chatting with the elderly publisher (hi, I'm Ed) who was probably the only reason this town still had a print newspaper. He admitted he held onto it because the locals loved having it, and he knew if he sold the business and brought in younger blood, they would only put everything online and a lot of small-town spirit would be lost forever.

He vividly remembered the accident and walked straight to a backroom archive where he pulled out the bound issues of the paper for that year. Placing his thumb near the end of the hardbound book, he only missed the Thanksgiving week edition by three pages. He flipped straight to it and showed me the stories, the biggest to hit his news desk, before or since.

"Yep, the only bigger story around here was probably

when Billy the Kid escaped from the courthouse." He lifted his chin toward the building I'd just come from, across the street.

At my startled expression, he laughed. "Sorry, that was just a rumor. It was actually the Lincoln County Courthouse."

I turned my attention to the oversized book in front of me.

"Take your time, read all you want." Ed went back to his desk.

I pretty much knew what I would find, having already been through the news at the statewide level, but I had to admit his writing gave it the hometown flair. The Torres family had taken in a couple whose car was totaled, housing and feeding them until the insurance company sent a rental car from Albuquerque. Two kids whose parents had been hospitalized were cared for at home by one of the police officers' wives. Every motel along Old 66 opened its doors for free rooms to anyone who couldn't get home. It was Thanksgiving, after all.

The spirit and generosity shown by these people, many of whom had nothing to spare except a bed or a bowl of chile on a cold night, was amazing. The paper had done a good job of reporting the facts and bringing out the emotional aspects of the tragedy without becoming maudlin or overdramatizing. We didn't often see this kind of thing in the big city where it was expected that some government agency would handle it all, and people got lost in the shuffle of officialdom.

Closing the bound book of newspapers, I picked up my purse and walked out of the archive room to find Ed pecking away at his keyboard. He looked up and held out the two photos of Jenny Blake.

"Want me to do a story about her?" he asked.

I thought of Linda's concerns over the cartel and her fear that someone out there still had harmful intent toward her daughter.

"Let me check with the family first. It's not really my call."

He nodded. Then he stabbed a bony finger at one of the pictures. "I know this girl. I'd swear it. But not from that accident. It's something else." His forehead wrinkled in concentration. "Aw, rats—it's hell getting old and not remembering things. Maybe I should be selling this place and getting myself off to some retirement home."

I thought back to my visit with Detective DeAngelo in Phoenix. The facility was nice enough, but the man had faded to a shell of his former self. I shook my head at Ed. "Don't do it just yet. You've still got a lot of stories to write."

He chuckled and handed the photos back. "Yeah, you're right. I'd go nuts if I couldn't cover the latest cattle auction or what the ladies book club is currently reading."

I left the office with a smile on my face. But that faded as I walked back to the spot where I'd parked my Jeep. I had pretty much exhausted the somewhat-official channels where I could get information about the accident and the missing Jennifer Blake. So, now what?

I got in the car, turned on the AC to cool it down a bit, and then began to meander. It was an interesting little town, filled with older homes and those longtime shop fronts, interspersed with bright spots of color in newer restaurants and the very few chain stores—a Napa Auto Parts and a Family Dollar store. Motels tended to be mom-

and-pop operations rather than those of the bigger chains. I cruised east on 66 until it climbed a steep hill and led to an entrance for I-40 where I spotted the golden arches and a scattering of well-known hotel signs, and I knew this, too, was a little town that couldn't completely escape the modern world.

Rather than getting on the interstate, I made a left turn into an abandoned parking lot, where something once stood before it got bypassed by progress, and wheeled around to get back on the main drag through town, this time westbound. Following a side street, I came upon a lake surrounded by ancient trees, a pretty oasis with picnic tables and families out for a day of fun. And all this time, circling on back toward the center of town, passing three churches and a library, I thought of Jenny and felt stumped.

Why was I making no progress toward learning the truth about what happened?

The afternoon was growing late, and I could feel my energy lagging. I checked into one of the mom-and-pop variety motels away from the solid noise of the interstate. I'd hoped the proprietors might have been around long enough to remember something from the past, but they turned out to be a young couple from India or somewhere like that. The room was squeaky clean, though, and that's all I wanted. Next door was a pizza place where I got myself a small pepperoni and a big Coke, which I carried back to my room where I could sit in one of the two chairs and stretch my legs out on the other.

I'd taken my second bite when my phone rang.

"We're in the Honolulu airport," my brother said. "Vacation's over. Thought we'd see if you want to meet up when we get in." I had forgotten Ron and Victoria would be returning from their Hawaiian vacation, and I would have enjoyed treating them to a meal and catching up on news, but I could do that any time.

"Um, isn't that going to be either the middle of the night or some ungodly early hour tomorrow?" When was he ever going to figure out how to convert time zones?

I filled him in on where I was, keeping my eye on the goal here, while I munched down two slices of the pizza. After we hung up, I finished off the rest. Hey, it was a small pizza.

Of course I slept like a person who'd eaten a whole pizza by herself, bloated and restless all night long. When I woke up in the early hours to take an antacid, I discovered a text from Cassie Blake had come in while my phone notifications were turned off.

Found someone in Santa Rosa who might have info.

Okay … but how was I supposed to reach this person? I composed a quick text back, well aware that four o'clock in the morning is not the time to expect an answer. With nothing better to do, I fell back into bed until I felt the vibration of my phone a couple hours later.

Her name is Tina Patterson. She'll call you this morning. Hope it was okay to give your # 😊

Sure. In case she doesn't call, can I get her #

It came back a moment later but before I'd decided whether it was too early to call, my phone rang.

Tina Patterson introduced herself in a sweet, little-girl voice. "I hope this isn't too early, but I gotta be at work in an hour. Cassie said she thought it would be okay."

"Yes, absolutely. She told me you might have some information about a case I'm working on, but she didn't exactly say how she found you."

"Ah. Instagram."

I wasn't quite sure how that explained anything, but okay.

"I am a huge mystery fan. Anytime a hashtag with 'mystery' comes through I just have to check it out. And so this one had *mystery* and *Santa Rosa*, so of course I was hooked."

Good thinking, Cassie!

"Did she tell you we're looking for a missing woman, someone who was in this area about fifteen years ago?"

"Well, kind of. She posted an old picture, with a caption something like 'Do you know this woman?' and well, I sort of think I do."

She used the present tense. "You know where she is now?"

"Yeah, well, the friend I'm thinking of, yeah I do. I'm just not sure. She looks kind of different from the picture."

"It's an old photo."

"True. So, would it help if I introduce you?"

I'd been wondering how I would approach Jenny without scaring her into running again. "That would be great. Do you think she'd be available today?"

"We meet for lunch pretty often. I'll give her a call and suggest that. Bring a brown bag or whatever you want and meet us at Park Lake at 12:30."

I told Tina I'd be there and described my Jeep so she would recognize me.

Chapter 44

The morning dragged by. I'd planned on leaving town, but with this new lead I had no idea where it would take me. I could end up staying a couple more days, or I might hit another dead end and leave right after lunch. A hum of excitement tingled at me, knowing I could be this close to Jenny. Or it might have been raw nerves, not knowing how she would react. She surely couldn't have been living this close to Albuquerque all these years without being sorely tempted to get in touch with her mother and Cassie.

Or maybe she had—the new thought edged in. Maybe she'd secretly made the drive and watched them, wanting to know they were all right. About fourteen such *maybes* filled my head as I walked around the central part of town, until at last it was noon. I got a sandwich to go at the café where I'd eaten breakfast and then headed to the lake.

I spotted them right away, two women in their thirties sitting at a picnic table. When I parked the Jeep and got out, one of them waved me over.

Tina introduced herself and then turned to her friend. "Charlie, this is Crystal Gutierrez."

She'd changed her name and Tina was right, her appearance had changed—rich, deep brunette hair, a noticeable scar on her upper lip, and the shape of her nose was different—but I thought this could definitely be Jenny.

We exchanged a little smile and I sat down across the table from her. And here's where I became a lot more unsure of how to approach the subject. So, at first, I didn't. We three just chatted. Tina told me she'd lived in Santa Rosa all her life, she and Crystal were the same age, and they'd met when Crystal lost her parents and came to live with her uncle.

"I was in a bad accident," Crystal said, touching the scar. "They took me in while I figured out what I wanted to do with my life. Apparently, I had a knack for accounting, so that's the path I took. Online courses, testing out of some classes, and then I got a job with Rory."

"Rory Martin, CPA," Tina supplied.

"A few years later I got certified and opened my own office."

"Where did you live before the accident?" I watched her face carefully as I asked.

Crystal's expression turned sad. "Puerto de Luna is what I'm told, but I have no memory of it at all. I woke up in the hospital and didn't remember anything. Ismael and Maria filled in the details for me once we got to their house."

I took a bite of my sandwich, mainly to mask my

churning thoughts. She'd been in the accident but lost her memory. That could explain so much. But the new name, the invented past—it didn't seem to be coming from her but from things others had told her.

"So, Ismael and Maria ... they're relatives?"

"My aunt and uncle. They both work at the hospital. I was so lucky they recognized me and even luckier that they took me in and helped me adjust." She gave a wink toward Tina. "Cause I'm *so* well adjusted now, right?"

They laughed at their own inside joke and the conversation turned to their plans for the upcoming weekend, from which I gathered both were single and unencumbered by children. I decided I needed to talk to these surrogate relatives before I jolted Crystal out of her comfortable world.

"So, what brought you to Santa Rosa, Charlie?" Crystal asked.

"Looking for someone who has family back in Albuquerque." But this wasn't something to spring on her over lunch so I switched topics. "Actually, I'm an accountant, too. Interesting that we have it in common."

"CPA?"

"Yes, but I actually only do the work for my brother's firm. It's tricky enough keeping up with the tax law for one type of business. How do you manage knowing all there is to know for a variety of clients?"

From there the conversation turned into enough obscure terminology that I caught Tina yawning at one point. And then the lunch hour was over. While Crystal gathered everyone's trash and carried it to a barrel across the park, I asked Tina not to say anything about our investigation.

"Until I'm absolutely certain it's Jenny, I don't want to scare her."

She promised, although by the gleam in her eyes I knew she would want to know how the mystery turned out.

We exchanged contact information and I told them both if they ever visited Albuquerque that I could send them to the best Mexican food in town. Tina set off walking—her job was at the nearby fish hatchery—and Crystal got into a little Ford. I drove straight to the hospital where I asked my buddy, the administrator, for a meeting with either Ismael or Maria Gutierrez—or preferably both.

He looked at a schedule on his computer screen before saying, "Sorry, it looks like this is their day off. They both normally take the same days."

While pretending to consult my own calendar on my phone, I did a search and found their home address. The other beauty of a small town is that it wouldn't be hard to find.

The house was built of the same sandstone as the courthouse, in a style I'd noticed was prevalent with the older homes all over town. Reddish rock, white trim, a covered verandah on two sides. The front yard was fenced with a low wall of the same rock, and a short iron gate led to a flagstone walk that went straight to the front door.

Maria Gutierrez answered my press at the doorbell, and the look on her face told me she'd seen me yesterday. She was the nurse who'd ducked into the ladies room when Mr. Baca had tried to get her attention. She started in with, "Sorry, we don't want to buy anything."

"Maria … I think you know why I'm here. I need to speak with you and your husband."

Without a word she stepped aside and let me in.

Doctor Gutierrez stepped through an archway into the living room. She looked up at him, this tall gray-haired man with a kindly face.

"Maria overheard the other nurses talking yesterday, saying that someone was asking about a girl, from the time of the accident."

I showed him the photos I'd been carrying with me. He nodded.

"Yes, she is the girl. We stayed up late into the night, talking about this." He gestured toward a grouping of chairs and a sofa. "Please. Sit down."

"I think I've figured out why Jenny Blake never showed up on any lists as a Jane Doe. But I'd like to hear the story from the beginning."

He nodded gravely. "We were on the road that night. If we had been only a few hundred yards farther in our journey, we most likely would have been involved. I was able to avoid being hit, but we both realized the situation was bad. We found one person alive among the vehicles we checked, and we brought her here, to the hospital."

"At first she was unconscious but she came around," Maria added. "But when we asked her name, she didn't know it."

"I treated the deep cut on her lip and several others. And I set her nose as best I could. She has always had sinus problems since then. I should have called a specialist."

"I watched her so carefully," Maria said. "But soon, very soon, the hospital was overwhelmed with people."

"Most of the injuries were worse than Crystal's—I'm sorry, you said her name was Jenny?" The doctor's gaze met mine and I nodded. "She wasn't in good shape to discharge, and where would she go. But there were no relatives to take her. Maria and I—no, I take full responsibility—I suggested we bring her to our home. Our housekeeper could watch her when we were not home, and we could see that she received proper medical care. I filled out the paperwork, listing her name as Crystal Gutierrez, and put myself as her next of kin. It was on the spur of the moment, but I said she was a niece, that my nephew's brother was her father but he had been killed in the accident. No one checked, no one cared to check. You must understand—everyone in the hospital was running at full speed that night."

"So you brought her home to heal. That was very kind of you. But I don't understand—didn't Jenny eventually remember who she was? Did she just quietly accept that you called her Crystal?"

They glanced at each other, and it was Maria who spoke. "At first she was very confused. Sometimes she would say that her name was not Crystal. But she never spoke another name, and when we asked, thinking someone would be missing her, she became frightened and confused. But there were the nightmares—she would call out names in her sleep."

"What names?"

"Most often it was Cassie … sometimes Ricky."

"But one thing stopped me from trying to find these people," said the doctor. "I will never forget this. She was in one of her nightmares. I went into the room to check on her and she cried out, so frightened, 'Ricky! No! He's going to kill you. He'll kill me!'"

He shrugged. "I have no idea who she was talking about but she was terrified. And that's when I knew she had been running from something, something very bad."

If I'd had any doubts about the photos matching, those

names made me certain I'd found her.

"We think it was the Chaco cartel, out of Espanola," I said.

His face turned pale. "*Dios mio!*"

Maria crossed herself. "We have seen the work of those men. They have a long reach, even to this part of the state."

I could well imagine, drug trafficking along the interstate highway corridors must be relentless.

"But it's been such a long time," Gutierrez said.

"It has, and the connection was a tenuous one. Jenny's ex-husband had become involved. He … well, he died a long time ago. There's nothing to make the cartel want to come after Jenny now."

"Good. I am happy to know that."

"But she has made a life for herself here now," Maria said. "She has many friends, a business."

"I know. I wouldn't expect her to leave, but there are important reasons I would like for her to know the truth." I went into the story of Linda's illness and how badly Cassie wanted to know that her mother was alive. By the end, Ismael and Maria both had tears in their eyes.

"If this mother could know, before she dies, that her daughter is alive and well—this would mean so much to her," Maria said.

"It would. I would like your blessing, but I plan to talk to Jenny anyway."

"It will be easier if we are there, all of us. She trusts us, but I sense there are things she has not told us."

I had a feeling that could be the understatement of the decade.

Chapter 45

Maria called Jenny at her office and suggested she come by their house rather than going to her apartment after work. I went back to the motel and paid for another night. This evening could go late. And I gathered all my case files to show the family. In a way, this was going to be sad—the Gutierrez couple literally had begun to feel as if their Crystal were their own niece.

I arrived around four and showed the older couple the file. They were astounded that word of the search for Jenny had never reached them. But I sensed that they both somehow knew; they had grown fond of her and didn't want to let go. When it came to revealing all this to Jenny, they agreed to let me do the talking.

The little Ford pulled into the driveway and Jenny—Crystal—came bounding up the sidewalk and through the front door.

"*Tia Maria, lo que es para la cena?*" she called out.

Maria answered, and I caught enough to understand that dinner would be enchiladas. The two bantered in Spanish a little more until Jenny looked across the living room and spotted me. A puzzled expression crossed her face.

"*Chiquita*, there is some news," Ismael told her.

"Before dinner, or after?" Maria asked, always practical.

"Before," Jenny said. I could see she was worried.

"At lunch I mentioned I was here looking for someone."

"Right." The light began to dawn.

I went through the whole story, pulling out photos and the police report Linda had filed when Jenny went missing. She listened quietly, taking it all in, probably filing it in her orderly accountant-brain. She pointed to the pink sweater she was wearing in the photo, the one where she was holding Cassie.

"I remember this sweater." She looked up at Ismael.

"You were wearing it when we found you. Unfortunately, it had a lot of blood on it. We threw it away."

"So my real name is Jenny Blake?" She looked toward Ismael and Maria. "And I have a baby?"

"We didn't know. *Chiquita*, honestly, we had no idea and no way to find out. There was no child of that age among the accident victims."

"Your daughter is called Cassie, and she is alive and well with your mother in Albuquerque. She's in high school," I told her.

Then Ismael went into his story about the night they found her and why they'd given a fake name, simply to be able to check her out of the hospital without a lot of questions. He admitted they had not tried very hard to learn her identity, as she was clearly very afraid of something from her past.

At some point, I closed the folder and Maria pressed us all to go to the table before the enchiladas became overcooked in the oven. We ate sparingly, everyone digesting the information we had all shared.

We were about to start on Maria's homemade flan when my phone rang. When I saw it was Cassie, I excused myself to take the call.

"Charlie, can you come over?" I could tell she was crying.

"Cassie, take a breath. I'm not in town right now, but tell me what's wrong."

"It's Grandma. She's taken a turn for the worse. The hospice nurse is here now. They say she might live only another day or two. I don't know what to do."

My mind raced. "Okay, for right now you just do whatever they suggest. I can be there tonight."

I walked back into the dining room and faced the Gutierrez family. I had mentioned already that Linda was ill, which was Cassie's reason for hiring me. Now I had to tell them the awful truth, that the timeline had suddenly moved forward.

"Jenny, I'm afraid it's now or never for you to see your mother again."

Her eyes darted back and forth between the aunt and uncle who had been her only family these past fifteen years.

"You can ride with me. I'm heading back to Albuquerque tonight." I hated pressing her this way; she'd received a shocking amount of news in the last couple of hours. But it was the only way Linda would get to see her again.

Ismael squeezed her hand. "Go, *chiquita*. You owe your mother this."

"And Cassie," I reminded. "She's a sweet, well-adjusted kid, but she needs the reassurance that you didn't willingly abandon her." I felt my own voice cracking slightly. With a deep breath, I went on. "You don't have to make a commitment to stay there or to leave your life here. But for now, for tonight …"

"This is the right thing to do," Maria said, taking Jenny's other hand. "Go to them now. We will be here for you, no matter what you decide later."

Jenny gave each of them a tearful look before she stood up.

"I'll need some clothes, enough for a few days," she said. "Follow me to my apartment."

I was already on my way to the living room to pick up the folder and my purse.

An hour later she'd tossed a small bag into my Jeep, I had grabbed my few items from the motel, and we were on the road. While I concentrated on the highway, she phoned her secretary and asked her to cancel all her appointments for the rest of the week. Then she settled back in her seat, a little dazed.

"This has all been a lot for you to take in, hasn't it? I can't even imagine."

She nodded. "For years now, I've had the strangest dreams."

"Ismael and Maria told me you used to call out names in your sleep."

"Scenes would flash through my mind, even when I was awake. Things I couldn't make sense of. Sometimes there was a baby—but I could never remember any specific details, could never make sense of it."

"Are you remembering now?"

I hoped, with some of the facts, it would all come back

to her. But she shook her head.

"Not really. It's like I have these details you've given, and the pictures, and I can accept that they're true. But right now, it just doesn't feel like it's me we're talking about. Does that make sense?"

In a way, it did.

Chapter 47

It was after ten o'clock when I pulled up in front of Linda's house, but soft lights glowed from most of the windows. I parked in the driveway, behind the minivan. A vehicle I didn't recognize sat at the curb, probably the visiting nurse.

Jenny stared at the house, taking in details. "The trim is green—it used to be brown. And the trees have grown so big."

Her gaze swept the front of the house. "These flowerbeds. Mom always planted pansies in the ground and petunias in hanging baskets. So funny that she's still doing it."

She knew the place. I felt a huge surge of relief. Until this moment I'd had a nagging doubt about what I would do if I had, in fact, found the wrong person. But that was dispelled completely the moment we walked into the sickroom.

Linda looked toward us and her haggard face lit up. "Jenny! Oh my god, you're here." She tried to sit up but couldn't quite manage.

Jenny rushed to the bedside. "Mom? Oh my gosh, I can't believe I'm here." She reached out to take Linda's hands, ended up bending over and holding her mother in a tight embrace.

Cassie, standing aside, looked at me. I moved over and put an arm around her shoulders.

When Jenny straightened up, Linda held both her hands and studied her. "I'm glad you went back to your natural hair color. It always suited you. And your face … you've got some little …"

Jenny touched her lip. "The scar. I know. It happened in the accident. I don't know much more than that." She turned to me.

"We can catch up on the details later. I want you to meet the most amazing young lady—she's the one who came to me because it was so important to her to find you." I ushered Cassie forward as I spoke.

Cassie suddenly became shy. The reality of the woman she'd heard about all her life … the emotion seemed a little overwhelming.

Jenny sensed her daughter's hesitance. "Oh, Cassie. I'm so amazed at how you've grown up. I don't quite know how that happened."

She laughed. They both laughed.

"I have so much to learn about you and about what happened. We don't know each other now, but we will." She was staring into Cassie's eyes, memorizing her face.

Then Cassie said the thing all teens use as a way of getting acquainted. "Want to see my room?"

Jenny took her hand. "Yes, absolutely."

It was my cue to leave.

Chapter 47

I fell into bed and slept like a dead person until my phone rang. A glance at the screen showed it was 8:05 a.m. and the caller was Ron. He may have said something in the way of a greeting—I don't know. I was still ninety-percent asleep.

"So, Kent Taylor called," he said.

I must have mumbled something like 'what?' but he went on talking.

"I guess you didn't mention that you and he were actually in on a case together … something more than simply checking out some fingerprints …" Did I hear some kind of envy in my brother's voice? "He wanted me to pass along to you that they found arsenic among Jeffrey's things at Iris's house. What's all that about?"

I'd been so wrapped up with Linda, Cassie, and Jenny

that it took me a second to remember.

"A friend of Elsa's. She married the wrong man and he tried to poison her."

"Okaayyy… At least this next bit makes a little more sense. Taylor says the whole family has pulled this kind of thing before." I could tell he was reading from notes. "In a few cases they've bilked the older women out of their life savings and then disappeared, but there was another poisoning, nearly identical to this. And, he says, Mark was in on it."

Wow. Iris had been lucky. We all had been lucky, since Jeffrey was trying to fix Elsa up with his so-called cousin.

"Thanks for passing along the message. I need to get with Gram today and we'll probably swing by to visit Iris, see how she's doing." I ended the call, sat up and realized it was full daylight.

Speaking of Gram, she'd surely been up since the crack of dawn, and by now she would have noticed my vehicle back in the driveway. I should relieve her of dog sitting duties.

"Iris is home now, and the slimy Jeffrey is gone," she told me when I walked over and we began to catch up on things over a cup of coffee at her kitchen table. "She's still kind of sad about it, though. Several friends tried to warn her about him. I think she's a little embarrassed that she didn't listen."

She stood up and picked up a small wrapped gift from the countertop. "I want to go by for a little visit and take her this."

"Yes, I'll drive you. I'd like to see how she's handling everything."

The plan became that we would drop by Iris's house

mid-morning. The sky was clouding up when we arrived to find a crew busily mowing, trimming, tending all the plantings. I wondered what it would be like to have such a perfectly manicured yard with all the work done by someone else.

Iris greeted us at the door with more bounce in her step than I'd seen since the day of her wedding. She led us through to the kitchen where she'd set out a plate of pastries and the scent of freshly brewed coffee filled the room. She exclaimed over the scented candle Elsa had brought and insisted on lighting it immediately.

I quickly filled her in on the information from Kent Taylor this morning.

"Well," she said, while pouring for all three of us. "I cannot believe what an old fool I was. Really, now that my mind isn't so foggy, I can see what all my friends tried to make me see. As soon as I got home from the hospital, I gathered all of the big rat's things and I had the security guards haul it all to the dumpster, including that seventy-something-inch TV set he bought. Can't believe I went for that."

"Everyone makes occasional bad decisions," I said.

"Not this bad. This debacle turned into a life and death choice. I was really shaken when the doctor told me how close I came to dying."

"And Charlie says his cousin Mark was part of it. He sure was trying his best to rope me in," Elsa offered. "Although once he saw the level where I live, compared to all this—" with a wave of her hand "—he must have known there were a lot bigger fish than me."

"Well, I think you both have done the right thing," I said, raising my coffee mug in a little toast.

"Men—who needs 'em," Elsa said. "Well, except for Drake. You've got yourself a winner there, Charlie."

"My lawyer says I can get the marriage annulled," Iris told us. "I'm lucky she's even speaking to me. She was absolutely livid when she found out Jeffrey had talked me out of signing a prenup. She'd drawn one up and everything, but he poured on more of the smooth talk. Said when people were as much in love as we were, we didn't need a bunch of silly paperwork like that. And I fell for it! Stupid, stupid, *stupid*."

"Don't beat yourself up too badly, Iris. Consider it a lesson learned."

"A mistake I'll never repeat," she said with a smile.

Chapter 48

The rain began that afternoon. After months with no moisture, we New Mexicans pray for and look forward to our late-summer seasonal rains. In those parts of the world where *monsoon* means *deluge,* the people may laugh at us for using the term, but we're always grateful and happy to see the much-needed water soak into our parched ground.

On a purely selfish level, I was most grateful to have my husband back. The rains had quenched the forest fires, to everyone's joy, and he was home. We made the most of the first few days with lots of togetherness. His work until October would consist of photo shoots, a music video filming he'd lined up for some big country music star, and whatever other odd work came in. Then the autumn wildlife counts for Fish and Game ... Anyway, he was pleasantly busy and I was happy that he would be home in the evenings.

My two cases had wrapped up—the official one and the unofficial. I'd settled under the gazebo in the back yard, reading a book and listening to the rain on the roof, when I got the call. Linda Arnold had passed.

Cassie told me the news in a stoically grown-up voice, although I knew she was hurting deeply. She invited me to the memorial, which was to be a small gathering of friends at Linda's house. Much as I detest funerals, I agreed to go. This girl who had walked into my office, weeks ago, still touched me. I wanted to know that she would end up in a good place in her life.

Thursday came around. I spent the morning at my office and then walked the two blocks to Linda's home. A dozen cars lined the block on both sides of the street, including one I noticed with Colorado plates. I saw Cassie staring out the front window, and she met me on the front porch as the first drops of this afternoon's rain began to fall.

"I'm so glad you're here, Charlie. There are so many people."

I pointed to the Colorado car. "Your uncle?"

"Yes. Come in and meet them. They've been locked away a lot in a separate room with Mom ever since they got here."

I noticed the ease with which she referred to Jenny as Mom. She caught my smile and guessed why.

"We've gotten really close since she came here. I'm amazed at how she's built a good business in Santa Rosa and how well she coped with losing her memory for all those years."

"She had good mentors there, the couple who became another family to her. And she's a strong person."

I hesitated to ask what Cassie's own plans were, guessing that's what the adults of the family had been locked away to discuss. Although most of us at sixteen aren't really capable of making those life decisions that are in our own best interest, surely it had to be tough for her to watch everyone else plan her life.

Inside, I met Ted and Myrna Arnold, who seemed like decent people, although somewhat stodgy considering they were only in their late fifties. That was just an impression and I didn't say anything to Cassie. We took seats in the living room, where a nice urn held Linda's ashes, and the minister from her church said a lot of good things about her. I ignored the scent of the flowers and most of the words—the parallels between this girl's life and my own still felt fresh.

I watched Cassie's expression, seated now beside her mother, and wondered if I would ever be able to face the death of a loved one with any degree of detachment. Probably not.

The official part of the quasi service didn't last long, and then Myrna stood to invite everyone to stay for food. A glance toward the dining room when I arrived told me the hospital bed was gone and a long table had been tastefully laid with a buffet.

While most of the guests helped themselves to tea and little sandwiches, I sought out Jenny.

"How are you doing?" I asked.

"It's been such an adjustment," she said. "Once I was here, inside this house, memories came flooding back. Mother and I talked, as much as she was able, and she verified most of what I remember."

"Ricky?"

"Yes, my marriage and him leaving. I took her car and drove by my old house, the one on Sixth. Details are hazy for me, but I remembered the house. And there was that nosy old neighbor who used to watch everyone. She still lives there." She chuckled at that.

"I suppose Cassie told you Ricky had died, a long time ago."

She nodded. "I'm surprised I don't feel more emotion over that. It was just so long ago, and I suppose a high school sweetheart … well, the attachment for us didn't last."

She said it with little regret, which seemed healthy. She had moved on with her life.

"So—leaving the past behind and facing the present," she said, "we've decided we're going to give Cassie the choice of where to live. Ted and Myrna are still very willing to take her in. Her final two years of high school will have to be spent somewhere other than Albuquerque, and that could be challenging for her, but she seems accepting. Denver is a much larger city with more opportunities."

Her face began to take on a new excitement. "On the other hand, my apartment in Santa Rosa is small, but I've had my eye on a house I'd love to buy. It's an older house, very similar to Maria and Ismael's, close to the lake. If my daughter decides she'd like to try small town life, I want her to see it and approve before I make the offer."

"Oh, Jenny, that sounds so nice. If you need help convincing her what a great little town Santa Rosa is, let me know. I was really impressed."

She shrugged. "She'll have to decide. Little communities

can be cliquish but I had an easy time fitting in, and we do have more than a few connections there now."

Cassie came up to us. "Mom—Mom! Have you tried these cookies, the ones with the nuts and chocolate filling? They are *amazing*."

Jenny laughed and picked one off the plate her daughter held out. "Ah, kiddo, you already know my tastes, don't you?"

When they laughed and bent forward to touch noses, I knew the bond was complete. I had a strong feeling that Cassie would, indeed, end up in a good place in her life.

Thank you for taking the time to read *Sweethearts Can Be Murder*. If you enjoyed it, please consider telling your friends or posting a short review. Word of mouth is an author's best friend and is much appreciated.

Thank you,

Connie Shelton

There's more coming for Charlie and family!
In the meantime, if you've missed any…
Turn the page to see the list of all my books.

* * *

Next up, The Heist Ladies!

It's Amber's turn to call upon the Heist Ladies for help in this wrap-up to the series. The team's youngest member has taken a computer programming job and is on her way to a promising career. But a business trip to Europe with a fun side jaunt in Paris ends badly when Amber's luggage is searched by authorities and discovered to contain contraband. Even if she can convince them she's innocent, Amber knows she's been taken in by a con artist, and, well … that's the specialty of the Heist Ladies. Will the women be able to catch this oh-so-charming bad guy before he can pull the same sleazy con on someone else?

Get *Show Me the Money* at your favorite online retailer, available spring/summer of 2021

Books by Connie Shelton

The Charlie Parker Series
Deadly Gamble
Vacations Can Be Murder
Partnerships Can Be Murder
Small Towns Can Be Murder
Memories Can Be Murder
Honeymoons Can Be Murder
Reunions Can Be Murder
Competition Can Be Murder
Balloons Can Be Murder
Obsessions Can Be Murder
Gossip Can Be Murder
Stardom Can Be Murder
Phantoms Can Be Murder
Buried Secrets Can Be Murder
Legends Can Be Murder
Weddings Can Be Murder
Alibis Can Be Murder
Escapes Can Be Murder
Old Bones Can Be Murder
Sweethearts Can Be Murder
Holidays Can Be Murder - a Christmas novella

The Heist Ladies Series
Diamonds Aren't Forever
The Trophy Wife Exchange
Movie Mogul Mama
Homeless in Heaven
And watch for *Show Me the Money*, coming soon

The Samantha Sweet Series

Sweet Masterpiece

Sweet's Sweets

Sweet Holidays

Sweet Hearts

Bitter Sweet

Sweets Galore

Sweets Begorra

Sweet Payback

Sweet Somethings

Sweets Forgotten

Spooky Sweet

Sticky Sweet

Sweet Magic

Deadly Sweet Dreams

Spellbound Sweets – a Halloween novella

The Woodcarver's Secret

Children's Books

Daisy and Maisie and the Great Lizard Hunt

Daisy and Maisie and the Lost Kitten

Sign up for Connie Shelton's free mystery
newsletter at connieshelton.com
and receive advance information about new
books, along with a chance at prizes, discounts and
other mystery news!

Contact by email: connie@connieshelton.com
Follow Connie Shelton on Twitter, Pinterest and
Facebook

Made in the USA
Columbia, SC
21 February 2021

33332621R00183